THE FINAL FANTASTIC INTERGALACTIC ADVENTURES OF SIR LIVINGSTON

* * * * *

UK AND COMMONWEALTH EDITION

To the Garvock House
The best Hotel/Restaurant
in Fife

Marco Palmer
Nov 2010

Published by Rodney Matthews
Studios Publications

THE FANTASTIC INTERGALACTIC ADVENTURES OF STANLEY & LIVINGSTON

* * * * *

BY MARCO PALMER
& RODNEY MATTHEWS

VOLUME 1

THE LONG SHADOW OF PLAGUE ISLE

WRITTEN BY

MARCO PALMER

IN COLLABORATION
WITH ARTIST AND ILLUSTRATOR

RODNEY MATTHEWS

BASED ON AN ORIGINAL CONCEPT BY

RODNEY MATTHEWS

CONTENTS

AUTHOR'S PREFACE

PART ONE

THE PERILS OF PLAGUE ISLE

PART TWO
NEW BEGINNINGS

AUTHOR'S PREFACE

SOURCES

It has been an honour and a privilege to be entrusted with the journals of Stanley and Livingston, and though I will narrate events myself some of the time, I primarily used the first hand accounts recorded in these journals to tell the extraordinary story of these two great explorers of the galaxies.

Volume One has adventures from the outset, but the adventures are not intergalactic to begin with. Rather, each adventure is a stepping stone toward the intergalactic. In fact, the story of how Livingston became an explorer in the first place is the main concern of Volume One and it is for that reason that I predominantly used Livingston's journal entries.

Stanley's journal, detailing some of the same events, was perfectly adequate, but I made the editorial decision to use Livingston's account first and foremost, and only used Stanley's diary when his experience was somewhat different to Livingston's experience.

A DESCRIPTION OF
STANLEY & LIVINGSTON

Most readers will find Stanley and Livingston altogether alien in appearance, especially if they have picked up this book in a different galaxy.

Stanley and Livingston are from the mucky misshapen planet of Cessestial, a distant world where people are both similar and dissimilar to humans from Earth; they walk upright on two legs and are more or less just as intelligent as your average earthling, and yet they have all kinds of features that are characteristic of rodents, reptiles and many other kinds of animals.

To most people in the universe, Livingston would look like a possum – a possum sporting a red handlebar moustache that is.

Livingston would not describe himself in this way and so I do so here, and nor would Stanley compare himself to a venerable walrus – minus the tusks.

In the text, you will note that Livingston refers to himself as 'tall and dashing', but 'tall and gangly' is probably a more accurate description of Livingston, and I warn the reader not to be fooled by Livingston's inflated views of himself.

THE PLANET CESSESTIAL

The reader will understand that simple words to do with time such as "day, month, year and hour," will have different lengths and names on the planet Cessestial.

The months on Cessestial, for example, are not named after ancient Roman people like Julius and Augustus as in Earth's July and August, but are instead all plumbing terms, and that is because plumbing is central to the culture, the art, the architecture and even the religious life of most of the civilised nations of Cessestial.

As for the flora and fauna of Cessestial, it took forms that would make a scientist want to slap you should you describe how these otherworldly creatures actually look. Therefore, when you read about animals with common names such as cat, dog, horse, cow, chicken and so forth, do remember that these words have been translated from the Cessestian tongue into your tongue, and these creatures will be a different model and type than the version you are used to.

The living creatures of Cessestial have also adapted to a high level of radioactivity that would be poisonous to people from Earth. The very different rocks and minerals of Cessestial, formed under pressures that the planet Earth never dreamed of enduring, are the source of the higher levels of radioactivity.

PART ONE

THE PERILS OF PLAGUE ISLE

CHAPTER 1

THE GREETING OF SKULLS

EXCERPT FROM LIVINGSTON'S JOURNAL
Ballvalver the 6th

With only the ghostly light of the three moons to show us the way, Stanley and I braved the rough sea, tugging hard at the oars of our raft as we made our way to the shores of Plague Isle.

The island's dead volcano and the skeletal trees of its jungle cast their shadow over us as we entered its coral lagoon.

Upon disembarking from our rubber dinghy in the shallows, Stanley and I picked up our raft and then carried it over our heads as we marched out of the sea and up the beach.

The dark shore was littered with sharp foot-piercing stones. And as if that wasn't enough of a natural "Keep Away" sign, there was the unwelcome sight of a dead welcoming committee assembled for our arrival. There were skulls, dozens upon dozens of skulls. These faceless faces with their leering grins and empty eye-sockets looked down at us from the tall spears they were impaled upon. It was a fence composed of (or should I say decomposed of) at least two hundred spears and two hundred skulls. Each spear was taller than a man and planted upright in the gravel while the skull atop each spear tip mocked our appearance on the shore with a macabre smile, as if to say, "Welcome fools to Plague Isle. If you don't want to end up like us, then turn back now, before it's too late!"

For me, it was a warning that sent shuddering waves of bladder-weakening terror through my body that almost caused me the embarrassment of wetting my khaki uniform trousers.

"St-Stanley" I stammered, "I th-think we should obey the No Trespassing sign – maybe come at the island from a different angle – you know, where we aren't stepping on anyone's private property."

"Pish posh," answered Stanley with a dismissive "Humph!" This was followed by an insult (which only he thought was witty). "Livingston, when you applied for this job, you told me that danger was your middle name. If I had named you however, I would have named you after a two hundred-year-old bottle of vintage port…"

I waited for the punch-line………

It wasn't worth waiting for.

"You see, my boy, you're nothing but an old wine."

I didn't laugh.

Gesturing up to the skulls, Stanley chortled, "You see, Livingston, even they think it's funny!" He then Ha Ha'd and Ho Ho'd until the awkwardly slanted raft wobbled like jelly above us.

I should point out that the reason for the uneven tilt of the raft was that there was a marked difference in height between Stanley and myself. Instead of being tall and dashing like me, Stanley was several feet shorter than I and shaped like a bowling ball. I therefore held the back end of the raft up high, which naturally created a downward slope of yellow rubber that descended to Stanley's much lower head as he led the way, carrying the front end of the raft.

Despite being tempted to drop the dinghy, turn around and run whimpering back into the lagoon, I pulled myself together, and with bravado that wasn't entirely convincing, I said, "These skulls don't bother me in the slightest. I was just questioning your choice of landing site is all, Stanley. It'll take more than a couple of hundred severed heads mounted on razor-sharp spears to scare me away. Plague Isle-Shmague Isle! This is just another day at the office for the world's greatest explorer, Stanley, and his new partner Livingston!"

"Temporary partner. Not quite partner my boy. An assistant perhaps – or bag carrier, latrine-digger and boot-shiner maybe. And just until Alvin recovers from that terrible tumble he took. Beastly luck I say, Livingston. My faithful assistant, Alvin Updike, braved peril at my side through many an adventure suffering no injuries to speak of, and yet as the fates would have it in their cosmic sense of irony, poor Alvin fell down the stairs in his own apartment building."

"Or maybe, just maybe, the fates didn't want Alvin to come here, but sent me instead?"

"And I repeat, the fates must be joking!"

Quickening his pace, Stanley led the raft and I past the gruesome skulls and up on to level ground that was covered in wild grasses and prickly plants.

Cold ocean water squished inside my leather hiking boots and dripped from my stiff khaki shirt and trousers, though my head remained dry underneath my pith helmet.

Stanley was just as wet as I was, and his soggy adventurer clothing (a wide-rimmed hat decorated with colourful bird feathers, a brown leather jacket, a casual beige shirt and matching shorts) clung to his roly-poly body, while water sloshed out of his boots.

"These diamonds had better be worth all this misery!" I groaned.

Countering with sagely wisdom, Stanley replied, "Ah, but Livingston, truth is treasure. Green diamonds the size of dinner-plates might just be native nonsense."

"You mean I could be risking my neck for nonsense! I've been sea-sick for the last week! I've never been so cold, wet and wretched in all my life and it's been impossible to keep any food down on that teetering tug boat of yours!" (The tug boat I referred to was actually a research vessel called the Porcelain Porpoise, a bowl-shaped boat on pontoons that was presently anchored beyond the hazardous reefs that surrounded Plague Isle). Really rubbing it in, I said, "On my expeditions, I did all within my power to avoid stormy seas, cyclones, singing whales and the like. And why did we have to come to this stupid island in the middle of the night? I still say we should have waited until morning before setting off."

"My boy, I thought it would be profoundly foolish to cross the territory of the Klawd Tribe in broad daylight."

"Kl-Klawd Tribe? Are they the p-people that put the skulls on those big long spear-thingies?"

"Indubitably, and that is because they are a jolly lot of head-hunters. Oh and did I happen to mention they were also cannibals?"

"C-c-c-cannibals?" I gulped.

"My boy, if you don't wish to meet them, then the crude phrase, 'Shut Up' comes to mind. We are approaching the Plague Isle rainforest, and I would hate it if you accidentally woke up the Klawd Tribe or any ferocious man-eating beasts within earshot of your incessant moaning."

The warning had the desired effect and I did 'shut up,' and not a moment too soon because it was then that we entered the island's suffocating jungle.

CHAPTER 2

THE NIGHT HAS A THOUSAND EYES

Blindly, we stumbled a few yards into the pitch-black forest, using our raft to push aside leaves and branches.

Stanley stopped and whispered, "Here. This seems as good a spot as any to conceal our craft."

Quickly we covered the raft in whatever vegetation our hands could find as we groped in the darkness.

When we were finished, Stanley said, "You'll be delighted to know I put radio-tracking devices in both our backpacks that can home in on the beacon sewn into the lining of our raft so that we might locate it again."

"Well, I would hope so," I snapped. "But I..."

"But what?"

"I just wish we had laser guns is all." I paused, gulped, looked nervously around, tried to see but couldn't and added, "On my expeditions I used to always take laser guns into such perilous places."

Stanley was stern and solemn. "You should

know by now, Livingston, that I have a moral aversion to guns."

"But why? I don't get it! It's madness! It's suicidal!" I stopped speaking in order to listen. There were subtle sounds I couldn't identify; a quiet rustling movement of some sort that unnerved me.

"Maybe I have a soft spot for living things that have not yet been turned into wisps of vapour," answered Stanley. "A laser against the Klawd People – primitive natives armed with stone age weapons? It's grotesquely unfair, I say! Why, with just one laser gun, we could vapourise everyone and everything living on the island, march straight up Mount Fluepipe and look for the legendary green diamonds without anything to bother us except our consciences. You and I know that no diamond is worth that!"

"What about two diamonds?"

I was met with stony silence; though I couldn't see Stanley's facial features, I sensed his reproving stare.

"Right. No guns. Have it your way."

"My boy, the only gun we need is my flare gun, packed safely away in my backpack. Believe me, a simple flare gun can frighten off attackers, be they the indigenous natives or the wild animals of this island. It shoots phosphorescent chemicals, not matter–melting laser beams. I prefer to use a little ingenuity to get myself out of fixes. It is much less bloody all round. No, give me a knife, a length of rope and..."

"See-in-the-dark-goggles?" I suggested.

"Quite right," agreed Stanley.

We proceeded to rummage around in our backpacks until we found, retrieved and placed our infrared night-vision goggles on our faces. It took a moment for our vision to adjust to their distorted green glow.

Slowly, I began to recognise the shapes around me: there were fern leaves, palm fronds, vines, twisted mangrove roots and large plant-eating insects. I then glanced upward and what I saw above me made me scream like a frightened little girl.

In the tree branches round about me I saw thousands of glowing eyes. Each beady pair of eyes was slanted in anger and stared down at us.

The horror hit me like a hammer over the head and when I tried to scream again there was suddenly no air in my lungs to fuel my shrieking.

When a hand touched my shoulder, I jumped two feet into the air.

"Oh, do get a hold of yourself," pleaded Stanley. "I cannot believe you would make such a fuss over a few harmless bats."

Unable to speak, I pointed up at the myriad eyes.

"Yes, the bats," whispered Stanley. "The trees around about us are their roost; Great South Sea B-flat Bugle-Bottomed Fruit Bats. With a wingspan of twelve feet, they are the largest bats in the world and they have a peculiar funnel shaped bottom, which really does look like some kind of musical horn. The musical note B-flat emanates from this bugle bottom, giving credence to the old adage, fruit makes you toot."

A pent up time-delayed shriek finally left my mouth in a long, drawn out, "AAAAAAAAAAAAAAAAAAAAH!"

This upset the bats and they began to raise a huge commotion, dropping from the trees in a furious flurry around us.

"Stand still!" commanded Stanley.

I tried not to move but couldn't stop shaking like a hula dancer in a hurricane. Nor could I stop screaming while I endured the thousands of fluttering wings near my face. The multitude of flapping bats sounded like a thunderstorm, while the noise coming out of their bugle bottoms was like a symphony in B-flat.

"If we calm down, they'll calm down," shouted Stanley.

Instead of calming down though, I crumpled under the weight of terror, and in an act of unhinged desperation, I began to run into the tangled vegetation of the jungle, my arms beating the air in a vain attempt to fight off the plague of B-flatulent bats.

CHAPTER 3

THE CRATER

I wasn't sure if Stanley was following me or not. I wasn't sure of anything, least of all where I was going. All I cared about was getting away from the bugle-bottomed beasties.

Instead of leaving me however, the bats swarmed in rage. They were a living, breathing, black cloud, following and harassing me while I hurtled haphazardly into the unknown.

Amidst the rat-a-tat-tat B-flats and agitated wings about me, I didn't see the gaping hole ahead, so when the ground abruptly disappeared, I tumbled headlong into a crater.

I slid, yelled and rolled down its slope until I plopped unceremoniously into the – I didn't know what it was – some of it was like a dry, putrid powder – and some of it was wet and felt like mud, although mud wasn't usually the colour white – but whatever it was, it filled the floor of this pit and I fell face-first into this gloppy gloop.

The only positive thing about this experience was that the bats gave up on me and didn't follow me into the hole.

With good reason I was to discover!

It took me a few seconds to realise where I was and what had happened to me. I was dizzy, winded, bruised, bloodied and now covered from head to toe in the white whatever-it-was, and dear Saint Valveless, did it ever stink! How can I describe the strange stench? The rancid fumes from the reptile enclosures at the zoo come to mind, although this smell was ten times worse. And so, not only was I trying to recover from the shock of falling into the putrid pit, but I was immediately confronted by an overpowering odour that made my eyes well up with tears..

Lifting my head out of - what I then started to realise was some kind of horrid animal poo - I wiped my goggles, looked around and saw that I had not only tumbled into some kind of hole, but I had fallen into a nasty nest of abnormally large lizards.

"S-S-St-Stanley," I whimpered.

I pulled myself out of the lizard manure and slowly rose to my feet.

To my great relief, a sideways glance revealed that Stanley was picking himself up out of the crud just off to my right.

"STAN..."

"Hush!" warned Stanley.

"You came after me?"

"Foolishly fell after you actually. My boy, we've had the dubious dishonour of dropping into a nesting site of Giant Blind Spitting Stinky Skinks."

These skinks, as Stanley called them, were indeed large, looking to be around fifteen-foot long from the tip of the tail to the steel-trap of their mouth.

They were all mothers. Each of the forty to fifty lady skinks was lying near a pile of eggs inside the spacious crater and each monstrous mama was fiercely guarding her patch of reeking real estate along with her horrid horde of eggs.

Their slimy, slick shine intermingled with dark speckles and spots. (I don't know what colour they actually were because through the goggles everything looked green.) The four squat legs of the lizards ended in feet attached to long and terrible claws. But the strangest thing about these creatures was their eyes, or the lack there of. Talk about a blank stare. Their whole head was a blank. There weren't even sockets for the absent eyes. I found this eerie and unsettling.

"Your flare gun" I squeaked. "Scare them away with your flare gun."

"A measly flare will not frighten a creature when said creature cannot see said flare."

"Then perhaps they won't see us while we climb out of here?"

"They can still hear us and smell us! They know ..."

Without warning, an accurately aimed barrage of jelly-like saliva rained down on us as the skinks spat in agitation.

"...exactly where we are," finished Stanley.

He then shouted, "RUN!"

Stanley and I turned about face and attempted to scurry up the slimy slope of the crater. The bath of skink spit made the climb even more slippery, and so we both resorted to frantically crawling upwards on our hands and knees.

With the gait of gators, scampering on their four lethal feet, the lizards made quick time. They had none of the problems that we did while climbing the crater slope.

The skinks were only a second behind us as we cleared the rim of the crater.

Stanley and I leapt to our feet and began to sprint. There was no choice but to dash straight ahead, further and deeper into the jungle.

Meanwhile the skinks poured over the crater-rim in a slithering flood, picking up speed. With surprising momentum, the lizards rapidly gained on us, nipped at our heels and lunged for our legs, before drenching us in a new onslaught of spit.

"THE TREES!" Stanley shouted.

Without hesitation, we leapt for the nearest overhanging tree branch, and with adrenaline-induced strength, we were able to pull ourselves up and out of harms way.

The eyeless monsters surrounded the tree. They gnashed their teeth in frustration, hissed furiously, and sent frothy ooze flying in every direction.

In the midst of the spit storm, an angry

chorus of hoots erupted from the trees around us. Sticks and branches began to fall on the lizards in a rain of violence until the reptiles retreated, slinking back to their hole in the ground.

As we pondered this strange turn of events, Stanley and I were suddenly snatched from the very branch we were sitting on, and with the speed of an express elevator, we were lifted high up into the tree.

CHAPTER 4

TERROR IN THE TREETOPS

Whatever had taken me high into the tree had a powerful grip and fearsome strength. So shocking and sudden had this been, I hadn't had time to cry out.

I was roughly tossed from one tree to another. Tough leathery hands passed me from tree to tree until I came face to face with what looked like a demon; a leering, green-glowing gargoyle. OK, the green and glowing bit was because of my goggles but there really was some kind of hideous monster glaring at me with the most evil eyes I had ever seen.

In the next moment, I was tossed like a rag doll to yet another tree and another green demon, all the while shrieking in a manner unbecoming to a great explorer.

EXCERPT FROM STANLEY'S JOURNAL

Abominable luck! After the initial shock of being lifted into the jungle canopy and being thrown back and forth from tree to tree, I finally recognised our captors. They were Bimpboonzees – big, hairy muscular apes with wicked fangs and crinkly bottoms that made the brutes look like they had a grotesque cushion tied behind them. Had I not been wearing infrared goggles, the apes would have appeared gray in colour instead of green. The other colours I could not see (but knew were there because of photographs I'd seen of these beasts) were painted streaks of vibrant blue, red and purple in the face while the swollen bottom was an indecent pink.

The few fragmented facts I had gathered from scientific journals about Bimpboonzees did not allay my fears in the slightest. To paraphrase the scholarly literature: "Bimpboonzees are twice the size of a man and have the combined strength of twenty men. They also possess a savage blood lust and find it a thrill to kill any weak and unfortunate thing they get their hands on."

Logically, I deduced that once the apes tired of their cruel game, they would most likely pull our legs and arms off for the fun of it, pick the raw meat from our bones, and make a grisly meal out of us.

The only hope for Livingston and I was to somehow escape, and so with that in mind, I took a life-risking gamble. After being tossed to yet another ape in another tree, and while I was being shaken and hooted at by the malevolent monkey, I held out two of my fingers and jabbed the ape hard in its cruel eyes. Immediately, the Bimpboonzee let me go as it screamed, screeched, shrieked – perhaps all three noises combined – the point being, it was one of the most awful sounds I had ever heard coming from an animal.

For a millisecond of a millisecond I was overjoyed at my new found freedom and proud of my great escape. In the next nanosecond, the great weakness in my plan suddenly and terribly became apparent. I had no place to go but down.

Impersonating a two-hundred pound pinecone, I fell from the arboreal heights. I had no choice but to crash through the foliage, take the bumps and scratches like a man, and grasp desperately at every breaking branch. Finally, there was nothing remaining but the ground to break my fall.

It occurred to me that this was going to hurt badly and might result in many severe injuries; fractures, broken bones or quite possibly death.

Strangely the ground did not behave like the ground when I finally hit it. In fact there was a muted splash. What had looked deceptively like the forest floor was in reality quicksand.

Monster monkeys! That's what they were! With a brain that was being rattled and shaken, it was no wonder that I didn't figure it out right away.

Pleading and bawling, I flew from one ape to another like a ball in a dangerous game of catch until one of the creatures decided to keep me all to itself.

Gripping me by an ankle, the monster monkey dangled me upside down and held me aloft for every other monster monkey to see. It was a childish, taunting gesture as if to say, "Look what I've got and you don't! Nyah! Nyah! Nyah!"

The other monster monkeys in the vicinity hooted in protest, before rising to the challenge and giving chase.

The game had now become "Keep Away" and the monkey flipped me over its shoulder like a sack of potatoes, while it swung on vines from tree to tree.

Unpleasantly, this meant that my face was now bouncing along on the monkey's humongous bottom. In desperation, I fought back the only way I knew how. I bit the monkey's butt!

The playful primate was in the middle of a mid-air maneuver when this happened, and while it shrieked in painful distraction, it missed the next vine. The catastrophic result was that the ape and I fell straight down to the forest floor together. The big brute crashed face first on its belly with a thud, breaking all its bones. Its life's breath escaped in a hiss from its surprised mouth. It lay dead.

CHAPTER 5

SINKING SAND

With a grunt, I rolled off the dead monkey, picked myself up, took two wobbly steps forward and hoarsely called, "Staaaaaaanley!"

There was no response.

"STAAAAAAAAANLEY!"

This time there was a response of sorts. Several yards in front of me, a muddy head burst out of the forest floor and yelped, "Help!" before submerging beneath the ground.

"What the, hey...?" was all I could say.

Suddenly the head appeared again.

"Help me!"

"Stanley, why are you in the mud?" I asked.

"Quicksand, Livingston! Get me out of here! And be quicker than the sand!"

Once more he sank beneath the muck.

I had no idea how to help him. I panicked, danced about hysterically and cried, "What do I do? What do I do? What do I do?"

Upon resurfacing, Stanley shouted, "Throw me a branch," and then gurgled, "Hurry!"

Frantic, and unsure of myself, I ran

forward, took one step into the quicksand, felt my foot sink and then withdrew my foot in the nick of time.

After this near fatal blunder, I tiptoed around the perimeter of the patch of quicksand while searching for a fallen tree branch or anything that could help Stanley.

Spitting and gargling, Stanley broke the surface yet again.

"For the love of Saint Valveless, Livingston! I'm drowning!"

Stanley went up and down like a muddy yo-yo for the next five minutes or so as I searched the area for something suitable with which to rescue him. Despite the "hurry ups" and insults at my expense, I refused to give up and at last I found the perfect stick. I tossed it to Stanley and said, "Here!" and then, "Oops!" as the stick clobbered Stanley over the head.

"Not like that, you blundering boob!" cursed Stanley before going under for the umpteenth time. Next, he resurfaced for the umpteenth and one time, spat gritty sand out of his mouth, and yelled, "You have to hold on to the other end of the stick in order to pull me out."

He went under yet again. When he came back up he screamed, "Don't just stand there. Find something else you – you – epito-mee of stupid-i-tee!"

In a tizzy, I turned around and spotted an unusually large flower. It was all green. Sorry. No.

That was just the goggles. I don't know what colour it was. Blotches and mottled specks decorated its petals while hundreds of long, leafy vines extended from its stem in all directions.

Picking up several of the vines, I tested them with a tug. They seemed strong enough, and so I tossed the vines to Stanley, saying, "Here! Pull yourself out!"

Stanley took hold of the vines, but instead of saying thanks, he yelled, "Watch out behind you!"

I swerved about only to find that the vines of the bizarre plant were moving; grasping, and reaching for me.

The petals of the flower opened like the jaws of a carnivorous beast.

Its sticky prickly arms snagged me, wrapped around me, reeled me in and in the very next moment the flower swallowed me.

EXCERPT FROM STANLEY'S JOURNAL

While my foolhardy companion was so indisposed, I continued to extract myself from the sludge, holding on to the vines of the ferocious flower for dear life. With a final heave ho, I found the safety of solid ground, crawled forward, fell on my chest and took the necessary time to catch my breath. My breathing somewhat restored, I then wearily stood to my feet, wiped the grit off my face and goggles and assessed the situation before me in a calm and rational fashion.

I could see that Livingston was trapped inside the petals of the carnivorous plant; he was upside-down with his feet kicking the air, while the rest of him slowly slid down the throat of the voracious angiosperm.

"Curious?" I said to myself. "It is either a mutated variety of Caryophyllales or an Oxalidales, a botanical marvel I would love to identify if other matters were not so pressing."

Against all my yearnings to stop and study the flower; to take photographs and cuttings of the plant for analysis, I instead set about the business of rescue, and my hat was the first thing that needed rescuing.

Why? My Journal-Keeping computer that recorded all my thoughts and experiences was in my hat and the information contained therein was invaluable. That I had worn the beat-up old thing on many an adventure gave it a certain amount of sentimental value, and the fact that I just liked it with its wide-brim, its feathers, its perfect fit, its leather feel, its wild style that said "Explorer!" – These factors made its retrieval a top priority.

Thus, I found a long stick and fished my filthy cap from the surface of the quicksand, before returning it to my dirty head. Once in place, I felt the wires and electrodes of the computerised Journal-Keeper reconnect to my brain so the diary recording could begin anew.

Exhausted and famished, the next order of business was to have a bite to eat. I took off my backpack, rummaged around inside, found a peanut-butter and jelly sandwich, removed the plastic wrap and ate the sandwich slowly, relishing the sweet taste of each bite. I then ate a banana, took a swig of water from my canteen and for dessert I had a chocolate bar.

By this time, Livingston's feet had almost disappeared down the flower's stem, and it was then that I reached into my backpack, found some water-proof matches, lit one of these matches, walked straight up to the plant and set the ghastly thing on fire.

The formidable flower hissed and shrieked like something out of a garden centre from Hell, emitting a high pitched whine as it whipped violently about.

It spat Livingston out of its mouth as flames engulfed it.

Livingston made the quick flight from the flower to the ground, and landed with a belly flop at my feet. He staggered to stand upright, coughed repeatedly and somewhat ungrateful, he said, "What took you so long?"

I ignored the question, and instead listened to the noises of the night. There was a rustling in the vegetation.

"Drat! It was just as I had feared would

happen!" To Livingston, I said, "My boy, turn around, stand still and do keep quiet! We are in something of a pickle!"

"Not another pickle!" groaned Livingston while spinning about face. "Please tell me it's not worse than the man-eating daffodil, or the monster monkeys, or the lizards or the bats!"

It was worse. The foliage parted and a circle of monstrous masks emerged from the jungle.

The large people behind the beastly faces wielded spears and stone axes that were aimed at us and ready to be thrown. We had no choice but to raise our hands in surrender and give ourselves up to the Klawd Tribe.

CHAPTER 6

DR. SLUICE'S LABORATORY

AUTHOR'S NOTE

The crimes recorded in this chapter took place seven months prior to the events on Plague Isle. These criminal acts and the fairly unpleasant individuals who committed them have bearing on the entire history of Stanley and Livingston, and so I thought it best to pause, back up and report what happened in the laboratory of Dr. Sluice.

My narrative is based on the

confession of one of the criminals.

I have researched this incident carefully, but I was not actually there, so I have taken artistic liberties in my narration, trying to imagine what must have taken place.

Like most structures in the smoke-stack belching,
city, (an industrial metropolis of pipes and basins
known as Septo City) Dr. Archibald Sluice's
laboratory had the look of a kitchen sink that
had been dropped from a great height before
crashing on to the ground upside-down. In other
words, it was a white, porcelain dome, grimy
with soot and splattered with specks of green
mildew.

Such an ugly building (and it was the size
of a supermarket I might add) was not out of
place in Septo City where vulgar was in vogue
and bathroom meant beautiful. In fact, it was the
in-door plumbing look and lavatory-esque
designs that had the greatest influence on
respectable Cessestian society; it was this crazed
hoity-toity toilety trend that the people of Septo
City (and almost everywhere else on the planet)
considered stylish and pleasing to the eye.

Inside the laboratory, occupying a spacious
upper room was a state-of-the-art holograph
machine that projected three-dimensional images
of stars and galaxies on to the domed ceiling
above as well as into the very air.

Dr. Archibald Sluice appeared god-like in
the midst of an animated sea of galaxies, stars
and planets courtesy of the holograph projector.
His aged mop of silver hair, bushy white
eyebrows, beard and moustache did nothing to

discourage the ideas about what God might look like.

Moving to the very centre of the room, Dr. Sluice found a gigantic star burning up with red light. This he walked past until he found the fifth planet away from the star, a lopsided ugly brown world full of smog clouds, continents, islands, polar caps and oceans. Encircling this planet were three moons, and creeping toward this planet from directly above, was a star-destroying black hole that was leaving a trail of destruction during its slide through the projected universe.

Dr. Sluice stood before the lopsided planet, poked at the ghostly sphere with his finger (his finger passed through the insubstantial image), cleared his throat and said, "And here is our planet Cessestial. This is what Cessestial and her three moons might look like from space – though we've never been to space – not because we don't have the advanced rocket technology..."

Looking up to the ceiling and the holograph projector suspended there, Dr. Sluice croaked a command saying, "Simulated rocket."

An animated rocket then left the miniature version of Cessestial and just before it passed Dr. Sluice's nose he explained, "This is what would happen if we left the confines of our planet in a rocket-powered vessel – of course the scale is totally wrong. For the purpose of my illustration this rocket is the size of a firefly, but that would of course be like sending something the size of a mountain into space and to be true to scale, a correctly simulated rocket would have to be microscopic..."

"Get on with it!"

The catcall had come from the billionaire businessman, Sigmund Looz, son of the richest man in the world, the toilet tycoon, Armitage S. Looz.

At present, Sigmund, was standing impatiently near the exit and acting as if he could not wait to leave.

Accompanying Sigmund was a tall muscular mass of a man that stood brooding silently beside him. He had been introduced to Dr. Sluice as an associate named Mr. Coop.

"Is there a point to all this?" complained Sigmund, clearly irritated by Dr. Sluice's deviation from the main point.

Just as the lecture had gone off course, so too did the animated rocket. It began to wobble in its trajectory and turned toward the black hole. Trapped in its gravitational pull, the rocket spun out of control and flew apart. Its remains were then sucked into oblivion down the throat of the dark inverted star.

"Right, well as you can see...." continued Dr. Sluice, his voice sounding raspy and uptight. "This is what would most certainly happen to any real rocket ship we sent up into space. As you know gentlemen, any attempt to leave our planet by this method would be certain suicide. The most powerful rocket we could build would not be able to escape the gravitational pull of our star-destroying cosmic neighbour, the black hole, and the rocket would be sucked into it..."

The animated black hole arrived within the bounds of the giant red star and her solar system. This sun and all her planets, including Cessestial with its three moons suffered the same fate as the rocket. The whole of this solar system was ripped apart by the coming of the black hole.

"...So you see, just like the rocket, our planet will soon be destroyed when the black hole finally reaches us in its slow crawl through our galaxy."

Again Dr. Sluice directed his voice upward, commanding, "Lights up. Projector off."

Harsh white lights flooded the laboratory and all the holographic images faded from sight. So did the illusion of Dr. Sluice's god-like appearance. Under the colour-draining fluorescents, the scientist looked frail and altogether mortal. There was anxiety in his withered face, underscored by the furrows of wrinkles around his aged gray-eyes. His dirty white laboratory jacket was dishevelled like his hair. His ill-fitting brown sweater and wrinkled beige trousers were a sign that fashion was an after-thought, if he thought about fashion at all, and this topic was certainly less important than the other weighty matters on his mind.

Sigmund Looz and Mr. Coop approached Dr.

Sluice. They both wore identical black and gray pin-striped business suits.

Sigmund was a striking young man, dapper in dress and dashing in appearance. His thick mane of black hair rolled forward in a sculptured wave above his long reptilian-face, and the grin he wore was just as oily as his hair gel.

Mr. Coop was just as striking, but not because he was young and good looking. Rather he was a hairless hulk, a gorilla of a man with a bald head and strange unblinking yellow eyes with no eyebrows to frame them.

"Well thank you for that explanation, Dr. Sluice," said Sigmund, "and for wasting ten minutes of my life. I thought you were going to show us your latest invention – not give us an astronomy lecture."

"Forgive my blustering," Dr. Sluice apologised. "A habit from my days as a professor of astrophysics. Your patience will be rewarded when you see what I have to show you. Please follow me."

Dr. Sluice led Sigmund Looz and Mr. Coop out of the projector room and down a metallic spiral staircase to a massive mechanical workshop that occupied the floor below.

The round room was crowded with every conceivable robot and automated device that could be used for welding, cutting, building and constructing.

These machines were dwarfed by the

largest thing in the room however, an immense, diamond-encrusted, obtuse object attached to a diamond-lined hose.

Dr. Sluice approached the colossal machine, turned to his guests, gestured up toward it and said, "Gentlemen, I present the Space Vacuum Cleaner."

Exchanging dubious looks, Mr. Coop and Sigmund Looz joined Dr. Sluice beside the contraption, and after Sigmund gave the Space Vacuum Cleaner a quick once-over, he began to laugh.

"You invited us here to show us an abnormally large household appliance that is covered in tacky costume jewellry?"

Wounded by the remarks, Dr. Sluice protested, "This is not a joke! We all have a very bleak future unless something is done about the catastrophe that will destroy us all."

Sigmund dismissed Dr. Sluice with a bored yawn. "You mean the black hole swallowing our planet? Yeah, yeah, tell us something we don't know. I mean is there a point to your senile, demented rambling?"

"Yes, there is a point!" snapped Dr. Sluice as he trembled in frustration. "I have been working on another method of traversing the cosmos and this is it!"

Calming himself down, he continued.

"In theory, it is possible to create tunnels through the very fabric of time and space – hence this device which I call the Space Vacuum Cleaner. Using nuclear fission, this machine could suck a hole through time and space thus creating a tunnel, a short cut if you will, to other worlds. We could bypass the black hole all together."

With piqued interest, Sigmund raised a sly eyebrow. "To other worlds, you say?"

"Theoretically," replied Dr. Sluice. "This machine is only a mock-up, a model of what I intend to build. But there is no reason why my machine shouldn't work. All the calculations add up"

"Show me the calculations!" demanded Sigmund.

Dr. Sluice hesitated.

"Well?"

"Very well," he finally answered. "But only if...if you will back me and fund my research."

Sigmund Looz and Coop smiled at one another before turning to grin at Dr. Sluice. "Tell us what we can do for you," offered Sigmund.

"I need an unlimited supply of Cessestian radio-active diamonds," blurted Dr. Sluice. Taking a deep breath, he proceeded to explain. "Diamonds are virtually indestructible. Also their radio-activity makes them a power source that can be harnessed. You can well imagine the resulting heat and pressure such a diamond powered machine will create. Only Cessestian radio-active diamonds forged in the violent crust of our planet and by the gravitational tug of war between our sun and the black hole – with our planet caught in–between you see – I mean to say that only such diamonds will be strong enough to withstand the astronomical forces and pressures exerted."

Sigmund's smile had not changed. "You've convinced me of the merit of your little science project, Dr. Sluice. It is the way of the future. After all, there will be no future to speak of, when, as you say, the big, bad, black hole arrives and destroys our dear little planet. So yes, I will agree to your conditions. Now show me the calculations."

Dr. Sluice studied Sigmund. Cautiously he reached into his jacket pocket and then pulled out a computer memory stick. "All the data is here. The schematics for the Space Vacuum Cleaner and all my research. But you will not see any of it until you sign a legal contract that is ratified in the presence of lawyers."

"And is there any security surrounding this data? A fire-wall perhaps? Secret codes? Passwords? That sort of thing?" asked Sigmund.

"Of course," answered Dr. Sluice. "I'm not a fool, and my security is tamper proof."

Sigmund gave Dr. Sluice a charming smile and said, "It's fantastic! We'll sign the contract! Mr. Coop will represent me and act on my behalf. Now if you will excuse me, I will leave you in Mr. Coop's capable hands to thrash out the details."

Without warning, Mr. Coop pounced on Dr.

Sluice. One massive arm held the old man in a steely embrace, while the other arm, and more specifically the hand attached to that arm, silenced the muffled cries of Dr. Sluice.

Addressing Mr. Coop, Sigmund said, "Make him tell you the password and show you how to get past his tamper-proof security. Threatening his family should be enough. A broken finger or two could be persuasive as well. I don't want to know what happens from this moment onwards and I wash my hands of it."

A far-off dreamy haze entered Sigmund's dark eyes. "Father will be so proud – perhaps not of the method, should he ever find out – but of the results."

CHAPTER 7

THE GREAT WALL

EXCERPT FROM LIVINGSTON'S JOURNAL

Stanley and I were both naked and tied to wooden totem poles. For some reason these poles were decorated from top to bottom with grotesque feline faces. Speaking of bottom – well, I can't speak for Stanley, but my butt had slivers of wood in it. The tropical afternoon sun added to the charming experience; it burned and blistered our green-beige skin.

All about us, a fearsome spectacle was taking place. The Klawd People were dancing frenetically in a circle around us as thundering drums beat wildly in the background.

"I hate this island," I moaned.

"Pish posh! My boy, this is a lost world, one of the last true unexplored places left on our planet. Wholly unique and fascinating!" said Stanley. "Exploring here will add to our…"

"Yeah, yeah. yeah," I interrupted, "...add to our scientific knowledge and understanding. Blotty-blotty-blah!"

"I couldn't have said it better myself," laughed Stanley, while grinning as if he didn't have a care in the world. "A naturalist could spend years researching the abnormally large creatures of Plague Isle. They are perhaps an even greater treasure than the diamonds we've been sent to find. Then there are the unusual plants..."

"Don't mention the plants!" I snapped. "Stanley, do you have any idea what it was like to be swallowed by that ravenous rose or whatever it was?"

"Undoubtedly, a flower new to science," commented Stanley, before pulling a mock serious face. "I, for one, think it belongs in the pansy family, but I could say the same thing about you."

"Shut up!" I shot back. "I can't imagine anything worse than being swallowed whole and digested. I will suffer sleepless nights for years to come just thinking about it... That is if we somehow survive the day and aren't eaten by the Klawd People first."

"KLAWD, KLAWD, KLAWD," the Klawd People chanted over and over again as if in some kind of hypnotic trance.

As was the trend on the island, they were a people of gigantic stature, looking to be about ten foot tall on average. Their skin was a deep golden colour and each man, woman and child sported a wild head of long, white hair that reached down to their waists. Apart from their wooden cat masks, they wore very little in the way of clothing, although their lengthy hair made up for what they lacked in the way of garments. The men and women did wear a meagre loin cloth made of animal hide – an orange coloured fur with tawny, brown stripes. Morbidly, the people also wore necklaces of shrivelled-up, shrunken heads.

"KLAWD, KLAWD, KLAWD, KLAWD, KLAWD!"

"Stanley?" I gulped.
"Yes, my boy?"
"Er, when's dinner? I mean how long will this dance last before they get down to the business of eating us or cutting off our heads or whatever?"
"Oh, yes, right. Livingston, today is our lucky day," sang Stanley, as if he were cheerfully wishing me happy birthday. "They're not going to eat us or cut off our heads."
"Pheeeeew! That's a relief," I said.
"Not really, we just happen to be the guests of honour in their monthly Klawd Festival."
"Aaaaaaaand that's bad – how?"
"They are going to sacrifice us to their cat-god, Klawd. That is why they put out this enormous bowl of milk."
Right in front of us was a huge, hollowed-out wooden bowl filled with what looked like a

hundred gallons of milk. (Water buffaloes had the run of the Klawd People village and so my guess was that the milk had come from these lumbering beasts).

"It is an offering to Klawd," explained Stanley.

"I'm confused. I thought the people were called Klawd. So who is this Klawd?"

"No, the people are the people 'OF' Klawd," answered Stanley, "and their cat-god 'IS' Klawd. They will use the bowl of milk to call Klawd forth and then Klawd will eat us."

"KLAWD, KLAWD, KLAWD, KLAWD, KLAWD"

"So let me get this straight. Instead of the Klawd People eating us, they're going to feed us to this deified kitty-cat named Klawd?"

"Hence the immense wall they built with the enormous cat-flap," said Stanley.

Several hundred yards beyond the big bowl of milk was a fortified, eighty-foot high wall made from the logs of some very tall trees. I should also explain that the wooden wall bridged a gap between natural walls of rock that were part of the rising volcano towering over the island. So, between the natural walls of rock and the man-made wall of wood, the Klawd People were protected from whatever this cat-thing was on the other side.

Again, I could only guess what Klawd might actually be, but the art work in the wall gave me a clue. There were monstrous cat carvings and chiselled-out pictures of fearsome felines doing terrible things to people.

In the middle of this wooden marvel was a large square door, or cat-flap as Stanley had called it, that was shut at the moment, thank Saint Valveless, because the size of the door alone hinted at the dimensions of the creature beyond.

"It is incredible!" exclaimed Stanley. "A real engineering marvel as well as being a stunning work of art."

"KLAWD, KLAWD, KLAWD, KLAWD, KLAWD!"

"And look around at their village," continued Stanley.

With absolutely no enthusiasm, I craned my neck to look behind me and saw communal long houses located in a valley surrounded by steep cliffs on one side and bordered by jungle on the other side.

"You have to admire the craftsmanship of these log homes, which were made without any of our modern tools!" commented Stanley.

Frantically, I blurted, "Don't you get it Stanley? We're going to die!"

"KLAWD, KLAWD, KLAWD, KLAWD, KLAWD!"

Nonchalantly as ever, Stanley said, "Maybe – but maybe not. Relax, my boy! Everything is under control."

"Relax?" I hooted. "Under control? Look where we are! We're stark naked and tied to totem poles in front of a giant wall with a cat-flap, and..."

BANG! CRASH! BANG! Something hit the great wall and this silenced me as well as the whole Klawd tribe.

The wall visibly shook, and I heard a ROAR, which sounded like slow rumbling thunder.

The Klawd People fell to their faces, prostrating themselves in worship.

I began to hyperventilate and whimpered, "I'm sorry, Stanley! I'm sorry for everything I've done."

"Stiff upper lip, my boy. My dear Livingston, I've come to accept the fact that you are a thorn in my rather large buttimus maximus."

"I'm worse than that. Er, um, Stanley, there is something I need to tell you. I'm a – er – oh, this is hard. I might as well just come right out and say it. OK, I'm a fraud! A failure! A fake! A cowardly liar! An impostor!"

Not taking me seriously, Stanley said, "You are an amateur, a novice, a lousy explorer, I'll give you that, but really, Livingston, you are being too hard on yourself."

The cat-flap moved. Something was pushing at it from the other side. I trembled, closed my eyes and confessed my big secret. "My name isn't Livingston."

"I beg your pardon?"

"I said, my name's not Livingston!"

Stanley studied me to see if I was joking. Judging me to be serious, he too became serious. His wise eyes pierced into my soul demanding an explanation. "What ever do you mean?"

Hanging my head in shame, I said "My name's Vincent Sludgepool. Livingston is the name I adopted because it sounds more like an explorer's name. I'm a petty criminal. I've done time. Remember the Sir Randolph Tickets costume that was stolen from the Septo City Museum of Natural History? I was the one who stole it!

And you know how I was a last minute replacement for your assistant Alvin Updike who fell down twenty flights of stairs and broke every bone in his body? I was the one who dumped the ice cubes on the stairs and it wasn't punk kids like you thought, though I never meant for Alvin to break all his bones – one or two maybe, but not all of them.

All that stuff about two hundred previous expeditions – I made it up. You want to know who I really am? All right, I'll tell you. I was a ward of the Saint Valveless School for Wayward Boys and was raised by the nuns there, right after being abandoned by my mother. Yeah, I was left on the doorstep of the Saint Valveless Convent when I was only a few days old. Trust me, it wasn't an easy childhood.

To make a long story short, I ran away from the school when I was around sixteen–

years-old. After that, I entered a life of petty crime on the mean streets of Septo City, stealing just so I could eat. To be honest, I was a lousy thief and was picked up numerous times by the police and spent a year or two in jail.

It was in prison that I'd see your shows on the communal television screen, and I thought, 'Man oh man. If there is anybody I'd like to be like, it is that Stanley from Wild Cessestial. I mean I was a jail-bird right? You were free as a bird, travelling anywhere your heart desired and seeing things and going places I could only dream of." I paused, searching Stanley's face for understanding, for compassion, for mercy. "I thought you should know all that before this Klawd thing comes through that flap and eats us."

Stanley stared back at me in stunned silence. To be fair, I don't think he knew what to say or how to feel about it.

"Why?" he finally asked, and I could detect the reproach in his voice. It was as if he had stepped in dog poo and was recoiling, turning up his nose at the sight of what was on his shoe. Except it wasn't his shoe he was looking at – he was looking at me!

The cat-flap opened in a flutter of swings while I closed my eyes, not wanting to see what was coming through the door.

"I'm sorry," I sobbed. "I just wanted to fill up my pockets with a bunch of free diamonds."

✷ ✷ ✷ ✷ ✷

CHAPTER 8

SAM, NED and GRACE

I heard meowing and purring, and at last I dared to take a peek from behind my closed eyes. Something had indeed come through the enormous cat-flap, but instead of a horrible monster, I saw twenty to thirty little cats that were no bigger than - well, normal-sized pet cats.

They were all ginger-coloured golden tabbies, like the domestic kind, but with a tinge of something wild about them. They were just slightly bigger than the household variety, with more muscle built into their shoulders. Their teeth were longer, they had pointy ears and they also had hard little faces with battle scars.

Without fear of any people, the parade of felines made their way to the wooden bowl of buffalo milk, jumped up on to the rim of the bowl and then started lapping up the drink with their pink little tongues.

It was then that the Klawd People stood back up and resumed their chanting.

"KLAWD, KLAWD, KLAWD, KLAWD, KLAWD!"

"Phew! Well, that was anti-climactic," I laughed with a relieved sigh. "I probably jumped the gun on my dying confession there and uh..." The expression on Stanley's face was grim. "...And, er, yeah, I totally understand why you wouldn't see the funny side of all this. For what it's worth Stanley, I'm sorry I lied to you. It's not like I wanted to actually steal the diamonds or anything. I just wanted diamonds that I could pick up off the ground. I mean finders-keepers right? You were going after the legendary diamonds of Plague Isle and I wanted to tag along. Can you blame me for trying to break free from my criminal past, for trying to do something legitimate for once, for coming clean?"

"KLAWD, KLAWD, KLAWD, KLAWD, KLAWD!"

Stanley glared at me with a withering scowl. "Break free?" he growled. "Legitimate? Come clean? Sorry, I do not believe it Livingston or Vincent or whoever you are. So you are trying to tell me that stealing the historical uniform of the celebrated explorer, Sir Randolph Tickets is your way of breaking free? I thought there was a strange resemblance, but I honestly didn't think that you were actually wearing his clothes!"

"It's not like he needs them," I answered. "He's been dead a hundred years or...."

"That's not the point!" interrupted Stanley. "And then you caused grievous bodily harm to my assistant and took his place at my side in this fraudulent manner. Is this seriously your way of breaking free, trying something legitimate and coming clean?"

"Look, the only future for me was one behind bars!" I pathetically argued. "Yes, I lied, cheated and stole stuff to get here, but it really was my way of trying to stop!"

"KLAWD, KLAWD, KLAWD, KLAWD, KLAWD!"

"Everything you told me was a lie!" fumed Stanley. "You're nothing but a lie so how can I trust anything you have to say? I do not know you. I really should leave you here!"

"I don't blame you," I sniffed, while hanging my head in dejected shame. "If I were you, I'd leave me too. – Leave? Wait a minute. What do you mean, leave me here?"

Suddenly, my pith helmet, Stanley's feathered hat and both of our camouflaged coloured backpacks landed with a thud in the dirt beside us having been tossed from somewhere in back of us. This startled the cats and they jumped back off the bowl and scattered to and fro.

"Missin' somet'in'?" called a friendly voice.

"The robots!" I shouted.

Craning my neck to look around and behind me, I saw Sam, Grace and Ned approaching from about two hundred yards to the rear of us, marching right through the village of the Klawd People.

AUTHOR'S NOTE

Sam, Grace and Ned are three robots in the service of Stanley Siphonpipe aboard his vessel the Porcelain Porpoise.

Here is a brief profile of each of them as Livingston does not describe them for us in his journal.

SALTY SAM

Sam is the cook on board the Porcelain Porpoise. He is an agile mechanical-man with six arms.

Designed for multitasking, he can fry bacon, break eggs, make the coffee, butter the toast and flip the pancakes all at the same time.

It was Sam that had called out, "Missin' Somet'in?"

It should be pointed out that all the Porcelain Porpoise's robots are programmed to speak with a friendly, but coarse, seafaring dialect.

GREASY GRACE

Grace is the ship's engineer and mechanic, a lean machine with all manner of tools attached to her slender body. Her eyes double as flashlights and she is an expert at fixing anything mechanical.

NAUTICAL NED

Ned is the ship's navigator with the job of steering the Porcelain Porpoise through seas rough or calm. He possesses telescopic eyes and he has sensitive weather instruments built into his sturdy brass body.

RUST ROB

A fourth robot named Rust Rob remains aboard the Porcelain Porpoise.

Rust Rob does all the dirty jobs aboard the ship such as cleaning the toilets, mopping the deck and scraping barnacles from the bottom of the boat's pontoons.

Unfortunately the exposure to so much sea air and salt water has corroded Rob's square-ish metallic frame and having spent so much time submerged underwater cleaning the boat, he himself has become covered in barnacles.

Rust Rob does not feature in this part of Livingston's narrative but he does make several appearances further on in this history.

LIVINGSTON'S JOURNAL CONTINUED

"I told you that everything was under control!" said Stanley. "I told the robots that if they didn't hear anything back from us by noon, they were to take another dinghy ashore and follow the radio tracking signals left in our backpacks, find us and then rescue us from any pickle we might be in.

"KLAWD, KLAWD, KLAWD ... HUH?"

The chanting, drumming and dancing stopped.

The Klawd People had been so wrapped up in their ceremony, that they hadn't noticed the three robots traipsing through their village, but when they did finally see them, their reaction was decisive and fierce.

A volley of spears greeted the robots, and each spear was aimed with deadly precision. Had the robots been made of flesh and blood their vitals would have been skewered many times over. Being robots however, the spears merely bounced off their alloy torsos, and the hatchets that would have beheaded a real person rebounded off their steel necks.

The robots didn't react at all to the violent attack and nor did they need to. They continued

their merry stroll through the village as if
nothing had happened. When they were a
hundred yards away from Stanley and I, Salty
Sam shouted, "Yur jus' cannae keep out o' trouble
can yu?"

"ello Cap'n Stanley!" called Nautical Ned.
"ello Mr. Livin'stun. Oy, we found yer backpacks
we did, an' yer clothes an' all yer belongin's
strewn abou' one o' these 'ere log 'ouses."

Screaming threats and curses, the Klawd
People surrounded the robots and tried to stop
them. They stabbed them at close quarters and
hacked their mechanical legs with their axes.

Sam, Grace and Ned simply pried the axes
and spears from the hands of the Klawd People,
broke the weapons and then tossed the pieces aside.

Finally, the three robots arrived at the
totem poles and Greasy Grace set to work on
cutting the ropes off of us. To sever the ropes,
she simply transformed her hand into a
miniature saw.

While Grace was busy doing this, Ned and
Sam turned to face the Klawd People, deflecting
many a spear and axe in the process.

"I have never been so glad to see the three
of you!" said Stanley as the ropes fell away from
his wrists.

"Lube jobs all around!" I promised as several
more axes were batted away by Sam and Ned.

"Aw, 'taint necessary Mr. Livin'stun," said
Grace, in her chipper voice. "Jus' doin' our duty we

was. Oh, an' I put yer clothes back in each of your backpacks, so I did. I even folded 'em as bes' I could. Now you go on then and put yer clothes on an' I'll turn aroun' an give you some privacy, an' don'tchu worry. We'll stand guard aroun' yu while yu get yerselves dressed now."

I noticed that one of the cats was sniffing around my backpack and so I gently moved it with a gentle kick while saying, "Shoo kitty! Shoo! Scat cat!"

"These feral felines must smell the food in our packs," remarked Stanley. "I still have a peanut-butter sandwich or two left to eat."

"Aye," said Grace. "So sorry bou' that Cap'n! Some o' yer equipment was tampered with and yer chocolate and po-tater chips was opened, so they was. I gathered up what food I could and put it back in yer packs."

Grace then turned about face to give Stanley and me our privacy, and as she did so, she caught several spears.

Quickly, we put our clothes back on and threw our backpacks over our shoulders.

"We are ready," Stanley announced.

"OK Cap'n," said Salty Sam, "We're jus' gonna move real slow like an' walk outa 'ere. Yu jus' keeps in the middle, an trus' us ta watch yer backs."

Despite the flying weapons, I felt strangely safe.

Stanley and I then started walking back

through the cannibal village in the company of our robotic escorts.

After taking only three steps however, Nautical Ned accidentally stepped on the tail of one of the cats and it let out a mighty screech that echoed through out the valley of the Klawd People.

To my horror, something answered the cat's screech. We heard a loud ROAR, like the roar we'd heard earlier but had almost forgotten about.

I felt the ground shake and then through the flap of the great wall there emerged the monster I'd hoped I would never meet!

CHAPTER 9

CATASTROPHE

"KLAWD! KLAWD! KLAWD!" screamed the Klawd People, before retreating to the surrounding jungle.

The creature they fled from (and which I would have fled from had I not been a paralysed gibbering wreck) was a gigantic beast that made us look as tiny as mice by comparison.

"A giant golden saber-toothed tabby," whispered Stanley in awe.

I pointed up at the creature and though I tried to speak, my words came out as unintelligible mumbles.

Stanley was right. It was a tabby cat, and despite its size, it was still just a big version of the domesticated golden tabby, complete with the ginger colorations and the bronze stripes. Unlike a normal tabby, Klawd had a mane of bristly, untamed hair around its head, pointy ears and saber-teeth that protruded downward out of its mouth, extending below its tufted chin.

The saber-toothed tabby roared and the sound shook the valley. In response to the call, the smaller cats ran to it and clamoured around its front paws.

"Those cats are not just cats," said Stanley, "They are kittens and that creature is their mother."

"Mother of Klawd!" I gasped as the monstrous mother stooped down to sniff and lick her litter.

"Oh 'ow sweet," said Grace. "She's just a mama with 'er babies."

"Yeah real sweet," I sarcastically murmured.

"Turn aroun' an' walk out of 'ere real slow," insisted Sam.

Stanley and I nodded in agreement and then quietly set off with the robots in an attempt to tiptoe out of the cannibal village.

All of a sudden the giant cat lifted her head in agitation. She roared angrily, sniffed the air, looked wildly about and then spied the five of us. She snarled, hissed, arched her back, spit and threatened us with rumbling growls.

I was about to run, when Stanley grabbed my shoulder and whispered, "Stop. No sudden movements." To the robots and I, he said, "I suggest we all turn around slowly and face the creature. Perhaps if we are still, it will leave us be."

Stanley, Sam, Grace, Ned and I did turn slowly to face the monster cat, though I took the opportunity to cower behind Stanley, while saying the word, "poop," over and over again.

"It's bean a honour ta serve yas Cap'n Stanley an' Mister Livin'stun," said Salty Sam. "Our protection programmin' is kickin' in an yer safety is our highest prior—tay. So yas dos what we say now. Backs up reeeeeeeal slow like an' when I says run, you two run an' don' look back, yu 'ear?"

"What about you three?" I asked.

There was no answer.

The colossal mother cat continued to growl, while glaring at us with menace. She then unleashed her claws, and prepared to pounce.

"Now!" shouted Salty Sam. "Run fer yer lives!"

I turned around and ran shrieking, flailing my arms about, and prancing like a clumsy antelope away from the monster cat.

Stanley did well to keep up with me.

Looking over my shoulder, I saw the three robots split apart and head off in three different directions. Sam moved to the right, Ned moved off to the left and Grace marched straight up to the monstrous cat and faced it front and centre. All three of the robots then jumped up and down while waving their hands, yelling " 'ere! 'ere! 'ere!"

Whilst the robots distracted the cat, Stanley and I retreated into the deserted village of the cannibals. We ducked behind a long house just in time to look back and see the terrible tabby leap on top of Grace. It pounced on her just like a smaller cat might have jumped on a mouse and Grace was instantly smashed to pieces. With a swipe of its paw, the cat then batted the remains of Grace sideways into the cliffs of Mount Fluepipe, where she was irreparably broken.

"Over 'ere!" shouted Salty Sam from the far right of the ferocious feline. With its quick reflexes, the cat turned and jumped. It landed on Sam, pinning him to the ground. It scooped the robot up in its mouth, biting and shaking him viciously. Treating him like a toy ball, it tossed Sam high into the air, leapt up, caught him in its paws, smashed him down to the ground and crushed the artificial life out of him.

As we hurried off toward the jungle we could still hear Ned shouting, "Oy, look at me! Look at me!"

There was another terrible roar and then Ned's voice was silenced.

CHAPTER 10

FLIGHT INTO THE JUNGLE

EXCERPT FROM STANLEY'S JOURNAL:

A well-trod trail snaked out before us leading inland through a forest of large-leafed ferns, twisting rubber trees, strangling fig trees, bizarre lobelia flowers and bulging, bottom heavy cycad palms.

Somewhere behind us, we heard the roar of the giant saber-toothed tabby.

Asking a foolish question as he was prone, and with his chest heaving, Livingston asked, "Do you think we've lost her?"

"I doubt it very much," I gasped. "The faster and farther away we get from here the better – and we are not out of the woods yet! The Klawd People will not be too happy to see us leave either, especially since we were meant to placate their angry cat-god."

We rushed along the twisting jungle trail for several more minutes, when suddenly, a hurtling hatchet passed millimetres over my head.

Looking back down the trail, I saw a war party of Klawd People in pursuit, and this was followed by the terrible sight of spinning axes heading straight for us. Somehow I managed to catch one of the axes and I used this to bat the other spinning axes out of the air. Livingston was now much farther ahead and I had to sprint to catch up.

My stomach ached from the effort and perspiration streamed down my face, burning my eyes.

It was then that Livingston clumsily tripped over a tree root and fell flat on his face. The mishap turned out to be fortuitous because three axes came twirling through the air just above him, narrowly missing him.

I ducked and dodged several spears intended for me, while stooping down to lift Livingston to his feet.

We then set off running again when all of a sudden an axe struck Livingston in the back!

The wrath I felt toward my fraudulent friend melted into pity. His anguished cry was dreadful. It was the howl of a man doomed to die, and then he groaned, "Oh they got me! I'm bleeding to death! I can feel it!"

Still clutching Livingston's arm, I dragged him forward, even though Livingston was swooning and about to faint.

"Stanley," he croaked, "You've been a true friend, and I hope you can find it in your heart to forgive me for every wicked thing I've done. It wasn't just the diamonds. Well yeah, they would have been nice, but you know what I dreamed of buying with all that money?"

"You're forgiven," I blurted.

I don't think I'd worked through the process of actually forgiving him in my heart or head yet, but I couldn't deny a dying man a request for absolution.

"Stop talking. Save your breath!" I urged as I hurried him along.

"No, this is important!" Livingston insisted. "You know what I thought diamonds would get me? I wanted what you had. I wanted your life. I was a worthless man who wanted to be worth something, to have meaning and purpose...and I thought it was far-fetched, but I thought I could maybe even make a difference. Remember that about me, Stanley, when I'm gone. Don't remember the bad man I was, but remember what I was trying to be."

Like a priest from the Saint Valveless chapel back home, I heard Livingston's confession in order to prepare him for his departure from this life – but then I took a good look at Livingston's back and this is what I saw: The hatchet had not really hit him in the back at all, but instead, it had lodged in his backpack, striking his enclosed canteen of water. The supposed bleeding was nothing but water leaking from the broken canteen.

I was relieved to see this, but then relief was replaced by all the disgust I'd felt previously toward this pathetic man with the false name of Livingston.

Interrupting his death-throes farewell speech, I yelled, "They got you all right - in the canteen! You're going to live, Livingston. Keep moving!"

Behind us we heard the Klawd People shouting aggressively in their harsh language.

At that moment a second party of Klawd People stepped out of the bushes and on to the path in front of us, whooping in triumph.

The first group of warriors caught up with us, and so once again, Livingston and I were completely surrounded by the cannibals. Once more we had no choice but to hold up our hands in surrender. (I raised my hands while wisely dropping the stone hatchet I had acquired).

An old warrior then stepped forward and faced the two of us. I gathered that he was a person of some importance in the tribe and presumed that he was either the chief or the witch-doctor. There was decorative scarring all over the skin of his body and his mask was larger, more elaborate (and more ferocious) than the other masks. There were more shrunken heads on his necklace and his hatchet was ridiculously big in comparison to the many other axes present.

Pointing down at us, the chief/witch-doctor uttered something threatening in his language. My knowledge of their dialect was sparse at best, but I made the educated guess that he meant something to the effect of, "Off with their heads!"

"Can we talk about this?" I pleaded. I uttered one of the few words of their tongue I knew and said, "DANTO!" which was their word for "Talk."

In response, the witch-doctor shook his head in the negative.

The surrounding warriors manhandled Livingston and I and forced us to our knees.

The chief/witch-doctor circled behind Livingston and I. He pushed us forward, and we ended up on all fours like sacrificial animals with our necks exposed to his hatchet.

Livingston began to whimper pathetically and even I have to admit that I gave up all hope of getting out of the predicament.

The chief/witch-doctor raised his axe above our heads. Then, just as he was about to bring his hatchet down, he screamed, "KLAWD!"

I looked up just as the giant golden saber-toothed tabby pounced on the warriors in a sudden, swift attack, killing the witch doctor and nine others in one terrible strike.

The surviving Klawd People scattered in all directions, wailing as they went, and so left Livingston and I to whatever doom awaited us.

I observed that the cat pounced on anything it could see moving, killing several more Klawd Warriors with vicious swipes of its claws.

Seeing that the cat was occupied, I whispered, "Follow me."

I retrieved my new stone axe from the ground, and on my hands and knees, I led Livingston into the fern bushes in the hope that we would be concealed from the cat's roving eyes.

Having studied the geography of the island prior to our venture, I whispered, "If I'm not mistaken, there should be a swamp somewhere nearby, my boy. We' shall lose the cat if we can make it to this swamp."

A minute later, our journey through the ferns abruptly ended when our heads broke through foliage at the ridge of a slope.

Looking down, we saw a steep wet moss-covered incline, and beyond it, a depression of lowland jungle.

"On my map of this island it appeared as if the swamp was a short walk from the Klawd People village. It was in a low lying depression of land, due south and east, which to the best of my knowledge is the direction we are heading now – and – is it me, or does it seem unnaturally dark to you, Livingston?'

Simultaneously, Livingston and I realised that a shadow was hanging over us, blocking out the sunlight. Twisting our necks around to look up, we saw the face of the saber-toothed tabby directly above us.

Before we had time to yell in terror, the gigantic cat lowered its head, took a big whiff of Livingston and began to lick Livingston's back with a purr.

Livingston's mouth dropped open with a stunned, "Huh?"

The cat's behaviour was a complete enigma. After viciously killing people from the Klawd tribe, she left Livingston completely unharmed.

Before his luck changed, I knew I had to take action to rescue him from the giant saber-toothed tabby. I rolled discreetly away, I removed my backpack, fumbled though it, found my flare gun, aimed it up at the cat's face and pulled the trigger.

In an instant there was a loud "WHOOSH!" accompanied by an explosion of dazzling light.

The colossal cat took the hit and jumped back in fright while the fur of its face burned.

"Down the hill!" I yelled.

Livingston and I threw ourselves over the ledge of the incline and slipped down the slimy slope.

CHAPTER 11

THE SWAMP

The anguished screeches of the giant tabby diminished in volume as we hiked south-eastward across the soggy ground of the lowland jungle.

"I hope our saber-toothed friend back there doesn't hold a grudge," I said. "But if she does, I hope she doesn't like ......" I paused in mid-sentence as Livingston and I broke through a barrier of ferns, abruptly arriving at the banks of the Plague Isle Swamp. "...water," I finished, and there was indeed water and lots of it. A vast horrid quagmire stretched out before us with a forest of tangled mangrove trees growing out of its stagnant shallows, while lichens and fungus hung from the trees like green cotton candy.

"You have got to be joking!" protested Livingston. "Forget it! I'm not going in there!"

"Don't you understand, my dear boy? The cat is hunting you. I don't know why it is hunting you, but it is, and after licking its wounds it will be back. Did you think it was strange that she ignored me and went straight for you? If you want to get off this island in one piece, then you will have to enter this swamp."

"But it will be uh, er, – what's the word I'm looking for? – Er yucky," moaned Livingston.

Losing patience, I turned my back on Livingston and marched into the swamp. I sloshed forward in the muddy water and grunted, "You coming?"

Livingston folded his arms obstinately and said, "I'll take my chances on dry ground, thank you very much."

"I trust you will find your way off the island by yourself then?"

"But wouldn't that swamp be full of crocodiles or flesh-eating fish?" called Livingston.

"I have a greater fear of the giant cat we just shot in the face?" I called back.

"This swamp scares me Stanley!"

There was a loud roar somewhere close by and this changed Livingston's mind.

"Wait up!" he shouted, before entering the fetid water.

After catching up with me, he said, "Then again a stroll through the swamp could be just the thing I need to clear out my sinuses."

And stroll we did. The rhythm of our breathing seemed to coincide with each step of our march. Despite the drone of a billion insects, the swamp seemed to swallow up every sound – and not only the sound, but it felt as if we were being swallowed as well.

Through the haze rising from the water and the steady stream of sweat burning my eyes, I was assaulted by the sight of a thousand shades of green, brown and black that merged together into the blurry collage of countless trees, stumps, moss-covered branches, water plants and lily pads along with the dark soup underneath it all.

Puzzling over the riddle of the cat's behaviour, I said, "the cat was hunting you?"

"I know."

"You?"

"You said that already."

"But why you? Why is the cat hunting you?"

"Beats me," shrugged Livingston. "Gross. Yuck. Gross. Yuck. OO! Ick. Yuck. Gross," he groaned as he moved through the liquid muck.

"And it was licking you? Why?" I asked.

"You got me," replied Livingston. "Maybe it's my aftershave."

Suddenly the solution to the puzzle presented itself and I stopped.

Livingston bumped into me from behind, lost his balance and almost tipped over backwards.

"Open your backpack!"

Livingston removed his backpack and opened it up.

"Hey, who let the cat in the bag?" cried Livingston upon discovering a golden saber-toothed tabby kitten asleep in his pack.

Removing the kitten, he held it in his arms

and began to pet it. "How did you get in my bag, you little freeloading stowaway?"

"It most likely wanted the food in your bag," I suggested, "and so it crawled in your backpack while we were dodging spears and being rescued by the robots. That explains the behaviour of its mother and that explains why she didn't crush every bone in your body and tear you limb from limb."

"But why is it asleep? Wait. My sleeping pills!"

"What sleeping pills?"

"I don't do well with all this sleeping outside business," confessed Livingston. "Or on boats. I brought the sleeping pills just in case we had to, maybe, camp out or something."

"But should not sleeping pills be inside a jar with one of those child-proof lids so children are prevented from opening the jar?"

"Well, I tried to open the stupid jar for like an hour. It was not only kid-proof, but me-proof. We were on your boat travelling down here. I couldn't sleep. You know wind, waves, singing whales and all that. Anyway I thought I'd take a sleeping pill, but I got frustrated and I broke the jar and so...."

"Right. How many sleeping pills did you spill inside your backpack?" I asked.

"Lots."

"Oh, jolly good!" I said in exasperation.

"So what are we going to do with this little hair ball?" asked Livingston.

Decisively, I answered, "Here is what we are

going to do. We will leave it."

"Leave it?"

"What do you mean, leave it?"

"When we get to dry ground, we shall put the little monster kitten down and little monster kitten will wake up and cry for its big monster mother and monster mother will find baby monster kitten and they will live happily eeeeeeever after and if we are so fortunate, so will we."

CHAPTER 12

LIVINGSTON'S ULTIMATUM

EXCERPT FROM LIVINGSTON'S JOURNAL:

With the comatose kitten back in my pack, I trudged onwards behind Stanley in silence while he tried to navigate the way through the confusing maze of trees and fog rising from the steaming black sauna known as the Plague Isle Swamp.

Every step forward was exhausting, and to make matters worse, we had to fend off swarms of hummingbird-sized mosquitoes by repeatedly spraying ourselves with insect repellent.

I also started to catch glimpses of some of the undesirable denizens of the miserable marsh.

"Look!" I shouted, when I spied a mangy over-sized rodent peering out from behind a tree root. "There," I pointed when a warty snapping turtle surfaced off to our right and watched us pass by. "Did you see that?" I asked as something that looked like a floating log opened its eyes and then submerged. "Stanley, what kind of bird is that?" I asked when I saw a small bright blue water bird scooting across the swamp.

"It's a turquoise..." Before Stanley could finish answering the question, a large salamander popped up to the surface of the swamp like a torpedo and devoured the bird. "...tufted coot," he added after the fact.

"Not anymore," I sighed.

We carried on without speaking for several minutes and during the silence my thoughts turned to the lies I had admitted to Stanley. Hesitantly, I said, "Er, Stanley?"

"Yes?"

"Suppose we get out of here alive?"

"Yes?"

"I guess it's jail, right? You're going to turn me in when we get back to civilisation, right?"

Stanley thought about this. "Do you sincerely wish to rehabilitate, change your ways, turn over a new leaf?"

"I really meant it," I replied in earnest. "Yes, I did steal this costume and adopt a false identity, but the funny thing was, it felt like I was starting over with a clean slate. No longer was I Vincent Sludgepool, the small time crook. I became the explorer Livingston. I became something better than I really was and someone important, even though it was all a lie. Believe me, it was a lie I wanted to believe and I thought that if I could better myself with a lie, couldn't I also better myself by becoming an explorer for real. To top it off, I was hanging out with the world famous Stanley Siphonpipe, the guy from the TV nature shows. Yeah, I thought it would be nice to find a fortune in diamonds I didn't have to steal, but for the first time ever, I also found something meaningful to do with my life."

"If that really is the case, my boy, and you are not lying to me and just telling me what I want to hear, then this is what I propose: When we get back to Septo City, I will give you a choice. Either you can go to university and get the higher education you will need to become an explorer or I will press charges and have you arrested as an impostor. You will return the Randolph Tickets costume to the museum after having it cleaned and repaired, and I will make a donation to the museum for the trouble your theft has caused. I also suggest you keep your new name Livingston – a new name for a new start. What would you say to such an arrangement?"

I was taken aback by Stanley's wise and gracious answer, and I had no words to express my relief. The kindness on display forever endeared Stanley to me.

"I'm, I'm uh speechless," I stuttered. "Thank you Stanley. I promise – I know my promises are worthless to you – but I will do all that you've asked, even go to university – but, er, um, is there any university that would take me?"

"If I have anything to say about it they will."

"Where would I get the money?"

Perhaps we might just find that legendary horde of green diamonds on this island," said Stanley with a grin and a mad twinkle in his eyes. "and even if we don't, I am sure that something can be arranged. I do work for Armitage S. Looz after all."

"The diamonds? We're still going after the diamonds? After everything we've been through? After the bats, lizards, apes and that man-eating marigold? Didn't we just escape from the blood-thirsty cannibals and that giant monster cat? Didn't we lose our crew of robots who gave their artificial lives so we could get off of this island? Maybe we should forget about the diamonds and just go home?"

EXCERPT FROM STANLEY'S JOURNAL

My reply to Livingston was determined and emphatic. "I could care less about the worth of the diamonds, or how they sparkle, glitter, shine and broadcast my perceived station in society with our artificial system of values. What I do care about is the future of our planet."

For the next ten minutes of our slog through the bog, I attempted to explain the idea of a Space Vacuum Cleaner in simple non-technical terms, and why an almost unlimited supply of radio-active Cessestian diamonds was needed to develop the technology being developed by Looz enterprises.

I don't think he understood everything I told him, but I suspect he caught the gist of it.

"So the inevitable destruction of the world and rescuing as many souls as possible is a mission much more important than finding a treasure trove of diamonds for personal gain," I concluded.

In the heavy silence that followed, my mind drifted to an afternoon five weeks before, where I had looked on a model of the Space Vacuum Cleaner in the laboratory of my employer and benefactor, the billionaire toilet tycoon, Armitage S. Looz. My then assistant, Alvin Updike, was there with me, while Armitage Looz was shadowed by his two sons, Sigmund and Howard.

Hobbling on his shiny brass cane, Armitage Looz led his sons, along with Alvin and I around the gigantic diamond-covered machine.

"I am proud to say, that my son, Sigmund, and the team of scientists he leads have been able to build this amazing machine – this Space Vacuum Cleaner," said Armitage Looz.

"And can this Space Vacuum Cleaner really create a hole in the fabric of time and space?" I asked. "Amazing! I heard that Dr. Archibald Sluice was working on something similar before he died in that fire at his laboratory."

"Dreadful!" said Howard Looz. "What a loss to the world. There was nothing left of him after that inferno."

Howard was the older of the two Looz brothers, but had none of the younger brother's charisma or good looks.

Howard's younger brother, Sigmund, shook his head solemnly and said, "Yes we are indebted to Dr. Sluice and his invaluable research. We stand on the shoulders of giants and he will be sorely missed." Breaking into a grin, Sigmund cheerfully chirped, "However, where he fell short, we eventually succeeded."

Armitage Looz pointed his bony finger at me, and barked, "A new dawn of space exploration is at hand, Stanley, and you will be at the forefront of it. Think of it! This machine just might save the entire Cessestian race from complete annihilation. But, we will need an unlimited supply of radioactive Cessestian diamonds to operate this machine, and that's why I'm sending you and your assistant Mr. Updike to Plague Isle."

"You do realise the diamonds are only a legend?" I answered.

"A plausible legend and worth the cost of mounting such a speculative venture," croaked Armitage. "I want you to leave in a month, and we'll hold a press conference about your historic expedition in the morning."

My daydream bubble burst, and I was

forced to face the fact that I was still tramping through the marsh with Livingston whining in my ear like the insufferable mosquitoes that had plagued our trek thus far.

"So all this misery is so this stupid vacuum cleaner can suck a hole in space", whined Livingston. "Personally, I think the whole thing sucks."

CHAPTER 13

CREATURES of THE QUAGMIRE

EXCERPT FROM LIVINGSTON'S JOURNAL:

Another half an hour of stifling humidity, mosquito swarms and filthy marsh water passed by without incident, though it seemed to me that we were still nowhere near the other end of the miserable marsh.

As we wove our way around several mangroves and entered an open patch of water, I began to notice a sucking sensation all over my legs.

"OO, EE, OH, HOO, HA," I giggled. "Stanley, it feels like my legs are being kissed all over."

"Yes," Stanley laughed, "I feel the same ticklish sensations. Nothing to worry about. Probably just parasitic worms or blood-sucking leeches. Nothing a tropical disease specialist can't extract from our intestines once we return to civilisation."

"Parasites and leeches?" I groaned. "Ick! Intestines! Gross!"

"My boy, I cannot count the number of times I've been de-wormed," added Stanley.

"De-wormed? OOOOOO!".

I noticed shapes and shadows in the water.

"Tadpoles," announced Stanley.

Right on cue, squiggling and squirming tadpoles surfaced. To my amazement, each was the size of my backpack.

"Are, are th–they d–dangerous t–tadpoles?" I asked.

"It is not the tadpoles we need to be afraid of – they are perfectly harmless," explained Stanley. "It is their parents that we need to worry about!"

Monsters covered in warts emerged from the water round about us, rising up like enemy submarines that intended to sink a battleship.

"Meet the parents," whispered Stanley.

"Dozens of bumpy, warty yellow creatures the size of hippopotamuses gazed hungrily at us.

"Let me introduce you to the South Sea Carnivorous Man-Eating Terrible Tusked Toads."

"M–m–man eating?"

"Anything eating, but yes, they have been known to chew on a person or two. They certainly have the teeth for it – correction, the tusks."

The toads did indeed possess terrible tusks.

Long, sharp, curling teeth grew out of their mouths in all directions, up, down, forward, back, left, right, centre and sideways.

Breaking out in a chorus of croaks, the toads caused their mouths to swell like balloons with each swamp-rattling, "RIBET!"

My jaw dropped and I stared at the tusked toads in terror!

"S–S–Stanley?"

"Yes, my boy?"

"Last one to shore is frog food!"

EXCERPT FROM STANLEY'S JOURNAL

I tried to keep up with young Livingston but his long legs gave him a distinct advantage and the distance between us increased considerably with each passing second.

Suddenly a long sticky tongue wrapped itself around my person, dragging me backwards through the water toward a wide mouth full of terrifying tusks.

"Oh, no you don't!" I cried defiantly.

I raised my stone axe above the rope-like organ and forcefully swung it downwards. The hatchet connected and severed the organ in two, causing half of the tongue to fall wiggling into the water like a worm in its death throes.

Another tongue of yet another toad targeted Livingston. It hit him, stuck to him, yanked him off his feet and pulled him toward its own gaping mouth of twisted teeth.

EXCERPT FROM LIVINGSTON'S JOURNAL:

I was within inches from the tusks when a blinding flare whizzed past my head and exploded inside the toad's mouth. Fireworks erupted from inside the shocked toad, while a fountain of sparks issued forth from its mouth, ear-holes and bulging eyes.

With what little life it had left, it released me withdrew its tongue, and disappeared beneath the surface of the swamp.

I looked over at Stanley and saw him standing there aiming the flare gun with one hand while the stone axe dangled from his other hand.

"Can I have a flare gun too?" I asked.

Turning back to the toads, I saw them all abruptly submerge.

In gloating triumph, I shouted after the frightening frogs, saying, "That'll teach you to mess with us, you stupid, ugly toads!"

Stanley cleared his throat in order to get my attention.

"Yeah, run away why don't you! And do us all a favour and make an appointment with an orthodontist."

"Livingston," whispered Stanley.

"Even better. Go see a dermatologist!" Driven to distraction, I turned back to Stanley and snapped, "What?"

Stanley backed away while pointing up. I slowly turned around and looked above me. I then saw the real reason for the hasty departure of the toads.

A gigantic green snake descended from the trees and dangled it's massive head in front of me, flicking its forked tongue.

"Shoot it," I squeaked. My eyes followed the snake's long body upward to where it was wrapped around the branches of a tree.

The serpent hissed; it stared at me with hypnotic eyes and then in a split-second, it struck me, swallowing me whole.

EXCERPT FROM STANLEY'S JOURNAL:

It was a one hundred and twenty-foot Reticulated Tree-Master Python with a green body as thick as a tree trunk and with coils that could crush an elephant. And yet, I had no choice but to confront it.

I marched right up to the giant snake and struck it between the eyes with my stone axe. Again and again I hacked at the creature's head, until I split open its skull and was able to strike its small brain, thus killing the giant snake. Its elongated body went limp, its immense coils unraveled and it fell into the swamp with a mighty splash.

Using my axe like a meat cleaver, I sliced into the serpent lengthwise, causing a gaseous stench to escape from the stomach of the dead monster.

I returned the axe and flare gun to my backpack, before attending to the unpleasant business of pulling Livingston out of the belly of the beast.

Upon recovering Livingston and helping him to stand upright, I told him the honest truth and said, "You smell awful!"

He coughed, spluttered, gasped for air, and said, "I-I-I d-d-don't f-f-feel very good!"

"You're welcome," I said.

CHAPTER 10

THE SLOPES OF MOUNT FLUEPIPE

EXCERPT FROM LIVINGSTON'S JOURNAL

It was late afternoon. Stanley and I were now half way up Mount Fluepipe, having climbed out of the perilous lowland swamp and its surrounding jungle.

Plague Isle's dead volcano loomed above us, its cone aglow in the red light of the sun.

Scrubby bushes, heathers, glorious orchids, and primitive trees were abundant at this high altitude.

All the plants and animals seemed friendlier somehow. The sight of butterflies and colourful birds feeding on the nectar of flowers soothed my shattered nerves.

Sadly, my peace of mind was only temporary.

"A rash declaration made without thinking," admitted Stanley. "We are now responsible for,.."

"Little Klawd. I've been thinking. We should name him after his mother."

"Him?" inquired Stanley.

"The kitten. It's a him. I checked."

CHAPTER 15

THE CAVERN OF GREEN DIAMONDS

Upon reaching the summit of Mount Fluepipe, Stanley gestured down into a lopsided crevice near the conical peak of the volcano.

It was a gash, a scar, a deep, dark crack in the side of Mount Fluepipe.

Surrounding it were jagged rocks and boulders that featured crude painted pictures of winged, multi-armed demons.

"This is it!" Stanley announced.

I peered fearfully into the fissure, feeling queasy in my stomach. Needing to sit down, I plopped my rear end down on to the rocky slope, took off my backpack and said, "Why don't I wait for you up here?"

Stanley gave me a disapproving frown and said, "My boy, you haven't come all this way to quit on me now have you?"

"Yeah, but…" I objected.

"Why my dear Livingston, this cavern is the very reason you lied, stole, and replaced my injured assistant with your fraudulent self, and yet now that we stand upon the threshold of history, you succumb to the paralysis of fear?"

"Yeah but..." I persisted.

"Oh the graffiti on the rocks," Stanley laughed.

"Don't worry about that. The Klawd People just do not want anyone else to know about the sacred treasure of their volcano god or whatever the superstition is, so they try to frighten people away with these pictures of evil spirits."

"It worked! I'm too frightened to go down there."

Stanley let out a frustrated sigh and said, "Of the many trials I have suffered this day, I would have to say, Livingston, that you are by far the greatest trial. The tusked toads were an easy test by comparison. At least I don't have to endure their company day in and day out. Very, well my brave companion. Stay up here if you so desire. I'm beyond caring."

At that, Stanley prepared to descend into the crevice. Rope (retrieved from his backpack) was tied around a rock formation and dropped into the hole.

Wearing his night-vision goggles, Stanley took hold of the rope, walked backwards toward the fissure and said, "If you really want to be an explorer, Livingston, you're going to have to overcome your cowardice and take a few risks."

He then dropped out of sight, abseiling into the unknown.

There was silence for a few moments and then I heard the reverberating echoes of Stanley's voice.

"Marvellous! I can see light! Tremendous! Stupendous! Spectacular! This is incredible! My boy, you really should see this!"

"What is it?" I yelled.

"They were right!" enthused Stanley. "There was some truth to the old cannibal legends after all! Millions of glowing green diamonds! – As big and as round as a person's head – a pre-shrunk head that is. Come on down!"

"WE'RE RICH!" I shouted, and I forgot all about the fearful fuss I'd been making.

Quickly, I retrieved the night-vision goggles from my backpack and snapped them over my eyes.

Leaving my pack behind, I grabbed hold of the rope and let myself down into the chasm. Aside from the sudden darkness, I was struck by how hot and humid the crevice was, and also by the smell of ammonia. Diamonds dominated my thinking however, so I was able to brush these discomforts aside.

Less than a minute later, I dropped to the floor of the cavern and the sight that greeted me was more wonderful than anything I could have ever imagined.

The volcanic chamber was resplendent with glowing green light and there were countless luminous jewels lining the shadowy cave walls that looked like landing lights on a darkened runway.

"We're richer than Armitage Looz!" I

shouted, awestruck by the sight of so many priceless diamonds in one place.

"Maybe not," cautioned Stanley.

"What do you mean 'Maybe not? Look around you. We're millionaires or maybe billionaires or even trillionaires."

"I thought so too," confessed Stanley, "but I have a sick feeling in the pit of my stomach that I am mistaken. I do not believe these thousands of glowing green objects are actually jewels or gems." He paused to wipe his sweaty brow. "I mean this ammonia! This humidity! This is body heat Livingston, created by hundreds and thousands of bodies. What we are witnessing is bioluminescence – the light manufactured by living things, like fireflies and deep-sea jellyfish."

I thought about this and demurely said, "So we're not rich?"

All at once the glowing orbs above around and below began to move. An explosion of sound erupted in the cavern..

Two of the glowing green objects came straight at me, while something took hold of my body. I yelled out in terror as I was picked up off the ground and carried upward.

I realised that what I had thought were diamonds were in reality eyes, great big luminous eyes belonging to – what? I couldn't tell.

A myriad of other glowing eyes circled around me, casting just enough light to see the creature holding me and to my revulsion I saw that it was a gigantic fly, twice my own size!

I felt resistance. Something tugged at my legs, followed by another strong pull. Looking down, I saw with relief that Stanley was holding on to me by my feet and trying to pry me away from the clutches of the enormous bug.

Eventually, Stanley won the tug-of-war. I dropped into his arms before we both tumbled to the ground together.

Without a moment to recover, a monster fly landed on Stanley, while still another fly landed on me.

"Don't let it sting you!" warned Stanley. "They want to lay their eggs inside of us. We are perfect incubators for their larvae."

"Too late!" I yelled, as the fly injected its stinger in me repeatedly.

With what little wits I had left, I shouted to Stanley, saying, "Your flare gun!"

Rolling, fumbling, twisting, Stanley somehow managed to retrieve his gun, aimed it and discharged the flare.

With blink-of-the-eye reflexes, both of the giant flies shot upwards into the air like grotesque jump jets.

Light burned bright in the cavern and in an instant, I could see everything.

Beyond the swarming flies, I saw waxy hexagonal cones covering the walls, housing giant fly maggots.

The cavern floor was momentarily

illuminated and just a few feet to our left, the floor dropped away sharply where there was a ledge. Below the ledge, there was a seemingly bottomless pit with descending walls of waxy hexagonal cones, each housing the growing larvae, the next generation of monster flies.

In order to escape the dazzling light, the giant flies dove downward into the darkness of the abyss.

"The rope!" shouted Stanley.

Stanley and I stood up and started to sprint toward the dangling rope.

To Stanley's grave misfortune however, several of the fleeing flies hit him; the flare gun was knocked out of his hands and his hat was knocked off his head.

One fly after another bumped him, knocking him back toward the ledge. Then, there was no ledge and he fell!

I dove and grabbed Stanley's hand, saving him from the drop into oblivion. "GOTCHA" I shouted over the thunderous drone of the flies.

The light of the flare fizzled out, returning the cavern to its eternal darkness.

I strained to hold on to Stanley's hand, but could feel it slipping.

The flies that had descended into the pit now returned to the upper levels of their volcanic hive and I could see countless numbers of glowing orbs approaching from below Stanley's dangling feet.

Looking earnestly into my eyes, Stanley said, "If you make it out of here alive my boy, I want you to tell my dear Cesselia I love her and tell my son how proud I am of him. Tell him…"

Stanley's hand slipped again and I made a desperate grab for it and caught hold of his wrist. It took everything in me to support Stanley's weight and I knew, and he knew, I couldn't hold on for much longer!

Stanley's final words were, "Tell my son how sorry I am that I couldn't be there for him."

His hand slipped out of my grasp and to my everlasting horror I saw him plummet downward.

"Stanleeeeeeeey!" I cried, but my cry was futile.

PART TWO

NEW BEGINNINGS

CHAPTER 16

CONVALESCENCE

EXCERPT FROM LIVINGSTON'S JOURNAL
Ballvalver the 22nd
Septo City General Hospital
Ward C, Room 9

Stanley's dead and I'm depressed. What a miserable way to begin a new journal, but that's where my head is at. I can't even go to sleep now without reliving the horrors of Plague Isle. I can still see him there dangling over the bottomless pit of monster flies. The desperate look on his face says it all. It's that begging and pleading in his eyes that get me. "Tell Cesselia I love her," he says, "And tell my son how proud I am of him and how sorry I am that I couldn't be there for him," and then he slips out of my hands and falls. It happens over and over again in my dreams.

So here I am in the hospital. It's something

like two weeks later. I can't be sure. I'm still a bit disoriented. Days, hours, minutes – the whole "time thing" seems to have gone by the wayside. The good news is, I'm thousands of miles away from that dreadful place and I'm back here in my hometown of Septo City.

Much of what happened is a little blurry. It was probably dumb luck, but I did somehow escape from the cave of monster flies.

I contacted the robotic ship-hand Rust Rob aboard the Porcelain Porpoise (Thankfully I had a working walkie-talkie in my backpack) and then I waited for him to come ashore and find me.

It took a while, but Rust Rob paddled a rubber raft to the beach, made his way through the dangerous jungle, climbed Mount Fluepipe, picked me up, and carried me all the way back to the beach before returning me to the Porcelain Porpoise.

Little Klawd went with us of course, but he was still asleep in my backpack.

Like Little Klawd, I was dead to the world and too ill to remember if there were any more incidents with cannibals or wild animals, but I knew Rust Rob wouldn't put up with any nonsense from snakes, toads, lizards, apes, bats or man-eating plants – and being a robotic sailor, he could curse like a sailor and that alone would scare most things away.

Once aboard the Porcelain Porpoise, I promoted Rust Rob to navigator there and then and said, "Take me home!"

It took a week to get back to the port of New Poot from the South Zeolite Sea, though I don't remember much of the actual journey – well, actually that's not completely true. I do remember being sick as a dog and suffering from exhaustion, dehydration, burning fevers and hallucinations. When I wasn't in my cramped berth aboard the ship, tossing, turning, shivering, shaking, groaning and moaning, I was throwing what was left of my guts up.

Somewhere along the journey, Little Klawd woke up yowling for its mother. Fortunately Rust Rob was there to feed and look after the little guy.

As for all the other details though, the passage of time, weather conditions, arriving back in New Poot and being airlifted to Septo General – well, that's all a haze in my mind.

Anyway, I've been recuperating here in this hospital for what I think has been about a week, but this is the first day I've had the strength to sit up and do anything.

The doctors tell me that I've come down with some kind of tropical disease like malaria and I've been delirious most of the time. They also had to remove some nasty things from my body, including the growing larvae of the green-eyed monster flies. The doctors didn't know what they were and said they'd never seen anything like these parasites before and they were the biggest maggots they'd ever seen.

I unfortunately knew exactly what kind of

creatures had been implanted in me.

"Here's a souvenir for scientific analysis," said a robotic nurse, while presenting me with a large formaldehyde-filled jar containing one of the maggots. It was white, wormy and as long as my arm. Green eyes were just starting to form on its ugly little face.

The nurse told me that they'd found twelve of these suckers growing inside me.

I didn't ask where they found them because frankly, I didn't want to know.

Had I been braver, I would have told the nurse off, saying, "Are you crazy? Flush the gross thing down the toilet!" but then I remembered that I was the explorer Livingston, and I was supposed to be interested in all creatures great and small and horrid, so I mumbled, "Oh, thank you very much. Put it down on the stand beside my bed please."

I could have been a jerk and pretended to be over the moons about it, acting all sarcastic, and saying, "Gee Whiz, just what I always wanted, a monster maggot in a jar!" but then again the nurse was too frightening to give any lip to.

Speaking of this frightening robotic nurse, she and all the other nurse models working here in the hospital really do frighten me. The ten syringe fingers might have something to do with the fear factor.

Nurses are supposed to have a friendly bedside manner, and bring comfort and reassurance to the sick, anxious and suffering. Instead, these robotic nurses have the cold personality a refrigerator might have.

So anyway, after Miss Corrosionality put the jar down on my bedside stand, a doctor entered to check on me.

"How's our patient?" asked the doctor.

"Agitated and depressed," said the nurse before leaving the room.

In response to this prognosis, the doctor tried to cheer me up saying, "Look on the bright side, Mr. Livingston. You'll be back on your feet in a day or two. Spare a thought for the guy in the room next to yours. He'll be here for the next six months. Poor Mr. Updike slipped on some ice cubes and fell twenty flights of stairs, breaking every bone in his body."

What else can I say about today?...

I am reminded of how much I instinctively hate hospitals and not just because of the robot nurses and needles. It's not just hospitals. I hate all institutions. I hate the feeling of being trapped and confined in a dreary room with absolutely no colour in it beyond the gray linoleum floor, the four boring square walls painted with colour-sucking whitewash and the hideous fluorescent lights overhead. My institutional hatred probably has something to do with all the years I spent as a ward of the state at the Saint Valveless School for Wayward Boys. My bedroom there was no better than a prison cell. My journal became my best friend during the lonely years in that hell-hole and I'd write down every angry and depressing thought that came into my head. It's a good way to unload I suppose, and better than keeping all the misery to myself.

So tonight, the night of Ballvalver the 22nd, I now conclude my very first entry in a new journal and I will begin a new and a much better life as the explorer Livingston.

Some new start though. I'm still a fraud and the man who was going to help me with this proposed transition to an honest new life is dead – and so is the hope that I will ever be honest.

CHAPTER 17

CESSELIA

EXCERPT FROM LIVINGSTON'S JOURNAL
Ballvalver the 23rd

I feel strangely happy. Yesterday was all woe as me, self-pity, depths of despair, boo-hoo-hoo and sob sob.

Today the black clouds have lifted, the sun is shining, the birds are singing, the flowers are in bloom and I'm floating on air (and it's not because they've increased my dosage of painkillers).

At the beginning of visiting hours earlier this afternoon, I heard a quiet knock on the door and then 'SHE' entered. By "SHE," I mean Stanley's widow, Cesselia. She stood in the doorway appearing hesitant and wondering if she had come to the right room. Cautiously she said, "Livingston, I presume?"

I took one look at her – and – I'm trying to

find the right words to do her justice. How can I describe the impact she had on me? Looking at her was a religious experience.

The stunning creature that stood before me was like a tropical sunrise – warm and breathtakingly beautiful, and it truly felt like the birds outside my hospital window were singing in her honour.

My next thought was not so virtuous. I jealously thought, "Stanley, you dog!"

Unlike Stanley, she wasn't shaped like a beach ball. Where Stanley was stout, she by contrast was slender and the shapes, curves and angles were far more interesting than Stanley's obtuse geometry.

Her hair was a shimmering red, long in back, with curling locks over her ears that framed her friendly face.

Her sad green eyes were puffy and reddened from crying, but if what they say is true about eyes being a mirror of the soul, then you could instantly tell that she was the best kind of soul because there was purity there along with kindness, strength and dignity.

I, however, was anything but dignified. Inwardly, I was howling and frothing at the mouth like a rabid animal.

With a predatory grin, I sat straight up in my bed, rubbed my eyes, tried to comb my messy hair with my fingers and then said in the most charming voice I could muster, "And you must be Cesselia."

"May I come in?" she asked me.

"Please do," I said as my grin increased in size and spread further across my face.

Reigning myself in, I had to tell myself: "OK don't overdue it on the cheer. Can't you see she's a widow dressed in black. Look at her. She's in grief and way too young to be a widow. ...Oh and don't stare, and whatever you do, don't drool!"

She came over to my bedside carrying an arrangement of colourful flowers in a basket, along with a box of chocolates and a get-well card.

After the polite formalities of a "Here, I brought you these," followed by my reply of, "Oh thank you very much. I'll put this right next to my decorative fly larva," she then said, "I would have come sooner, but the doctors told me you were too ill to have any visitors."

"I'm over the worst of it," I said truthfully. "It's er, uh, really nice to meet you."

I didn't know what to say for a second or two and then I asked, "So is Little Klawd all right?"

"Rust Rob was able to pass Little Klawd on to me just as you instructed," replied Cesselia. "I don't know if Stanley told you, but I'm a veterinarian, so I do know how to take care of cats, even strange wild ones. Believe me, Little Klawd is being well taken care of and my son absolutely loves him. I do worry that this particular species of cat is growing too big too quickly though and that we'll have to give him away soon. I don't think my son could handle another terrible loss..."

She stopped speaking and her whole body started to tremble. Cutting through all the polite claptrap, she pleaded, "Please, tell me what happened! Tell me what happened to my husband!"

Trying to compose herself, she took a seat on the edge of my bed and for the next hour I told her everything that had happened to us on Plague Isle – although I did leave out the part about me being a two-bit thief and a lying toad – Oh, and come to think of it, I didn't mention how utterly lacking in courage I was every step of the way. Actually, in my version of events I came out smelling like roses – no, more manly than that. I smelled heroic and virile.

"...And his very last words were, 'Livingston you're the best and truest friend I ever had. You must tell Cesselia that I love her. Tell her that she's the most beautiful woman in the world and if she needs absolutely anything, you must look after her for me when I'm gone. I can't think of any person better than you to make sure my dearest darling is all right. And Oh yeah, please tell my son how proud I am of him' – and then he slipped from my hands and fell."

As I recounted these events real and imagined, Cesselia would cry and then she'd laugh and then her eyes would beam with pride.

When I told her how Stanley died though, she was inconsolable. She put her face in her hands and wept for what seemed like ages.

Trying to offer some words of comfort, I said, "He loved you with all his heart and regretted every minute he had to be away from you. You know he's in a better place, blazing a trail up there." I didn't say, "…and while he's exploring up there, I'll be on bathroom cleaning duty in the bad place for all eternity."

"Stanley always wore a hat that recorded all his experiences" sniffled Cesselia, "I mean the Journal Keeping computer inside the hat did. I presume this was lost along with my husband?"

"Yes," I lied.

The truth was I'd been able to quickly recover Stanley's flare gun and hat from the floor of the cavern and they were still in my backpack.

I reasoned that if I gave Cesselia the hat, my crimes would be exposed and off to jail I would go.

Just before leaving, Cesselia asked if I had somewhere to stay. At first I didn't know how to answer her. When I wasn't in and out of jail, I had lived rough on the streets or in the various charitable homeless centres around Septo City.

"I'm, er, in-between places at the moment," I answered.

"Why don't you stay with us?" she said and I was delighted to accept the invitation.

CHAPTER 18

STANLEY'S SON

EXCERPT FROM LIVINGSTON'S JOURNAL
Ballvalver the 32ndth
Explorer's Cottage

Today was Stanley's Memorial Service, which is a polite way of saying a funeral without a body to bury.

Right before the Memorial Service, I was hanging out with Stanley Junior, Stanley and Cesselia's ten-year-old son.

What's spooky to me is that Stanley Junior looks like his dad in miniature, but without the moustache.

His nose is more prominent perhaps, but he's got the same short, sturdy shape – yeah, the perfect shape to play crudby, the kid's favourite sport.

Everyone knows that if you're going to play a rough game like crudby (I mean running a ball up and down a field of muck, being tackled by guys as hard as cement), you kind of have to be built like a tank.

I've been doing a lot of hanging around with the little tyke (or should I say, tank?) and it's one of the ways I've been able to help out around here.

I've been company for Cesselia as well. She goes from needing to talk and to be around people to needing to be alone for long stretches of time.

It's the same with Stanley Junior. I don't know how a ten-year-old kid, or anyone for that matter, copes with this kind of loss, and the worn out old saying, "well, they just do," is cruelly inadequate to describe what really goes on.

Inside Explorer's Cottage

I've seen Stanley Junior in all kinds of moods these last few days, from sullen and quiet, to weepy and clingy, to angry and bad tempered.

When I could tell that Cesselia was in one of her "I need to be alone" moods, I'd say, "Hey Stanley, let's go throw the ball around," or "Let's take Little Klawd out for a walk." I'd then tell him all these great stories about his dad and clown around with him.

So there the two of us were, in the living room of Explorer's Cottage. I was seated on a bearskin throne from some ancient kingdom. Stanley Junior was across from me and seated on a fossilised tree stump stool (weird furniture I know, but this truly was the house of an explorer). Every room in the late great Stanley's house was like an annex of a museum with bizarre objects he had collected from around the world.

Little Klawd was straddled across Stanley Junior's lap, treating the kid's knees like a plush bed from a ritzy hotel. The kitten was already three feet longer and ten pounds heavier than when he'd first crawled into my backpack.

"So you see, your father's last thoughts and words were about you and your mother," I said to young Stanley.

He took these words in, choked back his tears and wiped his red eyes on the sleeve of his black suit.

I was also wearing a black suit, which was the appropriate way to dress for the sad occasion.

(More stolen clothes I'm afraid). The day before yesterday, I took a little wander into the Septo City Mall and came back with all the clothes I would need for the funeral, plus several weeks' worth of underwear and socks.

Stanley then sniffed, wiped more tears away on his other sleeve and then asked a question in order to keep me talking.

"So what did you do then? I mean after dad fell?" he asked.

"There was nothing I could do but try to escape," I answered. "I found the rope and climbed out of the crevice."

Stanley thought about this, sniffed again and asked, "But didn't the giant flies try to attack you?"

"They did and I almost fell off the rope several times. In fact, one of the flies stung me and implanted some fly eggs in me. As soon as I got back here, I was taken to the hospital and they had to take out at least seventy-five maggoty worms as long as my arm out of my body. I've got one preserved in a jar of formaldehyde. Remind me to show it to you sometime."

"What happened next?" asked Stanley. "I mean, after the fly laid its eggs in you?"

"Well, remember I said your father's flare gun was knocked from his hands? I forgot to mention that I picked it up on my way back to the rope. So, while I was being attacked, I fired the flare gun point blank at one of the attacking flies and that set the monstrous thing on fire and killed it.

(A half-true story. I did fire at random with my eyes closed and luckily hit one of the flies).

I put a stranglehold on one particular fly and twisted its head till I broke its neck.

(Not true. In reality the flies left me alone after I fired the flare).

I pulled the hideous arm off another fly and used it like a club to beat them off, as I yelled, 'Back you bug devils!'

While I was fighting off the last few extremely nasty bugs, I kept climbing for what seemed like forever until I somehow managed to pull myself out of that horrible hole.

I found Little Klawd right where I had left him, still fast asleep inside my backpack.

It was now the dead of night, and so under the cover of darkness and with the night vision goggles, I made my way back to the island beach, using my skills as a tracker to avoid all the cannibals, man-eating plants and ferocious animals.

(Again an exaggeration, because as I've recorded elsewhere in my journal, I was able to get a hold of Rust Rob, and it was his trusty-rusty self who carried me off the island.)

So after escaping from Plague Isle on the very same raft we'd brought to shore, I finally made it back to the Porcelain Porpoise.

I then ordered Rust Rob to pull up the anchor, set a course for home, and get us out of there as fast as possible.

As you can imagine, I was completely

exhausted and I was very sad because of – because, you know, what happened to your dad and all, and I–I I uh still am sad.

Anyway, I fell asleep as soon as my head hit the pillow of my bed aboard your father's boat. Plus with seventy five big worms in me and swamp fever to boot, I was miserably sick and as you know, I've only just gotten better.

I was really too sick to look after Little Klawd, but thankfully Rust Rob took care of him for me, and as you also know, Rust Rob passed Little Klawd on to your mother who then gave him to you."

After hearing the story, Stanley looked me straight in the eye and said, "When I grow up, I want to be an explorer just like my dad, and just like you."

Coolly I said, "Like me. Believe me, I know you can do better than me, and if you're anything like your dad, you'll be a great man."

CHAPTER 19

ARMITAGE S. LOOZ

It was then that I heard the quiet rumble of an approaching pooter. Looking out the window I saw a long, sleek, black flying machine – a Limoutrine – land outside Explorer's Cottage; and it was not just any Limoutrine. It was the Limoutrine of the world's richest man, the toilet tycoon, Armitage S. Looz.

I had almost forgotten; today was the day I was going to meet the famous gazillionaire.

He had been Stanley's boss, the man who funded all Stanley's expeditions and his nature shows and he was personally going to take Cesselia, Stanley Junior and myself to the Memorial Service.

A moment later there was a rap on the cottage door. I made my way out of the cluttered living room (I stepped over fossils, avoided a suit of armour and almost tripped over a wooden idol of some ugly has-been-of-a-god), entered the adjoining, equally cluttered, front entrance hallway (a hallway with wooden masks and butterfly collections) and opened the door to Armitage S. Looz.

Scary. Imposing. Intimidating. I knew instantly that this man could step on me like a bug.

He had a reptilian face like a wrinkled old crocodile. White strands of hair grew out of his ancient head.

Armitage S. Looz

Dressed in his funereal best, he wore a black and gray pinstripe suit with a solid-gold toilet-seat choker around his bony neck.

His belt buckle alone was worth several million putos because crisp green thousand puto bills were rolled up like toilet paper in his toilet-roll-belt-buckle.

"Livingston I presume," he growled, while extending his hand to shake mine.

He had a vigorous grip like a crab, and I felt like every bone in my hand had been pinched after the handshake.

"I read your report," he said. "I like your style Livingston. I could use a go-getter like you, but we'll talk later. I want you to come see me tomorrow."

"Y-Yes sir," was all I could say.

"Dirty shame all this," he grumbled.

"Tragic," I agreed.

"Tragic isn't the word for it. There weren't any diamonds in that blasted volcano, and so we're going to have to look elsewhere, but we'll talk about that later after we get this memorial business out of the way. My office. 2PM tomorrow. Be there."

"2PM tomorrow." I repeated with a forced smile.

"Well, don't just stand there like a moron. Invite me in."

"Oh sorry. Please come in."

The grim old man then followed me into

the living room, hobbled past me and went straight over to Stanley Junior.

Addressing the kid, he said, "Chin up young Stanley. You be brave like your father now."

Meekly, Stanley Junior said, "I'll try."

I softly said, "Stanley, go tell your mother that Mr. Looz is here."

Cesselia was in her bedroom, going through the heart breaking ritual of dressing and preparing herself for the toughest afternoon of her life.

Stanley stood up, straining to lift Little Klawd in his arms, and just before he went to get his mom, he suddenly turned to me and said, "Can we keep Little Klawd?"

"Well, er um, uh," I stammered, "That's up to your mom, not me. What'd she say?"

"She said that pretty soon we'll have to give him to the zoo, but not for a while." Tearing up, he said, "But I don't want to give him up. You and my dad brought Little Klawd here and gave him to me."

"The zoo! What's all this?" croaked Armitage Looz. "Why can't the boy keep the cat?"

Tempering my words, I answered Stanley. "Pretty soon Little Klawd will be bigger than this house and the best place for him will be the Septo City Zoo, but don't worry, you'll be able to go visit Little Klawd anytime you want."

"But mom's a vet. She knows how to take care of animals."

"True, but Little Klawd will be too big even for your mom."

"But my dad gave him to me. My dad wanted me to have Little Klawd!"

Stanley's lips quivered and even more tears flooded his eyes.

Armitage Looz repeated his question, saying, "Tell me Livingston, why can't the boy keep the cat?"

Replying to Mr. Looz, I said, "B–but he's a – I mean you should have seen the mother of this cat – I mean, she was gigantic – and hardly tame and it will cost a fortune to keep it."

"It's simple Livingston. Give the cat to me. I have a fortune after all and young master Stanley and I will share ownership."

Looking down into the boy's upturned face, Armitage smiled with the winning smile that had sold millions of toilets and related products around the world.

"Do we have a deal then young master Stanley?" he asked.

Stanley nodded in the affirmative, matching the grin of the old man.

"Then let's shake on it!"

Stanley reached up to shake the wrinkled hand of the billionaire.

"I'm counting on you now to look after this cat for me," said Armitage Looz. "Now run along and get your mother. We have a Memorial Service to go to."

CHAPTER 20

THE MEMORIAL SERVICE

Cesselia, Stanley Junior and I joined Armitage Looz in his chauffeur-driven Limoutrine.

After a short flight across Septo City, we landed in the parking lot at the Sitaspel of Saint Valveless. Its water-spewing spires, its rusting pipes and stark blue marble exterior towered into the heavens forming a cubicle large enough to seat 500 people.

I entered the polished marble shrine dedicated to the dead plumber of old.

Friends, family, dignitaries, the famous, the important and just ordinary people who had admired Stanley, gathered inside the Sitaspel to commit Stanley's soul to his builder and to the Life Overflow Manifold.

I must admit though, that my mind was not on the hereafter, but on what was taking place several cold porcelain seats to my right. I could not believe it! Sigmund Looz, The devilishly charming younger son of Armitage Looz, was making a move on Cesselia before the Memorial Service to her husband was even over.

As a matter of protocol there were seating arrangements in place, and it turned out that Sigmund was supposed to sit right next to Cesselia.

These were the seating arrangements: Stanley Junior sat next to me on my immediate right. Cesselia sat next to Stanley, and then there were three seats reserved for Sigmund, his father Armitage and his older brother Howard..

Sigmund had been the last official mourner to arrive and his footsteps disturbed an opening prayer, causing all eyes to look up at him.

"So sorry, excuse me, sorry," whispered Sigmund, while flashing his look-at-me-everybody smile (I hated him from the moment I saw him!) He was the spitting image of his father, albeit a much younger, better-looking model of his father, and instead of white cobwebby hair, he had a head full of wavy black hair with enough oil to power his dad's Limoutrine.

Both father and son possessed the smile that could sell someone anything, and like his father, Sigmund was dressed in a dark pin-stripe suit with yet another toilet-roll belt buckle full of money and a golden toilet-seat choker around his neck.

Sigmund's appearance didn't so much as say, "I'm in mourning," but rather, "Admit it, I look good and you wish you were me!"

Taking his seat next to Cesselia, he brazenly took her hand and said, "Cesselia, I am ever so sorry." He produced a handkerchief and wiped tears from her eyes and from the eyes of

Stanley Junior. "I can't imagine what you must be going through," I heard him whisper. "I hope you don't mind, but I've taken the trouble to arrange an extended vacation for you and your son. It's the least I can do and I would like you and your son to join me on my yacht for a cruise up the fjords of North Cessestia."

From then on, I didn't hear any of the gracious words and fine speeches made about Stanley. Instead, I watched him from the corner of my eye in a jealous rage.

I couldn't put my finger on why I felt so threatened. The hostility unleashed inside me was irrational. I was like an animal claiming a mate and staking out territory, even though Cesselia was not mine and I had no right to her.

Sigmund was bringing out the beast in me and while I imagined putting dynamite in Sigmund's underwear and many other horrible things, the remembrance service (which I didn't remember) continued apace around me.

Before I knew it, the ceremony was over and regretfully, I hadn't celebrated the life of Stanley or thought much about him at all. All my thoughts were about Sigmund and none of them were good!

CHAPTER 21

THE NEW MAN ON THE PAYROLL

EXCERPT FROM LIVINGSTON'S JOURNAL
Ballvalver the 33rd
Looz Towers

So today was my 2 PM appointment with Armitage S. Looz and this is what happened:

I made my way to the 199th floor of Looz Towers, the tallest building in Septo City, and the headquarters of a multiheaded, multi-tentacled monster corporation of Looz.

Wearing my newly cleaned and pressed Sir Randolph Tickets costume, I was ushered into the presence of the man himself.

I was shown to a seat in front of his desk, and what a seat it was! It was a white, high-back, leather-cushioned toilet, a piece of furniture consistent with all the bathroom-esque furnishings sold by the family Looz.

The normal flushing toilets were in the bathrooms, but thanks to Armitage S. Looz, the bathroom-look was the fashionable design influence for the must-have, in-vogue furniture for every other room.

Old man Looz was proudly sitting on an even bigger, leather, toilet-style chair, behind his grandiose white desk, which was made out of the finest glazed porcelain money could buy.

To his back, there were foggy windows that you couldn't exactly see through, and these acted like prisms, breaking down light into a rainbow of colours.

The floor and walls of Looz's office were made of blue ceramic tiles with pictures of starfish, sea horses and seashells, and overhead there was a brass chandelier of light-spewing faucets that dangled from the marble ceiling overhead.

Pith helmet in hand, I squeaked, "You wanted to see me Mr. Looz?"

Without looking up or acknowledging me, Looz slapped his intercom button and barked, "Howard hold my calls." He then peered over his desk at me and made his pitch.

"Exploration and Research," he croaked. "We back it. We invest in it. It keeps us on the cutting edge and ahead of our competitors in this rat-eat-rat business. Let me cut to the chase. Livingston, how would you like to take Stanley's place and head up my exploration division?"

I sat there speechless, but before I could try to answer he was already on to his next part of the sale.

"I'm sorry that Stanley's dead, but crap-ola happens, so you deal with it and you move on. I need someone out there yesterday making those important discoveries for us."

Humbly I replied, "I don't think I could ever replace Stanley."

Mr. Looz didn't like this answer. He lost his patience with me and snapped, "Let me put it this way, 'Somebody WILL replace Stanley, and it might as well be you!"

I fumbled my words, saying, "Well, er, um..."

He interrupted my inarticulate response and said, "Stanley was also the face of Wild Cessestial, the nature programs we backed – not that I ever watched the show or bought into his tree-hugging, save the environment, fruity-nutty-flaky granola-crap-ola message – but the nature show was good advertising and put over the message that we cared about such things here at the Looz Corporation.

So what do you say Livingston? Do you want to be a player on team Looz or not?"

I thought about this, hummed and hawed, hesitated, and then said, "What about Stanley's assistant, Alvin Updike?"

"What about him?"

"Well, wouldn't he be next in line for Stanley's job?"

Old man Looz rolled his eyes in contempt and grumbled, "For one thing, he's in the hospital and he'll be out of the picture for a long time. Secondly, he's a follower, not a leader. According to your report, you practically led that mission out on that island where all the crap-ola went down."

"I may have exaggerated just a little," I said.

"Don't be modest. Did you or did you not say you had nerves of steel and laughed in the face of certain death?"

"In hind sight, I should have been a lot more modest," I confessed.

Pointing his finger at me, Looz said, "You know who you remind me of? Sir Randolph Tickets. Don't ask me why, you just do – but can you imagine that Updike loser being the new face for Wild Cessestial? I don't think so! Talk about a crappy idea. Let me tell you what's going to happen to Mr. Updike. I'm going to pay him off, buy out his contract and let him retire to who-knows-where and I-don't-care's-ville."

Daring to make a request, I said, "But if Stanley had an assistant, shouldn't I have an assistant?"

Hitting the intercom again, Looz shouted, "Howard, send in the Directo-cam."

The door to Looz's office opened and in hovered a robotic movie camera.

Its body was flat-ish and square-ish, much like a brief case. Two large reel spools were positioned on top of its square body like mouse ears.

The camera even had a face in a mechanical sort of way. Its big outward-jutting lens looked like a pig snout while two pin-spot lights functioned as its eyes. For a mouth it had a funnel-shaped megaphone.

As for appendages, the Directo-cam had four arms, two mechanical arms on each side. One side of the robot contained boom microphones and movie lights and the other side was equipped with makeup and hair styling products.

Tiny rockets were placed all around the box-shaped body so that it could fly or hover in any direction.

After it entered the office, it came up beside me and floated there.

"Livingston, meet your new partner, Directo-cam," announced Armitage Looz.

"Er, um hello," I said to the robotic movie camera. "Pleased to meet you. My name is Livingston."

Directo-cam looked me over, sized me up disdainfully and griped, "What is this? Amateur hour? This is what you give me to work with? Mr. namby-pamby, Mr. Oh-I-broke-a-nail-and-want-to-call-my-mommy! Oh, this is going to be a barrel of laughs!"

"As you can see," said Armitage Looz, "Directo-cam will demand nothing less than perfection from you, and that is what I expect from you. It will be as if I'm directing you, although I'm much easier to get along with."

"So if he's my assistant, will he do things like carry my luggage?" I asked innocently.

The robot turned its glaring spot-light eyes on me. "I don't carry anyone's luggage pal! Let's get one thing straight from the get-go. I'm an automated auteur, not some stupid bellboy."

"We'll start you out at 100,000 a year," said Armitage Looz.

"A hundred-thousand!" The words echoed in my ears and a party started in my head with dancing, music, fireworks, explosions and confetti.

No one had ever hired me for anything ever in my whole sorry life, and here I was starting work for the richest guy in the world, earning a salary of a hundred grand a year!

"My son Howard will go over the contract with you, and take you through all the nitty-gritty details." Looz's wrinkled old face broke out in a dazzling sealed-the-deal smile and in a mood that was suddenly buoyant; he stood up and reached over the desk to shake my hand. "Welcome aboard, Livingston. Oh, by the way, tonight you and Directo-cam are leaving for the North Pole."

CHAPTER 22

VISITING HOURS

EXCERPT FROM LIVINGSTON'S JOURNAL
Flushuary the 27th,
Septo City General Hospital
Ward C – Room 9

It's been almost a month since my trip to the North Pole.

How it ended so successfully, I don't know, except to blame it once again on sheer dumb luck.

I'm over the worst of the pneumonia now. Most of the frostbite has healed and my broken leg is setting nicely so the doctors say.

I am finally well enough to have visitors and to my delight, my very first guests were Cesselia and Stanley Junior.

They came in and if my body hadn't been so incapacitated and riddled with pain, I would have flipped over three times in the air and landed on my feet like a champion gymnast at the thrill of seeing them both.

I must have appeared like a mummy to them because of all the bandages I was wrapped in, and this was in addition to the plaster cast around my broken leg that was winched at an uncomfortable elevation above my bed.

Being a medical doctor, albeit for animals, Cesselia wasn't squeamish about the way I looked and nor was Stanley Junior who seemed to have a morbid fascination about my injuries.

Cesselia's greetings were cheerful, humourous and completely lacking in sympathy. "Hello, Livingston. You know those bruises on your face really bring out the colour of your eyes and I think stitches suit you. The only things missing are bolts in your neck. Nice cast. Remind me to sign it."

She was standing there beside Stanley Jr. looking happier than I'd ever seen her before. She wore a rainbow coloured dress, trimmed in gold and spring flowers were braided into the tresses of her flaming golden-red hair.

After her little comedy routine, she proceeded to explain that since she was visiting Alvin Updike down the hall, and had a few extra minutes to kill, she thought she'd pop in and see me as well, but only because she had nothing better to do.

Stanley Junior then chimed in, asking, "So how was the North Pole?"

"Cold," I answered.

"And is it true you were really bitten by carnivorous snow weasels?"

"That's the interesting thing about snow weasels," I answered. "There isn't a lot of food to eat up there in the permafrost, so the weasels will eat almost anything they can get their grubby little paws on. They are three times the size of normal weasels, and they hunt in chattering coordinated packs. Yes, I was attacked and bitten all over my body by a pack of pesky snow weasels."

Stanley seemed to think that this was wonderful and he stared at me with widened eyes of admiration. "How did you fight off the weasels?" he asked.

"Fortunately, I had a robot movie camera with me, called Directo-cam, who sort of rescued me, though not really. I'll explain what I mean. It was the middle of the freezing polar night. I was sound asleep. Suddenly, the weasels ran into my tent and jumped in my sleeping bag with me, while other weasels carried me, sleeping bag and all out into the snow before starting to chew on me with their sharp little buckteeth. I am, of course, used to thinking on my feet in dangerous situations, and so I immediately came up with an idea that would save me from the vicious snow weasels. I shouted, 'Directo-cam replay the sound of howling snow wolves...'"

(Truth be told, it was actually the Directo-cam who came up with the idea. I was too busy screaming and turning the snow yellow).

..."That is the only sound that will frighten snow weasels away, you know, and so Directo-cam replayed the sounds, and the weasels immediately forgot about me and ran away."

"Smart," said Stanley, giving me his vote of confidence.

"The problem though was that the pre-recorded howls summoned every snow wolf for miles around, and while wearing only my thermal long underwear, I had to abandon all the gear and race away on my rocket powered skis to get away from the wolves."

(I didn't mention that I put the skis on backwards and rocketed away in reverse.) "It seemed like I skied for hours, and the wolves chased me across a frozen lake, up a glacier and then up onto a snowy volcanic plateau, but that's when I had my accident. While skiing across the plateau, the snow suddenly gave out beneath me and I fell into an icy crevice, breaking my leg. I also suffered frost bite on my nose, fingers and toes."

"Cool!" exclaimed young Stanley.

"That's one word for it," I quipped while sarcastically rolling my eyes. "But it was in that very crevice that I discovered a rich vein of glowing, radioactive Cessestian diamonds.

When Directo-Cam eventually found me, I had him call the Looz Corporation and ask them to send an emergency rescue team.

They didn't seem to be in any hurry because they said they'd come get us in a day or two.

It was only after I reported the discovery of the diamond mine that their tune changed and all of a sudden it was: 'Oh, you're in luck. It seems we can have a team pick you up in two hours.'

Cesselia took my bandaged hand in hers, looked into my eyes and said, "I'm just glad you're not a pet. In my line of work, I would have to put you down. I'm also going to have a word with your doctors, advising them to order you to stay at home for at least a year. I will be really angry with you, Livingston, if I hear you've gone on some dangerous, daring and stupid expedition any time soon. I wouldn't want you to miss my wedding after all."

"Wedding?" I said in shock. I could scarcely believe my ears! It was like she'd taken a needle and jabbed me in the chest, because I felt my heart deflate like a balloon before it dropped into the lower extremities of my body.

"Wedding?" I repeated in the same way a sick person says, "terminal brain tumour?" after the doctor gives him or her the bad news.

"Sigmund has asked me to marry him," announced Cesselia, while holding out her hand to show me her engagement ring, which was a horridly beautiful gold band dotted with a glittering array of fiery red rubies.

Quickly, I rallied my facial muscles into a forced smile and lied to Cesselia. "Oh that's er really wonderful. Congratulations," I said, parroting the polite things one is supposed to say on such an occasion. "When's the big day?"

"This Summer," answered Cesselia. "Sumpump the 6th. You'll be coming of course?"

"Oh I wouldn't miss it," I said through my false smile.

I glanced over at young Stanley, and his frown said it all. It was obvious that he wasn't too happy about this news either.

"When you get out of hospital, we really should all get together? I really want you to get to know Sigmund. He's nothing like the tabloid newspapers have made him out to be."

"Of course not. Those jilted women were just after his money," I said.

"It was so romantic!" gushed Cesselia. "Sigmund took Stanley, Little Klawd and I aboard his yacht and we toured the fjords of North Cessestia."

"Truly one of nature's great beauty spots." I lied, having never actually been there. "One of my favourite places to stop and smell the puffin poo. The lemmings committing suicide is also a treat."

(I felt like jumping off a cliff with the lemmings).

"To be honest," continued Cesselia, "I had hoped to someday visit the fjords with Stanley. He said North Cessestia was one of his favourite places to film his nature show and he wished that I could join him sometime. I suppose I'm still in mourning, and that's hard to explain to people who haven't lost someone they loved so dearly. So on my part, and on Sigmund's part as well, there was no intention of beginning a romance. The cruise was just a gift and was meant for a time of healing. I needed space to be alone instead and Sigmund allowed that. Gradually however, my melancholy moods would lift. I don't know. Maybe it was the sunshine on my face, or the ocean spray washing over me but I would suddenly cheer up, and that's when I began opening up to Sigmund.

We started to have the most wonderful conversations about almost every subject you can think of.

Did you know that he studied psychology before joining his father's business? I asked him why, and he said it was because he wanted to understand himself.

I said, 'So what conclusion did you come to?' and he said, 'I concluded after five years of intense study that the so-called science of psychology was no better than the magical mumbo jumbo practiced by witch doctors, because if I were to take seriously my own psychological profile, I would have to believe that I was as crazy as the people I was studying.

Anyway, we'd laugh and end up talking for hours. We seemed to cover everything that could be said about psychology as well as everything that could be said about being a veterinarian, and really that was the beginning of a more intimate friendship. He really is a brilliant mind, Livingston, and you should hear him talk about his desire to explore the universe. That would be right up your alley. He said the frozen underground diamond caverns you discovered in the North Pole will go a long way to achieving that end as the radioactive diamonds are needed for some experimental machine he's been working on that can punch holes in space and time or something like that."

"Diamonds that almost killed me" I said bitterly, "And it was these same diamonds that the Looz family sent us looking for that cost your husband his life" Quickly I said "Sorry," and apologised for being so insensitive.

Graciously, Cesselia replied, "Let's hope something truly good comes from your diamond discovery that is worthy of your hardship and my husband's great sacrifice." She paused for a sad moment, let is pass, and returned to the happier topic, (at least for her) of the proposed get together between myself and Sigmund Looz.

"Anyway, I'm sure another cruise on the S.S. Looz can be arranged once you've recovered.

Sigmund is an enthusiastic yachtsman and takes the boat out most weekends. In fact we'll be going out again this weekend."

"I wish I could be there," I lied.

Cesselia then said, "Well, we brought you a little something, didn't we Stanley?" and Stanley nodded.

"You shouldn't have."

"I know. People who fall into ice crevices deserve a good bawling out, not chocolates and a card."

CHAPTER 23

A CHILDHOOD FIEND

EXCERPT FROM LIVINGSTON'S JOURNAL
Effluence the 3rd
Septo City General Hospital
Ward C – Room 9

I feel like I've just seen a ghost, although it was much worse than actually seeing a shrieking transparent bed sheet.

I don't know what I did to deserve to be haunted by this ghoul from my past, but he was here and I'm still shaking from the experience.

I had noticed a shadow in the doorway and looking up, I expected to see a nurse, but instead I saw the cold eyes of Coop. Yes indeed, it was my old childhood nemesis from the Saint Valveless School for Wayward Boys.

The nuns there had been bad enough, but the Saint Valveless School was also a dumping ground for every unwanted juvenile delinquent the police could send our way, and there was one deranged kid in particular who really had it in for me, a big thug named Coop.

Maybe it was because I was such a weakling and so skinny and easy to pick on, but Coop and his idiotic entourage, singled me out for torment. I don't know how many times I was jumped, beat up, robbed or had my head flushed down the toilet.

I got my own back though the night I escaped from the Saint Valveless School. I made a stink bomb in chemistry class and threw it into Coop's dorm. When he ran out, I soaked him down with a fire hose.

He screamed he'd kill me, but I had no intention of sticking around to see him carry out his threat.

I ran away from the school, climbing out of my dorm on bed sheets tied together while disguised as a nun.

Now that same psychotic kid who had threatened to kill me all those years ago was looking into my room, although he wasn't a kid anymore.

Yes, it was unmistakably Coop. He'd always been a cave-mannish looking brute, but a few years out of Saint Valveless, and he had grown into something akin to the bimpboonzees that had attacked us on Plague Isle, except Coop lacked both hair and colour. His face had certainly taken a beating since our school days, and it was pitted and scarred like one of the crater-covered moons. His large nose had also been broken. It was now a crooked, twisted slab. His sadistic smile hadn't changed however, and it reminded me of the frozen grin of the giant green python before it swallowed me.

For a scary moment, I thought he'd come to make good on his childhood threat, a threat made all the more credible by what I'd heard on the streets; word had reached me that Coop had become a professional killer, an assassin, a hit man for hire if the price was right.

Thankfully, he didn't recognise me and that was probably due to the remaining bruises and bandages that covered me.

For whatever reason, he moved on. I heard the receding echo of his footsteps as he went to kill, stab, poison or smother somebody (that's what I imagined he was up to anyway).

I then heard him stop to talk to someone. I strained my ears to listen and I heard a scolding whisper from another person – who? – I couldn't be sure who it was – but this person hissed, "What are you doing here? Not in public I said."

Coop didn't bother to whisper. His voice was mocking and as chilly as an iceberg, just like I remembered it, and he said, "The good people in the fire department are starting to suspect foul play in the blaze that burned good Dr. Sluice and his laboratory to a crisp."

"What?" I felt like screaming. "Did I just hear what I think I heard or am I dreaming this?" I tried to remember who Dr. Sluice was and then I recalled the conversation about radioactive diamonds and the space vacuum cleaner – Dr. Sluice had been working on the project but died in a fire, and then the Looz family took over where Dr. Sluice left off – it was something like that. Wait. And now Coop is saying it wasn't an accident, but the fire in Dr. Sluice's laboratory was set deliberately?

The cold-blooded conversation continued.

"That's why I want you to disappear?" demanded the other voice.

"I would rather make the firemen disappear," was Coop's frightening reply.

"No!" was the emphatic reaction from the other person.

I couldn't hear what followed but it must have been some kind of discussion about money or payment because then Coop said, "If you want me to disappear, move to some far away land and acquire a new identity, it will cost you ten million putos."

"That's extortionate! I'd rather pluck out my right eye. I've paid you enough! Now leave. I never want to see you again!"

I heard quiet footsteps walking away. Shortly thereafter there was the ding of an elevator. Footsteps approached and then a female voice said, "Sigmund, there you are." It was Cesselia's voice. "I hope you weren't waiting long."

"Not at all," I heard Sigmund say, and to my horror I realised that it had been Sigmund who had been speaking to Coop!

"Why is Sigmund even talking with that psychopath?" I shouted inwardly. In my alarmed state of mind, I hadn't been adding two plus two, but after recalling what I had just overheard Coop say – the obvious conclusion was that Sigmund was somehow involved in Coop's crime. I mean, I never liked the guy but I never thought he would be mixed up with anything so shady and sinister."

Cesselia and Sigmund entered my room together. Gag! They were hand in hand. Vomit! And they were making lovey-dovey eyes at each other. Spew!

Somehow I managed to be cordial and say all the right things and smile at all the right times. Thank Saint Valveless, they didn't stay long!

CHAPTER 24

STANLEY JUNIOR'S VISIT

EXCERPT FROM LIVINGSTON'S JOURNAL
Effluence the 24th
Septo City General Hospital
Ward C – Room 9

Just after my tasteless hospital dinner, I was pleasantly surprised to hear a knock on the door and to see Stanley Jr. poke his head through the entrance.

"Come in," I said. "To what do I owe this honour? And where's your mother?"

Stanley Jr. slipped into the room and quickly closed the door behind him.

In answer to my question, Stanley made a sour face and gloomily reported, "Out for dinner at some fancy restaurant with Sigmund."

Frowning, I replied, "Oh."

"I said I wanted to visit you," explained

Stanley, "and Mom said if I wasn't too much of a pest that would be OK. Mom and Sigmund dropped me off and they'll pick me up in a few hours. Is that OK? She said if you get fed up with me, just tell me to be quiet, and we'll watch TV or something."

After this long-winded explanation, Stanley took a sullen seat on the edge of my bed and stared down at the floor in silence.

"No problem," I smiled. "Glad to have the company."

I thought a light-hearted approach might be the best way to proceed so I asked, "How's Little Klawd?"

"Big," answered Stanley. "He's grown six feet in the last three months. Mom won't let him in the house any more and he has to sleep outside and he's been banned from going aboard Sigmund's yacht, especially since he scratched Sigmund."

"Scratched him?" I smiled at the thought, thinking that no one was more deserving of being scratched. "How did that happen?"

"That's what I wanted to talk to you about." Raising his eyes from the floor, Stanley Jr. turned his face toward me. "Something bad happened last time we went out with Sigmund on his yacht. Both mom and I will be in danger if Sigmund finds out. He might even..."

"Might even what?"

"You'll probably laugh at me and say I'm just a dumb kid!"

"I promise I won't. I'm glad you trust me. I

don't think you're a stupid kid at all. You're probably the smartest kid I've ever met. So what do you think Sigmund might do?"

"Sigmund might kill us."

"I don't doubt that," I told the boy. "I have reasons to believe that Sigmund isn't the great guy your mother thinks he is, but you first. Tell me what happened."

"Well, um, so like we were aboard Sigmund's yacht. We were going out to the Psychedelic Sea. Mom and Sigmund were – they were having dinner out on the deck, and I was tired of searching for Little Klawd."

"Little Klawd went missing?"

"Not exactly. Little Klawd just has a habit of disappearing now and then, and on Sigmund's boat there are like a million places to hide.

Anyway, I decided to go into Sigmund's cabin and play 3-D holographic video games. Sigmund told me I wasn't supposed to go in there because of all the expensive equipment – mostly to do with the boat – but he had the best game console money can buy, and I figured that as long as I didn't break anything, it'd be OK.

I thought getting on to Sigmund's computer would be the hard part, but I cracked the password no problem. It was my mom's name. I then programmed the computer to warn me if anyone was coming.

After that I put on a helmet and virtual goggles where you feel like you're inside the 3-D graphics, and I put on the special operating gloves, and sat in the hydraulic motion chair and for about an hour or so, I raced rocket pooters around a really treacherous race course. I only crashed a few times, and I even won a few games, but then the computer's voice broke in, saying, 'Red alert. Sigmund Looz is approaching the ship's cabin.'

I ripped off the helmet, goggles and gloves, putting them exactly where I'd found them. I then said to the computer, 'Thanks for the head's up. Delete last entry. Computer off.'

Just as the cabin door was opening, I jumped into this closet, where all of Sigmund's suits were hanging and I hid in the back behind the jackets.

The first thing that Sigmund said was, 'Speaker phone on.' And there was a buzzing and crackling and then a voice said, "Siggy I've been rethinking our arrangement.'

Sigmund totally lost it! He cursed and swore and punched the wall, and I don't think I've ever heard anyone as mad as that before!

He shouted 'I thought I told you never to call me again .....Listen you greedy" ... er, he said a bad word. He then said, 'I paid you over ten million putos, and I will not pay you a puto more. Besides the police and fire department have no proof that Dr. Sluice's death was anything more than an accident. They can be suspicious all they want but unless they come up with actual proof...'

The guy with the spooky voice then says to Sigmund, 'And as for your belief that there is no proof of our misdeeds, I have recordings and bank transactions that say otherwise. I want another ten million for my trouble or I will confess to the authorities.'

Then Sigmund screams, 'Yeah, and they'll lock you up and throw away the key! You wouldn't dare and I won't be intimidated by you! I'd rather spend ten million more to hire someone to wring your neck in the middle of the night!"

Then I heard a smash, and my guess is that Sigmund destroyed his speaker phone. After that, all was quiet and I wondered if Sigmund was still in the room.

All that time, I stood still like a statue, but my legs started to hurt, so I moved just a little bit. It was a big mistake because I bumped into some clothes hangers and they clattered together.

'Stanley Junior is that you?' said Sigmund. 'I thought I told you this room was off limits. How much did you over hear? Your poor mother has already lost a husband. I'd hate it if she lost a son."

I kept quiet, but tears were running down my face I was so scared.

Then, WHAM! Sigmund jerked the closet door open!

I nearly jumped out from behind the jackets, but Little Klawd beat me to it. I didn't know it, but Little Klawd had been hiding on the top shelf of the closet right above me. Little Klawd screeched and leapt right on to Sigmund's face, and that's when he gave Sigmund the scratch I told you about, and then he shot out of the room and ran away.

Sigmund slammed the closet doors, shouted some bad words, and screamed, 'I SWEAR I'M GOING TO KILL THAT CAT SOMEDAY!'

I then heard him stomp out of the room.

I waited for about five minutes, and then I snuck out of the closet and out of the cabin. As far as I can tell, Sigmund never caught on that I'd been in the room.

From then on, he was all smiles and he acted like he was nice and friendly but I knew different. I was scared to say anything to my mom, because if she ever mentioned these things to Sigmund, he'd probably murder her and murder me as well."

After Stanley Jr. told his story, I in turn told him what I'd heard in the hallway outside my room – although I didn't go into the bit about me knowing Coop, because as far as I was concerned, Stanley Jr. didn't need to know anything about my real history.

"So what do we do?" asked Stanley Jr.

"Believe it or not, I' have already been doing something about it! I've been in touch with a detective on the police force named Lieutenant Commodo, and I know he'd be anxious to hear exactly what you told me."

✳ ✳ ✳ ✳ ✳

CHAPTER 25

NIGHTMARE NUPTIALS

EXCERPT FROM LIVINGSTON'S JOURNAL
Sumpump the 6th
The Saint Valveless Sitaspel

Cesselia's wedding to Sigmund Looz felt more painful than breaking my leg in an ice crevice.

With my left leg still in an itchy cast, I was forced to hobble into the Sitaspel of Saint Valveless on crutches, and there I took my seat next to Stanley Jr. in the front row of freezing cold porcelain chairs, the very same seats we had occupied for the Memorial Service for the late Stanley Siphonpipe Senior.

Glancing down at young Stanley's miserable face, I could tell he felt the same awful way I felt about the occasion. I therefore leaned over to the kid and whispered, "Hang tough. Soon your mom will know what we know and Sigmund will be out of your life for good."

"But when?" pleaded Stanley.

"I don't know. It's out of our hands. We just have to play along until it all comes out in the open."

We then stood to our feet as the shrine organ began to play a groaning, creaking wedding march.

Sigmund Looz took his place at the altar wearing a white tuxedo, as did his best man, his brother Howard.

The wrinkled old priest of Saint Valveless, the Right Reverend Abdominal Cramps, shuffled out of a holy off-stage, what do you call it? A cloister something? Slowly (we're talking turtle slow), he made his way to the forefront of the shrine and stood there in front of the groom and best man, while looking over the congregation as best he could through his thick bifocals.

Suddenly there was an intake of breath and many sighs were heard as the beautiful bride, Cesselia Siphonpipe, entered from the back and began her procession down the centre aisle of the sacred Sitaspel.

She was wearing a white gown and veil made of the purest of double-pleated toilet paper, the sort of paper blessed by the exalted plumber of old, Saint Valveless.

Everyone was smiling at the lovely sight except for Stanley and I.

Cesselia then took her place beside Sigmund

and they stood before the priest, while he mumbled through all the formalities and thanked the heavens for indoor plumbing and so forth.

Before we knew it, the service had reached the part we dreaded the most – the wedding vows!

Peering out of his thick glasses, the Reverend Abdominal Cramps looked to the bride in white and asked in his quaking voice, "Dooooooo yoooooooou taaaaaake thiiiiiiis maaaaaan tooooo beeeeeee yooooooour laaaaaaawfully weddeeeeeeeeed huuuuuuuuuusband?"

Before Cesselia could say, "I do," and pledge her hand in marriage to Sigmund, the sound of sirens invaded the ceremony.

The doors abruptly burst open and dozens of robotic policemen entered the sanitary sanctuary with their laser guns drawn.

Cesselia's mouth dropped open in shock as two heavy, ball-shaped robotic policemen made their way up to the altar, took hold of Sigmund Looz and handcuffed him.

"Sigmund?" she cried, expressing her hurt and confusion. "What's happening?"

Flustered and angry, Armitage Looz stood to his feet and shouted, "This is an outrage! Who's in charge here? This is a wedding for the sake of Saint Valveless! I demand to know the meaning of this!"

A scruffy little man in a grubby trench coat entered the shrine, puffing on a cigar.

His name was Lieutenant Commodo, a detective with the Septo City Police Department, and it was he that Stanley Jr. and I confided in when we reported what we had learned about Sigmund Looz.

Now after months of covert investigation, and on this day of all days, Commodo came to arrest Sigmund Looz.

The detective arrived at the front of the shrine, held up his badge for all to see and said, "Sigmund Looz, you're under arrest for conspiracy to murder, arson and theft."

The Reverend Abdominal Cramps slapped his forehead, cried, "Saaaaaaint Vaaaaaalveless Pluuuuuunge Uuuuuuus!"

"Preposterous!" shouted Sigmund.

"You're co-conspirator, an unpleasant fellow named Coop, just confessed to everything," boasted Commodo. "He said, it was his wedding present to you and it was the least he could do."

"Coop? Who's Coop? I don't know anyone named Coop!" lied Sigmund.

With tears in her eyes, Cesselia pleaded, "Sigmund is any of this true?"

"Of course it's not true!" Sigmund snapped. "How can you, above all people, doubt me? This has got to be some kind of mistake, a lie, a slanderous allegation, but Cesselia, don't you ever doubt me!"

Cesselia winced, stung by Sigmund's words and the tone of his raised voice.

"Lie my eye!" snorted Commodo. "We have witnesses. We have phone numbers and computer records tying you to these crimes.

"Why that lousy, good for nothing, lunatic!" cursed Sigmund.

"And we have you on tape instructing him to steal the blueprints for a Space Vacuum Cleaner from the laboratory of Dr. Archibald Sluice," Commodo continued. "Only Coop will go down for the murder of the good doctor, but we can prove that you knew about it."

As the charges were leveled, the terrible truth about Sigmund became more and more obvious to Cesselia. She took several faltering steps backwards, turning away from Sigmund with an expression of horror.

Stanley Junior ran up to his mother and gave her a protective hug.

"Son," she sobbed, "I–I think I've made a t-t-terrible m–m–mistake."

"You!" screamed Sigmund, glaring at Stanley Junior. "It was you, wasn't it? You've been playing a devious little game behind my back you fat little brat!"

Other language was unrepeatable.

Cesselia turned on Sigmund, slapped him across the face and shouted, "Don't you ever talk to my son that way again! And – And – I – I- don't care if you are innocent of these charges! The wedding's off! You're a fraud! An impostor! I don't even know who you are!"

At that, Cesselia removed her expensive wedding ring and tossed it at Sigmund's face. She left the altar with Stanley Jr. by her side, and they made an exit through one of the cloistered rooms at the forefront of the shrine.

"Read him his rights and take him away bots," barked Lieutenant Commodo.

As he was dragged off kicking and screaming, Sigmund called to his father, saying, "Dad, get me the best team of lawyers money can buy because I swear, I'm innocent of these trumped up charges!" To everyone else he shouted, "I've been framed! Do you hear me? Framed I tell you!

CHAPTER 26

CONCLUSIONS
AND REFLECTIONS

THE AUTHOR'S EPILOGUE

SIGMUND LOOZ

Sigmund was tried in the High Court for his part in the conspiracy to murder Dr. Archibald Sluice and to steal the blue prints for the Space Vacuum Cleaner.

His damning psychological profile and Sigmund's convincing insanity plea persuaded the jury that Sigmund had truly lost his mind, and so instead of a jail sentence, he was sent to the Septo City Insane Asylum.

COOP

Coop was convicted of murder, arson and theft, and just like Sigmund, he was declared insane. He too was hauled away and institutionalised in the Septo City Asylum.

ARMITAGE S. LOOZ

Armitage cut Sigmund out of his will, making Howard his sole heir.

He also took charge of the Space Vacuum Cleaner Project after paying out an astronomical sum in legal fees and damages to the family of Dr. Archibald Sluice.

Armitage died while running tests on the Space Vacuum Cleaner.

According to news reports, the whole laboratory imploded leaving only a crater in the ground. Armitage and his team of scientists were never seen again and it was as if they'd been wiped off the face of Cessestial. No body was recovered, and nothing was left of the laboratory.

HOWARD LOOZ & LITTLE KLAWD

Howard took over his father's vast empire, and therefore he became Livingston's employer.

Over the crater of the old laboratory, Howard built a new laboratory and put Livingston in charge of it.

All the deals made under his father Armitage Looz continued as if his father had never left, and therefore the special arrangement to help take care of Little Klawd fell on Howard's shoulders.

As the giant golden saber-toothed tabby kitten grew into an eighteen ton monster (that was even bigger than his mother back on Plague

Isle,) Howard purchased 500 square miles of wasteland outside of Septo City which Little Klawd could use as a cat-box. He also imported seven breeding pairs of rhinoceros-sized rodents called Rot-Rats and turned them loose in the arid kitty litter. The Rot-Rats and their numerous descendants then became the primary food source for Little Klawd.

CESSELIA

Though hurt and saddened by Sigmund's duplicity, Cesselia had the strength of heart and mind to put these events behind her and go on living a happy productive life.

Moving away from Explorer's Cottage and its memories, Cesselia and Stanley Jr. moved to the suburbs of Septo City and took up residence in a spacious, new home with a pool, front and back gardens and all the comfort, security and beauty that a family could ever need or want.

The sick animals of the city also continued to benefit from Cesselia's care and treatment due to her continuing practice as one of Septo City's finest veterinarians.

STANLEY JUNIOR

Young Stanley continued pursuing his dream of becoming a great explorer like his father.

He was outstanding in school, excelling in all his subjects.

He was a champion crudby player and when he eventually went off to Septo City University he became the captain of the university crudby team.

LIVINGSTON

After Cesselia and Stanley Junior moved out of Explorer's Cottage, Livingston took up residence there.

Livingston became a world famous explorer, the charismatic presenter of the natural history television program, "Wild Cessestial."

Little did he know that soon he would not only become the most well know explorer on the planet but also in the universe.

✳ ✳ ✳ ✳ ✳

TO BE CONTINUED IN VOLUME 2

VOLUME 2

THE STAR FLUSH

CONTENTS

AUTHOR'S PREFACE

PART ONE
THE OBJECT THAT FELL FROM THE SKY

PART TWO

THE HEROES AND VILLAINS ASSEMBLE

PART THREE

THE FIRST INTERGALACTIC ADVENTURE

PART FOUR

WHAT CAN GO WRONG, WILL GO WRONG

AUTHOR'S PREFACE

The events of Volume Two take place ten years after the incidents described in the previous volume.

I have carefully interviewed all concerned, and have downloaded the memories from the computers and most of the robots featured in this next part of the story.

As before, I have structured this record around Livingston's own words and the excerpts from his journal, though in this volume I found it necessary to interject my narrative in the crucial parts of the story that Livingston was not able to describe first hand.

If Volume One was about how Livingston became an explorer in the first place, then Volume Two is about phenomenal events on one hand and evil events on the other that push Livingston out of his comfort zone and give him the necessary means and motivation to become an intergalactic explorer.

* * * * *

PART ONE

THE OBJECT THAT FELL FROM THE SKY

CHAPTER 1

THE CAT AND
THE PORCELAIN RING

AUTHOR'S NARRATION
Ten years after the events in Volume One
Privy the 19th

The fully grown, eighteen-ton giant golden saber-toothed tabby, known as Little Klawd, was lazily excelling at what he did best, and that was being lazy. To be specific, the colossal cat was taking a cat-nap, lying on his belly and digesting three rhinoceros-sized Rot-Rats that he had partaken of earlier in the evening.

The setting for such inactivity was a vast desolate desert of top-heavy sandstone structures carved from the elements, treacherous Rot-Rat holes and kitty litter as far as the eye could see, piled up into great dunes of sand.

Above Little Klawd, the blood-red of the early evening sky bled into a darkening violet stain.

Amidst the stars, the three moons were in different phases from full to waxing to crescent.

The galaxy ripping black hole was there also, high up in the night sky, looking like an ugly puncture wound in the heavens.

Suddenly, Little Klawd was startled out of his comatose state by a dull, distant thud and a

muffled crackling sound from above.

Looking up, he saw a mushroom cloud of light escaping from the black hole.

Something like a comet rocketed out of the cloud and hurtled downward in a blaze of fire, which increased in brightness until it made the night appear like broad daylight. It tore into the skies above Cessestial, bursting into the atmosphere as if it intended to rip the heavens apart.

In a blinding flash, the object crashed into Little Klawd's cat-box, hitting the ground with a terrific, eardrum-smashing, eye-burning explosion! Fortunately for Little Klawd, this happened ten miles away from where he was.

Immediately, the wasteland around him started to rumble and quake, creating cracks and fissures throughout the cat-box. The giant feline was shaken from the tufts of his pointy ears to the tip of his bristly tail. The very ground beneath Little Klawd then opened up! Just before he was swallowed by the newly created chasm, he jumped to the safety of the far ledge that was forming in front of him.

A sandstorm of hurricane force swept through the cat-box and the great feline's first instinct was to run to the safety of nearby Septo City, where perhaps the buildings might protect him from the ferocity of the storm.

As is the fatal undoing of many a cat however, curiosity got the better of Little Klawd, especially when he saw a blue disinfectant light aglow in the distance. In his feline mind, this light also meant an incursion into his clearly marked territory and this enraged the tabby, especially since he had taxed his kidneys by purposely urinating around the perimeter of his property (five-hundred square-miles worth of scent markings would tax any kidney, even that of a giant cat). The explosion had been frightening and the sandstorm truly terrible, but storm or no storm, nothing was going to invade his territory without him having a say in the matter.

Running headlong into the wind, and with half-open sandblasted eyes, he travelled the ten miles toward the source of the light and arrived at the summit of a dune overlooking the crash site.

Below him was a slippery crater of hot black glass created by the element-melting heat brought on by the impact of the extraterrestrial object, and sticking out of the glassy sand was a half-buried, blue-green porcelain ring that was almost as tall and wide as himself.

From within this ring there swirled a fluorescent ultra-violet antiseptic light, which caused every colour it hit to glow like electrically charged neon, and under such light, Little Klawd appeared to be a glow-in-the-dark orange colour.

Prompted by his terrible territorial instinct and his cursed curiosity, he decided he would take a closer look at the alien ring, and so cautiously he began to prowl down the other side of the dune toward the object.

Walking down a hill of glass however was not a good idea, and Little Klawd's legs slipped out from underneath him, causing him to sprawl out on his belly and slide down the glassy slope like an over-sized bobsled.

Two seconds later, he hit the porcelain object sideways with tremendous speed and force. A stab of pain shot through him as his ribs absorbed the bruising impact.

While he yowled in agony, blinding blue light swirled round and round like an ocean whirlpool inside the circle of the alien object and sand was sucked from the surroundings, caught in the suction of the spinning light.

Little Klawd screeched as he was sucked toward the ring with an irresistible pull and with gravitation that could swallow the whole planet of Cessestial.

CHAPTER 2

MONT SNOZ

EXCERPT FROM LIVINGSTON'S JOURNAL
Privy the 20th

"I want more terror!" shouted Directo-cam. "Show me pain! Show me strain!"

The robot movie camera, Directo-cam, hovered above me, kept aloft by the rockets that surrounded its rectangular body.

It pointed its big snout of a lens straight down at my grunting face while shining its pin-light eyes into mine. Holding a boom microphone in one of its four hands and even more movie lights in its other hands, it hurled directions at me through its megaphone mouthpiece, shouting, "Your hand is slipping!"

The scene today was taking place on the cliff face of Mont Snoz. The precipice in front of me looked like purple glass, as did the mountain peaks in the surrounding area. Opaque and transparent, the amethyst cliff consisted of jagged clusters of crystallised quartz.

I was dressed like a real mountaineer with spiked boots, a red snow suit, a matching parka, woollen hat, gloves and yellow goggles.

Below me was a mile of air with only clouds of mist between me and the ground. I hung by one quivering gloved hand to the handle of a pickaxe that was lodged precariously into the snowy cliff ledge above me as wind and flakes of snow blew around my head.

In response to Directo–cam's directing, my hand slipped off the pickaxe handle, and I yelled out in fright. My spiked mountain–climbing boots kicked at the cliff face. My arms flailed and reached up.

"You grab the pickaxe again," bellowed Directo–cam.

I lunged for the pickaxe handle, took hold of it and sighed with relief.

"Line," said Directo–cam.

"Oh no the pickaxe is slipping," I shouted.

"EMOTE! Put more feeling into it Livingston. ARE YOU MADE OF WOOD? You're going to die if this pickaxe slips!"

"OHDEARSAINTVALVELESS!THISPICKAXE ISSLIPPINGANDI'MGOINGTODIIIIIIIIII!" I screamed.

The camera then reached down with one of its four hands and made sure the pickaxe slipped. It nudged the sharp tip of the tool off the cliff–

face and then it filmed the pickaxe tumbling in slow motion downward behind me into oblivion. In the meanwhile I fell with a scream as the camera flew down after me.

"You bounce against the cliff!" yelled Directo-cam. "You hit rocks on the way down!"

So then I bounced off the cliff face several times and cried "OO!" and "OW!"

"You then save yourself by grabbing on to some rocks."

My hands found a chunk of quartz jutting out of the cliff face, and I grabbed on to this, and held on with all my might.

"Smashing baby! We're talking ratings through the roof!" raved Directo-cam. "That's why we're the number one nature show on television and why you're a science channel superstar. This is action! This is excitement! Come on, show me agony! Let's see the veins in your neck throb! OK, now I want you to turn your head slowly to your right and there you see it...."

I followed the camera's instructions, glanced to my right, and there I saw a steaming green waterfall, (although it wasn't really water.) Actually, it was more like a gunk-fall because it was made of a sickly green slimy substance that had the sticky sweet consistency of syrup as it dropped in stretchy globs of goop over the cliff ledge.

"There it is! You look at the mean green cascade in wonder and awe."

"RRRRRING! RRRRRRING!"

Suddenly, a jarring telephone ring inside Directo-cam's body made the robot camera vibrate and rattle.

"Hey Livingston. You got a call! It's Howard."

"Tell Howard I'm busy."

"He says it's an emergency, and he won't take no for an answer."

"Alright, patch him through,"

That's when I stopped acting, relaxed my grip on the rock, effortlessly held on by one finger, and then let go of the rock all together. Instead of plunging into the chasm though, I dangled there in the air by the wires and harness I was hooked up to.

Howard's unpleasant frog-with-a-head-cold voice was then amplified from the camera's megaphone mouth, and his miserable face appeared inside the big lens-snout of Directo-cam.

"Good. There you are. Livingston, I need to talk to you," he said.

"Howard, can I call you back? This isn't a good time."

"I need you to drop whatever you're doing and get back here as quick as you...." Howard's voice trailed off and then he asked, "Are you floating?"

"Not exactly."

"You're rigged up to something aren't you?"

"Don't worry, the wires will be removed in post production."

"But doesn't everybody think you really climb..." Howard stopped, shook his head impatiently and said, "Oh never mind. The point is, Little Klawd found something! It's a porcelain ring made of indestructible porcelain and with strange writing all over it. My guess is that it fell from space. I could be wrong, but last night there were reports of a bright object falling from the sky, and then there was a quake, a sandstorm and guess where the epicentre was?"

"Haven't a clue..."

"That's right. Little Klawd's five hundred square-mile cat-box."

I screwed up my face, thought about this, and said, "And?...."

"And I can send somebody to pick you up in around ten minutes."

"Ten minutes? Ten minutes? But the Directo-cam and I have not finished making our documentary yet. I'm on the verge of a big discovery up here. I'm looking for the source of..."

Howard's tiny image in the camera's lens-snout blinked out.

"He hung up!" shrugged Directo-cam.

"...The River Vile," I finished.

CHAPTER 3

THE VILE RIVER

EXCERPT FROM LIVINGSTON'S JOURNAL

I stood on the banks of the steaming green stream that I'd seen tumbling, stretching, dropping and plopping from the top of Mont Snoz, not ten minutes earlier.

Speaking of the top, it was a flat rocky plateau with strange amethyst crystal formations rising out of its lofty surface. The river of green gunk snaked its way in and out of these bizarre crystal sculptures like slow moving Jell-O-gelatin.

I cleared my throat, flashed a dazzling smile at Directo-cam, and said, "How do I look?"

"If I told you you looked like the hind end of a horse, would you believe me?".

"Actually, I'm the handsome host of the highest rated nature show on television, and I need a touch up,"

Directo-cam hovered over to me and shouted "Makeup!" through its loud megaphone mouthpiece, causing several avalanches on some of the other mountains in the vicinity. One of its mechanical arms retrieved a powder puff from its side and it slapped, hit and pummelled my face until I was covered in powder. Its other arm simultaneously grabbed a brush, and proceeded to comb my red moustache.

After the touch-up, Directo-Cam backed away from me and announced, "Ready whenever you are."

Once again, its hands held up bright movie lights, while a fourth hand held up a boom microphone.

"On my count…One, two…and…"

"Good evening and welcome to 'Wild Cessestial!'" I said, while striking a heroic pose. The camera then zoomed in for a close-up of my face as I delivered my famous opening line. "The name's Livingston, and I'm an explorer, baby!"

Winking and grinning, I proceeded with my presenting duties. "I am standing upon Mont Snoz in the Amethyst Alps. This purple mountain of crystallised amethyst – which just so happens to be shaped like a mile-high nose – was created by cataclysmic forces when the world was first formed. It's as if the world blew its nose and Mont Snoz was the result. The reason I've freely climbed this previously unclimb-up-able peak was not merely to mark yet another milestone in the history of mountaineering – oh no; rather I've risked life and limb for another more important reason. It's up here that I believe I'll find the source of the Vile."

I turned away from the camera and began to follow the winding path of the green gunk stream. Looking back over my shoulder, I said, "Yes, the gooey green river was long thought to flow from the Amethyst Alps, but no one has yet discovered the source of the Vile.

I continued to trudge through the snow in my spiky boots, following the course of the Vile River. It oozed around one particularly large crystal formation, and there on the other side around the bend, I discovered the source of the green goo.

My jaw dropped open, I scrunched up my face in revulsion, and blurted out, "Oh, that's vile!"

Before me was a herd of mangy, hairy, diseased albino mountain mammoths. Old infirm pachyderms, with terrible flu symptoms, trumpeted weakly and discharged mucus from their trunks, thus creating a stream of snot.

"Yes, ladies and gentleman," I announced while screwing up my nose, "the source of the River Vile can be attributed to sick Albino Mountain Mammoths blowing their noses. This is a rare sight indeed. Albino Mountain Mammoths are terribly difficult to see in the snow. Usually their little pink eyes give them away, but here there are dozens of the sick elephants in one place. Could it be? Yes, I think it is! Not only have I climbed Mont Snoz unaided and discovered the source of the River Vile, but I have also discovered the legendary Albino Mountain Mammoth graveyard."

No sooner had I said all this then one of the ill elephants sneezed in my direction. The force of the flying phlegm knocked me backwards into the Vile River.

I squirmed, turned, flipped and kicked, but I was unable to pull myself out of the gunk stream. In the end there was nothing I could do but slide with the green tide.

In the meanwhile, the Directo-cam hovered over me giving me performance tips I didn't need.

"Show me disgust! Show me struggle!" shouted Directo-cam. "This is great stuff! OK I'm zooming in on your face! You suddenly realise you are being carried toward the mountain ledge in the slow dribble flow and can't do a thing about it! CUT and it's a PRINT! Now, I'll circle around so I can get the best angle on you falling over the – I'll call it New Boogera Falls. Yeah, that's catchy." Directo-cam then added, "Like a cold."

"Why don't you help me?" I screamed.

Directo-cam zipped away out of sight. I presume he positioned himself below the cliff so that he could film my death from the best possible angle.

"What and miss the scoop of a lifetime?" I heard Directo-cam shout from somewhere nearby. "This footage will give me favour with the academy come award season. I mean give me the Mario now."

A moment later, I slid over 'New Boogera Falls' while calling Directo-cam names that would have to be deleted in post production.

Suddenly, a search and rescue air ambulance interrupted my plunge. I landed on a stretcher conveniently located in the back of the craft after falling through the open top of the rocket-powered pooter. The only thing I could think of to say in my traumatised state was, "What took you guys so long?" I then fell backwards on to the stretcher.

The ambulance circled the chasm and ascended up and away from Mont Snoz. We zoomed off toward the horizon, while somewhere behind us, I heard the Directo-Cam yell "Hey wait for meeeeeeeeee!"

CHAPTER 4

THE SEPTO CITY PET CLINIC

AUTHOR'S NOTE

My humble apologies for interrupting the chronology of events. It will be important to back up several hours and recount Howard's morning prior to his conversation with Livingston (the conversation via the connection through the Directo-cam and taking place while Livingston was dangling over the side of Mont Snoz.)

AUTHOR'S NARRATION
5:20 AM, Privy the 20th

It was just before dawn (the morning after Little Klawd's encounter with the alien porcelain ring) and it was at this sleepy hour that Howard Looz entered the Septo City Pet Clinic.

Unhappily, his senses were assaulted by primary-coloured pictures of happy cartoon animals papering the walls.

Beyond his intolerance of all things cute,

Howard suspected the wallpaper itself was crawling with bacteria. To his anxious mind, there was nothing in the animal hospital that was free from contamination including the very air he was breathing. It was for this reason he had taken the precaution of wearing rubber gloves and had placed a surgical mask over his long, lizard-like face.

A door leading to the interior of the hospital opened. The veterinarian on duty, a woman with emerald green eyes and curling locks of red hair entered the reception room dressed in a white doctor's jacket and a smart dark-blue trouser suit.

"Hello Cesselia," said Howard.

A decade had done little to detract from Cesselia's beauty and it could be argued that her appearance had been enhanced by time. Even the natural weight gain that accompanies the aging process worked in Cesselia's favour, filling out her feminine figure.

The only noticeable imperfection to blemish Cesselia, was the severity of her current facial expression. Her warm smile had turned to a frown upon seeing Howard, and her normally kind eyes had narrowed into a frosty glare.

With a slight nod, she flatly said, "Hello Howard."

Intimidated by Cesselia's cheerless greeting, Howard broke eye contact and looked up, down, around and anywhere but directly into Cesselia's steady gaze. He mumbled through his mask, and said, "Nice to see you. Er, right, erm, um, you, er, said Little Klawd was in an accident of some sort?" Howard sounded like a frog with nasal problems at the best of times, but with his voice muffled, he sounded like a frog being suffocated under a pillow.

"Why don't you take off the mask, Howard? I can't understand a word you're saying."

"I'd rather keep it on, thanks," insisted Howard. Speaking up, he said, "Usually it is Little Klawd that causes the accidents. Every time he leaves his cat-box and comes into the city he costs me tens of thousands of putos in property damage and lawsuits. So what happened this time? Did something fall on his head in that quake we had last night?"

"I'll show you." Cesselia turned about face and said, "Follow me. Little Klawd's in the operating theatre."

Howard fell in behind Cesselia and they entered a long hallway filled with noisy barks, squawks, roars, chirps, growls, screeches, snorts, whinnies, bleats, moos, meows, and hisses. Glancing timidly to his right and left, Howard could see that both sides of the corridor were crowded with electronic animal cages (cages without bars that kept animals inside their open pens with invisible walls of electricity). These housed every kind of convalescing creature imaginable, from fanged hamsters to enormous Rot-Rats.

At the end of the hallway and after stopping in front of a sliding glass door, Cesselia said, "We need to be decontaminated before we can go on."

"Thank the plumber," sighed Howard. "Yes, please!" He then remarked, "Sigmund's doing better now, so I'm told."

Howard let the words hang in the air, while he studied Cesselia to see what kind of hostility these words might cause.

She was silent and showed no reaction beyond a serious frown.

"I was ashamed of what my brother did," continued Howard. "He disgraced the good name of Looz." A shower of decontamination mist and spray fell on Cesselia and Howard from sprinklers overhead. "You should know Cesselia that Sigmund was treated for the mental illness that made him do those horrible things – you know, take part in the conspiracy to murder Dr. Archibald Sluice – steal the plans for the Space Vacuum Cleaner and so forth – of course I can understand how hurt and upset you were to find these things out – on your wedding day of all days – and I don't know if you know this or not, but Sigmund made a full recovery. Sigmund actually became a psychiatrist. He now works up at the Septo City Insane Asylum where he started out as an incarcerated inmate. We were all high achievers in our family, but you got to hand it to Sigmund. He worked his way up from patient to doctor." The decontaminating spray ceased and was replaced by drying blasts of hot air and flashes of bacteria zapping radiation. "...Now he's doing his part to help others so..."

'That is such nonsense!" interrupted Cesselia. "I clean cages that smell better than your brother's lies. This goes way beyond being bitter or holding a grudge. Sigmund should be in prison. Those high priced lawyers your dad paid for got him off with a slap on the wrist and some time in counselling up at the asylum. Little good it did him though. He sends me at least three letters a week telling me that he's a changed man and that he's still madly in love with me! It's obsessive Howard! Do you call that cured? He's one letter and bouquet of flowers away from a court restraining order. Every time one of those sickly perfumed letters comes through the door, I either throw it away or burn it."

"Oh," said Howard. Feeling awkward, Howard changed the subject and asked, "Er, so uh, how's young Stanley?"

Softening, Cesselia replied, "Headstrong as ever. He graduated from Septo City University last summer, specialising in you name it – Let me see, biology, zoology, anthropology, archaeology, comparative religions and probably a dozen other subjects I can't recall at this moment in time. Needless to say, he did remarkably well and I'm very proud of him."

"And what is he doing now?"

"That's what I'd like to know. Two months ago, he took off for the Psychedelic Sea in order to dive for sunken treasure. I haven't heard from him for three weeks, and to be honest, I'm worried sick."

"I'm sure he's fine Cesselia."

"He wanted to work with Livingston, but Livingston told him he was too young and inexperienced. Now I think he's trying to prove Livingston wrong."

"Is that so? I'll have a word with Livingston," promised Howard. "Livingston works for me after all so I think I should have the last word on who does and doesn't work with him. Besides, I think young Stanley would make an excellent explorer. Leave it with me and I'll see what I can do."

Cesselia smiled. "Thank you Howard. I'd appreciate that."

The drying and zapping finally stopped. Glass doors then slid open and Cesselia said, "This way. The operating theatre is just through here."

CHAPTER 5

THE ALIEN OBJECT

"Little Klawd managed to get himself stuck inside that, erm, gigantic ring machine object over there," said Cesselia as she and Howard entered the gallery overlooking the high-tech operating theatre.

The arena below was just big enough to hold an eighteen-ton cat and the massive machine Cesselia was talking about.

Little Klawd was spread out flat on his back in an anaesthetised catnap, snoring, snuffling and purring as he dozed.

Beyond Little Klawd, on the far side of the theatre, the mysterious porcelain object sat like a legless chair (ringed seat on the floor with a perpendicular ringed back standing upright behind it.)

Light flooded down from the ceiling above, which made the object look like a holy relic blessed by Saint Valveless.

"I say machine," continued Cesselia, "because it was built with some type of unknown function – I mean, lights, video panels with animated writing, and as you can see, there is a column jutting upward from the ring base with a handle and what looks like a coin slot for money. The steps you see leading up to the base can be withdrawn into a panel that will open in the underside of the base when it is off.

The lid is interesting. You will notice that it is the same size and oval shape as the base. It is mounted on hinges at the base and it stands at a ninety degree angle to the base, and yes, it will close when the machine switches off. I haven't a clue what the machine does, but the biggest mystery is the foreign– I think it's foreign – it could be coded – anyway, the writing that you see appearing."

The writing Cesselia referred to filled video panels lining the inner circle of the lid. The panels were lit up with a blue light while the dark–green stick–figures danced about like the participants of an aerobics exercise class.
"It is as if those little pictures are all shouting, trying to get our attention," explained Cesselia, "but I haven't had time to try to decipher their message. The machine is on now, but when you pull down on the handle, the machine will switch off, the video screens go blank, the lid closes and the stairs are withdrawn. Pulling down on the handle again will then switch it all back on. We didn't find any of this out though until after removing the object from around Little Klawd. He was actually stuck in the base ring and so the machine was upturned and on its side when Little Klawd was discovered.

Luckily for him, some seismologists from the university had gone out to Little Klawd's cat-box to investigate the source of last night's quake. They found Little Klawd stuck in the machine and called the clinic.

I was alerted to Little Klawd's predicament and arranged to have him airlifted to the hospital by a military heli-pooter.

It wasn't easy, but with a lot of lubrication we were able to pull the ring off Little Klawd – well that is with hydraulic robotic arms pushing and pulling.

But before that, we tried to cut the, the whatever it is, off with a surgical saw. We couldn't cut it though. The density of the porcelain was murder on our cutting tools, shattering steel blades if you can believe that! We went through five different saws and couldn't put a dent in that thing. There's not even a scratch! I didn't believe it was actually porcelain until I had a chemical analysis done on it. Incredible! But yes, the machine is made of porcelain all right. Porcelain like nothing in this world, with elemental porcelain molecules so compact and dense that I wouldn't be surprised if this thing turns out to be indestructible."

"Indestructible porcelain!" said Howard.

"Don't quote me on that. I don't know if it really is indestructible," admitted Cesselia. "I've just never seen anything like it."

"Indestructible!" Howard repeated, pondering

the word. His face brightened as if he was experiencing a spiritual epiphany, a revelation, and it dawned on him that his cat had just stumbled on something absolutely amazing – something that could help him step out from underneath the shadow of his father and make his own mark for Looz Enterprises. "With Indestructible porcelain," Howard told himself, "I could revolutionise more than the family business. I could revolutionise the world!"

Trying not to betray his increasing excitement about the ring, Howard asked a diverting question. "Was Little Klawd hurt at all?"

"Apart from a few bumps and bruises, no. We had to anaesthetise him before we tried to remove the ring. Then after pulling him out of the object, we immediately gave him a cat scan and the results came back saying that he was perfectly fine, although I do want to keep him overnight for observation." As an afterthought she said, "Now all I have to do is figure out what to do with the machine. Do you know anything about it?"

"Of course," Howard lied. "Who else would have such technology? The machine made from indestructible porcelain is something that we have been developing over at Looz Enterprises. Unfortunately, Little Klawd just happened to wander into the testing area and got himself stuck."

Cesselia's eyes narrowed suspiciously and she searched Howard's face for the truth behind his words. Quizzing him, she said, "This isn't another attempt at developing a Space Vacuum Cleaner is it?"

In a hush, Howard replied, "All I can tell you Cesselia, is that it's a top secret project. I'll have my people pick up the ring and bring it back to our product testing laboratory and I'd appreciate it if you didn't discuss this incident with anyone."

He gave Cesselia a serious knowing nod, and tapped his masked nose as if to say, "This is our little secret." "Now how much do I owe you? – For the saws, the treatment, everything?" he asked. Without waiting for an answer, Howard began to unwind the paper money notes that were rolled up on his fancy, solid gold toilet-roll belt buckle.

CHAPTER 6

THE BUMLEY

Howard took an elevator up to the rooftop parking lot of the Septo City Pet Clinic and then rushed out on to the flat tarmac of the lot. There he ripped off his surgical mask and gloves and breathed a sigh of relief, grateful to be outside the germ-infested hospital.

The next thing he did was look for his Bumley.

Among the rocket-powered pooters, the Bumley made the other crafts pale into insignificance.

Like all pooters, it looked like a toilet mounted on a rocket engine, but the fifty-year old vintage Bumley was covered in real gold, and it made Howard feel like a king when he sat down upon its golden throne.

The Bumley was mounted on long conical rocket boosters and exhaust pipes, and like the rest of the magnificent pooter, these were also overlaid in gold.

Pulling out the ignition keys from his right trouser pocket, Howard turned off the alarms with a button on the keys.

He stepped up to his flying machine before taking his place on the leather-padded ringed seat.

He proceeded to check the gas gauge on the driving control panel, which was situated on a column jutting upward between his legs from the base. The gauge assured him that the bowl beneath his seat was full of the methane-based rocket fuel upon which the craft was powered.

He put the ignition key into the slot, revved the rocket engines, shot off into the air and pooted off towards his home, a penthouse suite on the 182nd floor of Looz Towers.

CHAPTER 7

LOOZ TOWERS

As he flew above the sprawling metropolis of Septo City, Howard's thoughts returned to the mysterious porcelain ring.

He smiled smugly, unable to believe his own dumb luck. Though he didn't know what the ring was exactly, he instinctively knew that he'd just come into possession of a treasure that was worth its weight in gold – or maybe twice its weight in gold or ten times its weight in gold.

"What is it?" He asked himself for the umpteenth time. "What is its function? Who figured out how to make indestructible porcelain?"

He was eager and impatient to find the answers.

"Maybe the strange writing on the ring reveals the object's secrets, its origin and purpose? But who could possibly decipher the strange writing?"

As the morning rays of the Cessestian sun broke through the overhanging blanket of smog and illuminated the plumes of yellow smoke rising from a thousand belching smoke stacks, so light broke in on Howard's thought processes. A name came to his mind, the name of the only person – perhaps the one brilliant man in the whole world who could possibly solve the mystery of the ring and its mysterious writing – and that name was Livingston.

"LIVINGSTON!" Howard said out loud. "Yes, Livingston," he thought. "Hadn't Livingston boasted of being a great linguist on more than one occasion? Didn't he say that he knew how to ask where the bathroom was in one-hundred-and-fifty languages and dialects? Didn't he announce on his nature show that he was very good at making sense out of gobbledygook writing that no one else could read?"

Howard put pedal to the porcelain as he pooted across the industrial heart of his city and he flew at break-neck speeds through the jungle of towering pipe apartment buildings, faucets, U-bends and gas-reeking, sludge-spewing chimneys. He knew that Septo City would soon be basin to basin with tooting pooters, but for the moment he could poot through its skyways unimpeded.

Upon taking a sharp left turn after the Septo City sewage treatment plant, Howard spied Looz Towers. It was a tower designed to tickle the upper reaches of the atmosphere, a two hundred story monolithic pillar, blackened by industrial soot.

On the two top tiers of the tower there was a neon sign saying: "LOOZ TOWERS, HOME OF MICROFLUSH AND HANDLES 95."

A gigantic statue of a toilet was displayed on the very top of the tower, and not only was it a famous work of art and an advertisement for the products of Howard Looz and Looz Enterprises, but it also served as a pooter-landing pad.

Howard leaned back as his pooter ascended to the height needed to land on top of the tower.

He circled the toilet statue before bringing his priceless pooter down on its lid.

He then got off his Bumley, walked over to the toilet statue cistern, descended a spiral staircase into the bowl of the toilet and pushed the button for the water-sliding elevator.

Two minutes later, Howard stepped out of the elevator on the 182nd floor of the tower and he entered his palatial penthouse suite, an apartment decked out in shiny, white marble tiles and filled with fine antique, furniture, magnificent statues and masterpiece paintings.

Howard aimed his voice at the ceiling and asked, "Tower Brain, where is Livingston?"

Audio panels and discreet cameras were mounted throughout the penthouse and these were the eyes, ears and mouthpieces of the Tower Brain Computer Network.

"Ding. Feeeeeel the Loooove," purred the voice coming from the ceiling speakers, "This is Tower Brain, the interactive computer network of Looz Towers, and I'm booting up just for you. What can I do for you today, Howard Looz?"

"For one thing, stop talking like a radio

disc–jockey on some head–thumping station I'd never listen to. You're too slick, cheerful, or something," complained Howard. "I don't want to feel the love."

"My programmers gave me a deep modulated voice, as slow and smooth as molasses, so I could purr like a panther."

"One cat is enough for me," said Howard.

"You know it. I wish I had arms so I could give you a big hug. You sound like you're stressed? Can I make you a latte? Maybe you should sit dooooown and relaaaaax."

"Shut up!" snapped Howard. "I'll have somebody reprogram the slang and platitudes right out of you. I have a task for you. I want you to find Livingston."

"Riiiiiiight oooooooon," rumbled Tower Brain. "I'm on it."

Howard then paced the tiles while the computer looked for Livingston.

Fifteen minutes later, Tower Brain's voice returned with a friendly 'Ding' and said, "Aw, maaaaan, no joy."

"Did you try all the usual places? His laboratory? His cottage? The museum?"

"Yeah, I checked all those places out," reported Tower Brain.

"Don't tell me he's out on another one of his scatterbrained expeditions somewhere on the planet?"

"Tower Brain is back on the caaaaaase! I'll

hook up with the rest of the networks around the world and checking .... checking...Nuh uh, nuh uh, nuh uh. Hmmmm? Let me try? ...Oooooooh, yeeeeeeah! Oh, I'm good. I found him. He's with Directo-caaaaam in some far away laaaaand. Connecting."

"Put the image through on my window monitor."

Howard's penthouse windows darkened. Static images replaced the panoramic view of Septo City. A picture came into focus. The celebrity explorer Livingston then appeared on the screen and he was floating in mid-air, suspended over a mile deep chasm.

CHAPTER 8

LIVINGSTON'S LABORATORY

I must have fallen asleep on the comfy laboratory couch, because the next thing I knew, it was morning, and Howard was outside making a racket.

"Yoo Hoooooooooo! Livingston! Knock, knock, knock, Livingston, I know you're in theeeeeeeeere! Open Uuuuuuuuup!"

I staggered from the sofa over to the door fumbled with chain-lock, opened the door and poked my head out. My eyes were bleary and blood-shot and so the morning sunlight nearly blinded me.

"Oh it's just you Howard," I said while blinking and yawning.

I knew without looking at myself that I was a mess, and since it was only Howard, I didn't care all that much. I stretched, scratched the back of my neck, massaged my face, flattened my hair with my hands, wiped sleep out of my eyes and tried to smooth out the wrinkles in my old Randolph Tickets uniform.

"Just me! Just me!" whined Howard sounding like a balloon being rubbed. "Only the sorry boob of a benefactor who pays for all this!"

My mind was still a bit foggy, so I said, "Pays for all what?"

"Look behind you. Only your multimillion puto state of the art laboratory. I mean, who is it that provides funding for you to do whatever it is you do?"

"Is this a trick question? And I've never called you a sorry boob. I usually just refer to you as the gloomy old toilet salesman."

"The point is, you must have a hundred or more computers in this laboratory of yours."

I didn't see Howard's point at all, and said, "Its eighty-eight super computers actually – Erm – I'm sorry. What was your point?"

"And I paid for all those computers! Did I mention that already? Yet, I can't connect with a single computer to get in touch. I can't call. I can't check on your progress. I had to pooter all the way down here just to find out whether you were alive or dead."

"I did-en wan be dis-urbed," I said while yawning once more. "What time is it by the way?"

"It is three days since I brought you back from the Amethyst Alps."

"Really? Has it been that long? I think I

Livingston

need a day off."

"Well?" said Howard.

"Well what?"

"Do you know what 'it' is?"

I still wasn't quite awake, and said, "Do you know what 'what' is?"

"The ring machine? The writing on it? What is 'it'?"

"Oh that! Yes I do know what it is."

"And......?"

"It's easier to show you than tell you. I've got it situated on the far side of the laboratory. Follow me."

Howard and I then started walking down the aisle between the rows of my bleeping, buzzing two-story high computers.

After the computers, we passed my big brass telescope.

"Discovered any new stars or planets?" asked Howard.

"Not lately," I said.

I didn't have the heart to confess that I'd only used the telescope to look into the windows of high rise apartments to see what everyone was getting up to.

"We really need to think about exploring beyond this planet of ours, Livingston. You know, try to get beyond the failed Space Vacuum Cleaner idea that my father and brother pursued."

"Funny you should mention that," I remarked, "because I'm just about to show you something that goes way beyond the Space Vacuum Cleaner."

Following on from the computer and telescope sections, we went through the chemistry area with its weird shaped glass beakers, workstations, tables, microscopes and all kinds of chemical stuff that I can't pronounce or spell.

"Do you ever use any of this equipment?" asked Howard. "It doesn't look like it's ever been used."

"Oh, I use it all the time," I lied. Truth be told, I'd mixed a cocktail or two in the lab, but I wasn't about to tell Howard that. "A clean laboratory is a happy laboratory," I chirped.

We then went through the specimen area, or in other words, the place with high wooden shelves stacked with thousands of jars, containing pickled samples of any creeping, crawling formerly alive thing that could fit into a jar and look totally gross.

Most of the specimens were horrible little monstrosities that the elder Stanley collected during his lifetime.

My only contribution was the jar with the monster green-eyed fly maggot that was extracted from my body after my traumatic little episode on Plague Isle. The maggot jar was on a shelf all by itself and was waiting for the many other jars that I was meant to fill with specimens.

Truth be told, the maggot was going to have a long, lonely wait for fellow specimen jars, because I had no intention of collecting anything I considered icky.

CHAPTER 9

CHARADE-OGLYPHICS

Near the very back of the laboratory, Howard and I arrived at the place where the ringed-machine thing was being kept.

A bathroom pink fur covering veiled the machine and so I directed my voice up into the air and called for my robotic arms, saying, "Arms, remove the cover."

One of the handy-dandy tools that had been built into my high tech lab was a pair of long, lanky robotic arms that moved around the laboratory on a circular track suspended from the domed ceiling above, and these robotic arms stopped just above the strange device. They then removed the cover, and unveiled the closed shell of a machine while floodlights shone down from above, illuminating the blue-green colours of its porcelain mass.

"Here, let me switch it on," I said.
Stepping up to the machine, I put my hands underneath the lid and began to lift.

"It's quite sensitive to touch," I explained.
The moment my fingers felt the inside of

the lid rim, the machine took over and the lid opened without any more help from myself. I then stepped aside as the underside panel opened and the staircase of six steps extended. At the same time the steps appeared, so too did the cylindrical column with the control handle. It rose up from the base like a tree growing out of the ground.

I ascended the stairs, stepped up to the control column and pulled down on the silver turn handle. The lights around the lid rim switched on and so did the video screen panels with their pictures of little stick-men (more like stick-frogs actually) that were jumping about.

"So what is it?" asked Howard.

"This is a Star Flush!"

"A Star Flush?"

"Yes, a Star Flush! Beautiful isn't it?" I said, while descending the stairs.

"Yes it is, and take this from someone who makes toilets for a living; it's a beautiful name too. Very catchy – so, er, what does the Star Flush do exactly?"

"I'm getting to that," I answered upon rejoining Howard. "This alien writing appearing in the video panels is called Charade-oglyphics … You need to start at the top left, read counter clockwise and let the pictures do the talking. I'll demonstrate. Each Charade-oglyphic completes a different part of the message. Start up there," I said, pointing to the upper left side of the lid rim.

A stick-frog in the upper left video panel was holding up one of its webbed fingers.

"The ugly little stick thing is pointing up for some reason," remarked Howard.

"On the contrary," I explained. "It isn't pointing up. It's saying 'First Word.'"

The Charade-oglyphic nodded its head in the affirmative, and then cupped its ear.

"Now he is holding his little stick hand to his little stick ear?" observed Howard.

"That means 'sounds like'."

Howard tilted his head backward and directed his voice up to the Charade-oglyphic.

"First word sounds like?..."

The Charade-oglyphic pointed to its back.

"Sounds like 'Back'?"

The animated stick-frog nodded its head "Yes" and gave Howard the thumbs up.

"I'm doing it! I'm doing it! Oh I like this. OK, sounds like 'Back?' Uh.. 'Sack'?

The Charade-oglyphic shook its head and waved its arms to say 'No!'

"Tack? No...Rack? No... Plaque? Book? Buck? Bag? No, - Oh I'm way off!"

The stick-frog kept gesturing "No, no, no, no, no, no!" and then in frustration it held up two of its webbed fingers.

"Livingston, I think the deformed stick-thing is giving me a rude gesture," whispered Howard.

"No, that means 'Second Word'," I said.

"Charade–oglyphics, give me the second word."

The stick–frog drew a circle in the air and kept moving its finger round and round.

"Circle?" shouted Howard. "Second word is circle?"

The stick–frog shook its head "No!"

"Round?"

The Charade–oglyphic kept saying "No," held up its arms to gesture, "Stop. Start over," and then began to mime digging with a shovel.

To himself, or maybe to me, Howard said, "I don't get it! Now it's trying to dig." Addressing the Charade–oglyphic, Howard said, "Second word is Shovel? No. Spade? Dig? Digging?"

The Charade–oglyphic flung its arms about saying "No! No! No!" It then turned its back, bent over and pointed at its bottom.

"Second word is behind? Bottom? Rear end? Derriere? ...Oh, I give up!" moaned Howard, feeling completely flustered.

"It is trying to say 'Hole'...like dig a hole, and the first word that sounds like 'Back' is 'Black.'"

"Black hole!" shouted Howard to the Charade–oglyphic.

The stick–frog jumped up and down in jubilation, gesturing "Yes! Yes! Yes!"

"Now you know why it's taken me three whole days to read the message." Pointing to the Charade–oglyphics on the left, I said, "This bit here is very technical. It's all about the black hole near our planet that makes space travel impossible.."

"Yes, yes, everyone knows that. Did these Charade-o-what's-its tell you anything we didn't already know?"

"Oh it gets better. Using black hole technology of shrinking time and space with extreme gravitation, the creators of the Star Flush have found a way to travel from planet to planet, or even galaxy to galaxy without rocket pooters or any type of spacecraft. It's called Black Hole technology."

"You were right. This is way beyond the Space Vacuum Cleaner we were working on."

"That Archibald Sluice was working on before he was murdered by Coop and your sick brother," I hastened to point out.

"Reformed brother. Sigmund, by all accounts is healed, but let's not get off the point. This Star Flush does what we wanted the Space Vacuum Cleaner to do."

"The Space Vacuum Cleaner was as primitive as a horse-drawn outhouse compared to this. This is perfection, Howard! This is everything your father and brother were trying to achieve. Where they failed, the Galactic Plumbers succeeded."

"Galactic Plumbers?"

"I'm getting to them. What all this means, Howard, is that we can be flushed through the plumbing of the universe!"

Howard was incredulous. "The universe has plumbing?"

"The physics are very complex, but I shall be as simple as I can."

I was now fully awake and as animated as the Charade-oglyphics. I then threw my arms about excitedly, as I proceeded to describe the inner workings of the Star Flush.

"You see, the Star Flush, the bowl in the base whirls and twirls and creates a miniature black hole, thus creating a pipe-way through time and space; we can be flushed to any other planet and any other galaxy!"

"Those little stick-fellows told you all that? How do you know we can trust them?"

While Howard's back was turned, the Charade-oglyphics stuck out their tongues and blew raspberries at him.

"Well, we'll have to test the Star Flush of course, but I for one believe them. Think about it Howard. We can travel to other planets! It's all true – and that's just the writing on the left side."

"Oh, what's it say on the right side?"

"Not as pleasant I'm afraid." I lowered my voice, and pointed to the right side of the lid rim. "This is the plumbing bill. Basically, time and space have been clogged by this black hole, and the Star Flush effectively bypasses the clog. And this has all been done courtesy of the Galactic Plumbing Service, a family owned business since 734652987, whenever the heck that was – this is a break down of the services rendered – parts, labour etcetera – and whoever uses this Star

Flush is going to have an astronomical plumbing bill."

"Plumbing bill? They, whoever they are, charge for using this thing? – And if we refuse to pay? I mean finders-keepers right? It's not as if we ordered this thing out of a catalogue and signed any papers making us obligated to pay? If this...this...?"

"Galactic Plumbing Service," I prompted.

"...Galactic Plumbing Service wants it back they can jolly well come and get it."

"Actually it says that they will take over the planet if they like it or blow it up if they don't like it, should the said silly planet refuse to pay their bills," I recited, reading the last few lines of Charade-oglyphics.

"Yeah, well I didn't get to where I am today without playing a little hard ball! We can always say the check is in the mail."

"I don't think it works that way," I cautioned.

"How does it work?"

"We have to tell the Charade-oglyphics where we want to go, they do the calculations and then we have to stick a thousand basic units of our currency..."

"You mean to say that every time we use this thing, this Star Flush, it costs a thousand putos?"

"Yes, in addition to the plumbing bill. Every time we want to use the Star Flush we will have to put a thousand puto bill into the money slot below the handle."

I pointed to the bottom right Charade-oglyphics and read the message out loud as each stick-frog mimed its word or phrase. "Make sure bills are facing up and the Star Flush doesn't give change."

"Then what?"

"Give a good down turn on this silver handle, and then jump into the Star Flush bowl and away you go through the plumbing of the universe."

Howard's eyes lit up. "Anywhere?"

"Anywhere that has another Star Flush. According to the Charade-oglyphics, there are Star Flushes on most planets, except some that didn't pay the plumbing bill, because the er, planets don't exist any more."

"This is incredible!" shouted Howard. "Just imagine the possibilities! This will do wonders for Looz Enterprises. Livingston, I want you to get everything you need for your trip into the universe! Hire porters. Get tents, sleeping bags, matches – whatever. Don't worry about any expenses! I will cover everything. You just go!"

"B-B-By m-m-myself?" I stammered.

"Directo-cam will be going with you, won't he?"

"Er, yeah, er, Directo-cam is good at filming things but when it comes down to it, he's not much help."

"Oh that reminds me. I've been meaning to have a word with you about Stanley Junior."

"Stanley Junior?" What about Stanley Junior?"

"I'd like to hire him and make him your partner."

"Yeah, but he's just a kid," I protested. "And remember my motto: I work alone! It's in my contract."

"We can tear up your old contract and draw up a new one. I'd even be willing to give you a raise, but you will have to take on Stanley Junior, train him up and teach him the tricks of the trade."

"Er, well, I already told him no."

"Tell him you've changed your mind."

"But, I don't know where he is."

"I do."

"Where?"

"Somewhere out on the Psychedelic Sea."

"I could use a vacation on the Psychedelic Sea, that is if you want me to go out and look for young Stanley. It could take a while though. It's a big place is the Psychedelic Sea."

"Vacation? You must be joking, Livingston. We have work to do. There's a whole universe waiting for you to explore!

I'll tell you what. While you make all the necessary preparations for a Star Flush expedition, I'll go find Stanley Junior myself!

Before I go on my little ocean excursion however, we need to talk about Star Flush security. Do you realise that there are whole armies that would fight to the death to get a hold of this amazing thing – this machine from outer space – this Star Flush? Can you imagine what would happen if the Star Flush were to fall into the wrong hands?"

❀ ❀ ❀ ❀ ❀

PART TWO

THE HEROES AND VILLAINS ASSEMBLE

CHAPTER 10

GROUP THERAPY

"You are in good hands," wheezed Dr. Sigmund Looz. His breathing was laboured and his gravelly voice sounded as if he had gargled with hot tar and ground up asphalt.

"For those of you just joining our group therapy session, I am Dr. Sigmund Looz, and your mental health is in my caring hands."

The psychiatrist rubbed his hands together looking like a praying mantis that was preparing to eat its own children. He smiled reassuringly at the group of mental patients surrounding him, though it was comparable to the reassuring smile a crocodile might give to a pond full of frogs.

The charisma and charm of his younger years were all but gone, and in its place was something more akin to frostbite. Gone were the handsome features of his youth. His face was now weathered and leathery like a pirate who had been out at sea too long, and the black eye-patch he now wore over his right eye did nothing to discourage the pirate comparison.

Sigmund was seated on a padded toilet-style chair, and he was wearing a white doctor's jacket, which had various surgical tools strapped on to it.

Thirteen patients were seated in a circle around Sigmund and they were all bound in straight jackets.

The glaring white room the psychiatrist and patients occupied was literally a rubber room with walls and floors padded with bright white rubber mats, and it was lit by harsh florescent lights.

Sigmund rose slowly from his chair, stood to his feet and looked from frightened face to frightened face before speaking.

"I was once a patient in therapy like yourselves and just look at me now. Sound in mind, cured of my mental disorder. I cried to the saintly plumber above, shouting 'how can I help others as I have been helped?' And then like a ray of light breaking through my mind's fog, I had a vision. I, Sigmund Looz, would become a doctor of psychiatry like those wonderful shamans of the mind who tinkered inside my head and helped repair my fractured soul. And now my dear lunatics, I likewise am here to fiddle with your damaged minds and see what I can fix. It is not easy to pull the daggers out of your psyches without doing irreparable damage to other parts of your malfunctioning faculties – yet here within our weekly megalomaniac group therapy sessions, some of you are making – and I use the word guardedly – progress."

Like a predatory beast stalking prey, he circled behind the thirteen patients.

"Megalomania is a mental illness, a psychosis, a pathological condition where the lunatic thinks he or she is some kind of all powerful monarch or omnipotent deity. The mad woman or man entertains wild fantasies of obtaining extreme power, domination and control. For example the megalomaniac may have silly notions that he or she 'rules the world. Tyrannical dictators and megalomania go hand in hand. The thirteen of you are all afflicted with this malady. What I enjoy about these sessions most is that I am the only one with real power. You are all powerless, completely dependent on my benevolence. You have delusions of power, yet I am the embodiment of power....And it is power over you!"

CHAPTER 11

FOUR ROBOTS AND A NEWSPAPER

Looz Towers Park
Privy the 24th

Within the grounds of Looz Towers Park and under the shade of a dragon palm tree, four robots stood together, huddled around a newspaper.

A hovering robot named Gigglebyte held the newspaper up for the other three robots to see and said, "I could have sworn that 'Help Wanted' ad was here some place."

One of the other robots, a feminine android named Pambot spoke to Gigglebyte and said, "In less then a millionth of a millisecond I have calculated what your problem is. Gigglebyte, you are holding the newspaper upside-down."

"Let meeeee seeeeee dat," said the biggest of the four robots. His name was Swatzanutter because he had been modelled after a famous weight-lifter. He was eight foot tall, solid as a tank, weighed a ton, and yet for all his size and strength he had a slower computer brain than most other robots.

Gigglebyte made no attempt to relinquish the paper so Swatzanutter ripped it out of Gigglebyte's hands, tearing the broadsheet in the process.

"Saw-wey 'bout dat," he apologised in his clipped, clunky voice.

Gigglebyte's electronic eyes flashed red with anger and he blew exhaust fumes out of his anti-gravity hovering base. "Now you've done it! You forget. I can read upside-down or right-side up or sideways."

Gigglebyte demonstrated this claim by extending his spring coil neck upward until his dented head tipped over and dangled upside-down.

"See, don't knock the inverted approach until you've tried it," he said.

The fourth robot, a tall silver mechanised-man named Brobot, spoke up and said, "Chill my ro-bros. I don't even know why I hang with you messed-up machines. Hand the paper over!"

Swatzanutter gave what was left of the paper to Brobot who proceeded to scan the newsprint with his shaded digital eyes. Small red blips of light chased each other through his inscrutable black eye-band as he read and then he said, "Here it is. It says, 'Porters required. Lift heavy stuff. See exotic far away places. Good pay. Apply in person. Livingston's laboratory. Looz Towers Park.'"

"Yeah, so where's the stupid laboratory?" complained Gigglebyte. He stretched his coiled neck upward as far as it could go and popped his eyes outward in binocular fashion. After looking around he said, "Nothing! Its just trees and plants and bushes and flowers for as far as my binocular-eyes will see."

"The map of the park in my memory banks makes no mention of a laboratory or has purposely left its location blank," said Pambot. "It is quite possible however, that one of the many pathways through the park, such as the path we are currently standing on will lead us to the laboratory, and if no bot has any objections, I suggest we follow this path eastwards."

The four robots then started down a dirt pathway that cut through the park in an easterly direction.

They whirred, hummed, stomped, rattled, clanked and hovered along the winding trail, which took them through a forest of weird succulent plants and bulbous bottom-heavy bottle-shaped trees.

After a half-mile stroll down the twisting trail, their path emptied into a clearing of grass, bushes and flower beds, and in the midst of this clearing was a building.

"This could be Livingston's lab," said Gigglebyte.

"That is indeed possible," said Pambot. "It could also be a person's home. Laboratories are generally found in industrial complexes and are functional buildings. Their aesthetic appeal is not the first concern of the designers of such structures. I assume that people would find this building nice to look at if my files about their psychology are anything to go by. It blends in with the environment of the park. Unlike most laboratories, it is not made of concrete and porcelain. Instead, this structure has been given a rustic look and is made of wood, reminiscent of pictures of log cabins I have on file. However, it is larger than most residences. It is approximately eighty feet high or four stories, and its large domed roof is in fact consistent with the architecture of most laboratories."

"Vat about small building?" asked Swatzanutter.

There was a smaller building, a tin shack with a corrugated roof sitting several hundred yards in back of the domed wooden structure.

"I am fairly certain that is a storage shed," said Pambot. "That is definitely not a laboratory."

"You're wasting brain power, ro-girl," said Brobot. "Standing around reciting endless facts about stupid laboratories will do no good until one of us goes to knock on the door and find out if it is one or not."

"OK, first one to throw their head on the ground gets to knock on the door," said Gigglebyte as his neck extended and his head dropped.

CHAPTER 12

COOP

"The power you think you have is an illusion, Doctor Looz?" mocked Coop, while smirking behind the bars of a protective face-mask.

Coop was seated in a chair just to the left of Sigmund's chair. Not only was Coop muzzled by such a mask, but he was also constrained by a straight jacket that was wrapped around his hulking body.

Sigmund gave Coop a hard stare and replied, "I don't think I'll dignify that with an answer, Mr. Coop."

Turning to address the other patients, Sigmund said, "For those of you who are new to the group, let me introduce our most infamous patient. This is the remorseless, murderous hit man, Coop. I partly owe the change of my life's direction to this man, because it was my innocent association with Coop that brought me to this place, and while it seemed an evil at the time, it has turned out for good.

I would not be here helping you today if it were not for Coop, and I long ago forgave this troubled man for all the harm he intended for me."

Addressing Coop, Sigmund said, "Why don't you tell the group about your megalomaniac desires?"

Coop threw the challenge back in Sigmund's face. "Very well, but first I have a question for you Doctor Looz."

He spit the word "doctor" out with contempt. "Don't you miss the power you once had, the power that comes from being from the richest family on the planet? Are you not upset that you were disinherited and disowned by your father, struck from his will and that your weak and undeserving brother now has all the wealth influence and power that you strived so hard for?"

Sigmund's left eye twitched and his voice became shrill and tense. "My b..b..brother...What family doesn't have their inward squabbles?" stammered Sigmund. "But, I don't want to talk about my broth... – sibling, any more than you want to talk about your – childhood!"

At the mention of "childhood," a fog clouded Coop's mind.

When the fog cleared, Coop was no longer in the padded cell inside the Septo City Insane Asylum. Instead, he looked down at himself as he once was, once upon a nightmare.

He saw himself as a child. Loveless yellow eyes formed a steely stare in the face of the boy. They were dry eyes beyond all tears and natural childhood emotions.

"You good for nothing little monster!" screeched the voice of a woman that he will not look at.

Her hand grabbed the boy's ear and twisted it. Coop felt pain but did not cry out, and nor did the boy that he was watching.

The woman dragged the child through the mud and led him to a wire-meshed cage filled with vicious roosters and hens.

Upon seeing the youngster, the poultry clucked angrily.

These were aggressive birds, armed with red fleshy layers of spiked body armour that covered their backs and wing tips.

They were also an enormous breed, close to an ostrich in size, having been genetically engineered by the military for use in combat missions.

Aside from being used on the battlefield, the birds functioned as watchdogs, guarding businesses and private property.

Before being pecked to death, Coop's father had been one of the genetic engineers involved in the covert military experiments that had transformed the poultry into such frightening fowl.

It had been left to the bereaved mother of Coop to bring up her troubled son on her own, and she was beyond the point of coping. For this reason, the woman of Coop's mind's eye, his very own mother, threw the young boy of his memory inside the cage with the deadly birds.

"To the coop with you!" Coop screeched, mimicking his mother's voice.

"Bad memories, Coop?" asked Sigmund.

Coop opened his eyes, but they were dilated and looked like the eyes of a bird. He started to bob his head and to cluck, while his bound body rolled on to the padded floor.

Violently twisting, jerking, and dislocating his arms, he freed himself from the straight jacket. Immediately, he jumped up to attack Sigmund. Screeching and crowing, Coop threw the long, loose sleeves around Sigmund's neck, and tried to choke him.

"Psychobot Nurse!" screamed Sigmund before Coop's stranglehold cut off all his air supply.

A padded door in the rubber room was thrown open. A terrible ten-foot robotic nurse stomped into the room.

Most of the patients visibly shook at the sight of the Psychobot Nurse.

The nurse had huge hydraulic arms with all manner of medical tools attached to them, such as head-shavers, conductive gel-squirters and hypodermic-needle-fingers.

Tiny concentrated beams of red light were aglow inside her cruel eye slits and her dangling elephantine trunk of a nose functioned as a water-squirting hose.

After entering the rubber room, the Psychobot Nurse marched straight over to the manic murderous Coop and injected all five of her hypodermic fingers into his buttocks, just before he slumped to the floor unconscious.

CHAPTER 13

THE PORTERS

Pambot, Swatzanutter, Brobot and Gigglebyte headed up the pathway to the bigger of the two buildings, and upon arriving at what they presumed was the entrance, Gigglebyte used his mechanical fist to knock on the wooden door in front of them.

After almost knocking it down, the door opened and Livingston presented himself to the robots looking frantic and distracted.

"Sorry!" he said to them. "Very Busy. Can't Talk. Come back later."

He slammed the door in their metallic faces.

They turned to look at each other in computerised incomprehension, before Gigglebyte knocked a second time. His knocking grew louder and more persistent. He knocked so hard that he accidentally punched a hole in the door and his hand became well and truly stuck.

All the racket caused Livingston to throw the door open once again, and because it was the outward swinging kind, Gigglebyte was slammed backwards into the bushes.

"Please go away!" pleaded Livingston. "I don't have time to sign any autographs today."

Livingston tried to shut the door in their faces again, but Brobot was ready, and he stuck his metal foot inside the door frame.

EXCERPT FROM LIVINGSTON'S JOURNAL

I could not believe the dogged persistence of these robots. My mind was fraught with all the preparations I had to make, and yet these robots would just not go away and leave me in peace.

The one with his foot in the door (I soon learned that his name was Brobot) must have broken every robot rule of protocol in the books. He was sleek, slender and silver with long spindly limbs. A dark visor stretched across his face with small red lights racing across it. Strands of curling electrodes extended from his head, and blue bolts of electricity jumped from one electrode to another.

"Listen man, we came to hook up with you, not look at the outside of your ugly door," said Brobot.

Somewhere along the assembly line a brash attitude had been programmed into Brobot. I could see he wasn't going to take no for an answer.

Brobot pointed at the door hinges and fired

a ball of laser light out of the tip of his index finger. The laser zapped the hinges and melted them, causing the door to fall out of its frame and tumble over on to the ground.

From underneath the fallen door, I heard a muffled voice saying, "Rebooting. Rebooting."

To Brobot I said, "You – you – broke my door! You – you – rude robot!"

The voice from below the door said, "Hey get this thing off of me! I think I broke my ball bearings!"

"After you hire us, I'll fix this door and put it back on its hinges," promised Brobot.

"Hire you?" I said in disbelief. "Why would I want to hire you?"

"Because, we're the best!" boasted Brobot. "Check out Pambot. That Robo-girl is one of the smartest bots they make – and check out my main bot Swatzanutter. He is one big bad strong machine – and nobody messes with me, because each one of my fingers shoots lethal laser beams and I will be your first and last line of defence. The name's Brobot."

I then remembered what this was all about. I had put out an ad in the papers looking for porters and these robots had come to apply for the job.

"So who's the robot underneath the door and what can he do?" I asked.

"Is some bot gonna help me up or what?" said the voice beneath the door.

With one of his massive hydraulic arms,

Swatzanutter picked up the door as if picking up a feather. A misshapen hunk of junk came up with the door, and dangled beneath the door by its hand, which had somehow gotten stuck in the wood.

Swatzanutter smashed the door into pieces with his other hand and the ugly robot fell on to a cushion of air beneath his hover base.

"Gigglebyte has an inbuilt anti-gravity rocket and can fly if the need arises," replied the pretty female robot called Pambot. "That is because he was not made in a factory like the rest of us. Gigglebyte was made by a man dabbling in amateur robotics. His parts were gathered randomly, piece by piece from a junkyard."

Gigglebyte then hung his head sadly and it fell off his body, though it remained attached to his stretchy hose-like neck.

"I'd understand if you didn't want to have a second-hand robot made from junkyard parts," sniffed Gigglebyte. "Go ahead! Send me away like everyone else has! See if I care."

He turned around and started to float sadly away. "I know when I'm not wanted," he snivelled.

"Wait," I called. "You don't have to er…"

Gigglebyte came back in a flash, and looked up at me with expectant electronic eyes.

"Yes?" he said. "You were saying?"

"Er, right, well, I'm sure there is something I could find for you to do."

"My homely-bot Gigglebyte here could

supply spare parts for the rest of us," suggested Brobot.

Taking offense, Gigglebyte retorted, "Who are you calling homely?"

He then backfired on purpose and oil spluttered from his hover base all over Brobot's shiny silver foot. "Oh, did I spill oil on you?"

Brobot lifted his foot and looked at it in disgust. He then poked his finger into Gigglebyte's back and electrocuted him, causing sparks, smoke and lots of shaking and clanking.

"Oh, did I shock you?" asked Brobot.

Gigglebyte's power cut out again and he fell flat on his dented face.

Pambot stepped forward and extended her hand to me, saying, "I do apologise for the behaviour of my ro-leagues. Just to clarify, we are speaking to thee Livingston, the world famous explorer?"

I was flattered and found Pambot to be the most courteous and gracious of the four robots. Despite having a see-through head with an electronic brain floating freely in gas, she had been designed to be pleasing to my flesh and blood male eye, and I noticed myself being more polite to her than the other robots.

"Well, as a matter of fact, yes, I am," I answered, trying to appear humble.

"I am very strooooooong," said Swatzanutter. "Do you want to feeeeel my hy-traaaaaaw-leeeek biceps?"

Before I could say, "No, that's all right,"
Swatzanutter took hold of me, picked me up, and
held me above his block of a head.

"See how strooooong I am?"

"Yo, check it out; remember the ad in the
paper? Porters wanted. See far away places and
carry heavy stuff?" prompted Brobot.

"You're all hired," I said from above
Swatzanutter's head.

CHAPTER 14

THE PSYCHEDELIC SEA

AUTHOR'S NARRATION

Howard's luxurious, golden poot-a-maran hurtled across the Psychedelic Sea at speed, while his one and only passenger, Little Klawd, attempted to fish from the side of the moving vessel. A large air propeller on the back of the poot-a-maran gave the craft its velocity, while the pontoons it was mounted on enabled the bowl-shaped boat to slice threw the swells and waves of the iridescent ocean.

It was a sensational day for a cruise. The Cessestian sun was high in the violet sky and no cloud obstructed its rays from reaching the multicolored surface of the sea. The radiance of the rays then refracted into millions of sparkles and incandescent flames of light.

Little Klawd's sharp eyes darted to and fro across the glimmering sea looking for the telltale shadows of the fishy residents beneath the glittering wake.

Upon detecting a conspicuous shadow amidst the ever-churning bubbling broth that was the sea, Little Klawd instantly thrust his paw into the brine and speared a fish (a five-hundred pound, long-haired mackerel) with his claws. In the next millisecond, the mackerel was tossed into the air and then batted backward on to the poop deck of the boat. Now that it was truly a fish out of water, the mackerel, with its pink scales and long pink hair, flopped about until Little Klawd was able to put it out of its misery with a bite.

"Hairy mackerel!" shouted Howard.

He was high up the ship's mast and inside the crow's nest, which from below looked like an upturned toilet plunger. This was where the captain's wheel and all the navigation equipment for the poot-a-maran was located. From the crow's nest, Howard steered the poot-a-maran while seated on a comfortable toilet-style chair made of varnished wood.

"Ahoy Little Klawd!" yelled Howard in an attempt to sound nautical. He also tried to look nautical, and so he wore a ship captain's hat sporting the words "S.S. LOOZ," which was superimposed over an anchor motif.

"Another fine catch matey! 'Tis good to be out of Septo City!"

Howard filled his nostrils with the invigorating ocean air. "Just feel that sea breeze on your furry face matey!"

Out of the corner of his eye, Howard spied another vessel off in the distance.

"Ship ahoy!" he yelled. "Turn hard forty degrees starboard!"

There was no one to listen to his instructions except Little Klawd, but he enjoyed giving the commands all the same.

Obeying his own orders, Howard then took hold of the wheel and gave it a spin to the right.

The boat swerved. This knocked Little Klawd off his feet and made him slide into the side rails around the deck.

As Little Klawd yowled angrily, Howard shouted, "Aye, sorry about that ye scurvy kitty!"

* * * * *

Fifteen minutes later, Howard caught up with the smaller boat, which was a quarter of the size of his golden poot-a-maran and much less ornate. It was at a standstill, anchored to the bottom of the sea, and so Howard slowed his yacht and brought it alongside the other craft, before stopping and dropping his own anchor.

"Here we are Little Klawd," announced Howard.

The words, "Porcelain Porpoise," were written on the barnacle-blemished side of the boat, and upon seeing the name of the vessel, Howard said, "Yes, this is Stanley Junior's boat all right."

A slurping, licking and chewing sound was

the only response to the statement. Little Klawd did not so much as glance upward at Howard. Instead, he concentrated on sucking the succulent meat off every bone of the mackerel.

Howard tooted the ship's foghorn and then yelled over to the other ship, shouting "Ahoy, Stanley!"

There was only silence.

Surveying the Porcelain Porpoise from bow to stern, Howard could see no sign of Stanley Junior, but instead saw a robot. One lone robot stood (If stood is the right word. Perhaps "propped up" is a better description, for what appeared to be only half of a robot) at the bow of the Porcelain Porpoise.

"Ahoy!" Howard shouted down to the robot.

The mechanical man's head turned slowly, causing a grating sound as rusty metal rubbed against rusty metal. Barnacles covered one of its electronic eyes like a patch, while even more barnacles seemed to form a beard on its corroded face. In addition to the rust and barnacles, there was a large nest of sticks on its head with a mother seagull in residence.

"Ahoy this!" it grumbled, while making a rude sound (achieved by squeezing its metal armpit down on its hand repeatedly).

Howard drolly said, "Charmed." He then shouted, "I'm looking for Stanley Siphonpipe Junior."

"Who be askin'?" asked the robot. "Don't ye

know it be rude to blast yer horn in such close prox–zimee–tay. You've shaken me bucket–o'–a–'ead and 'urt me blasted soun' sensers!"

"Er, sorry. The name's Howard Looz. I'm an old acquaintance of Stanley's. May I come aboard?"

"Please yerself me hearty. I could nay stop ye if me tried. Aye, Both me legs rusted off. I can nay move to chase a robot–wench with a wrench. I be planted 'ere like a wart on a whale's winky."

In an aside, Howard muttered, "I hope he's talking about the whale's eye–lid,"

CHAPTER 15

ELFLY

Septo City Insane Asylum

"I trust Coop's little episode didn't cause any unnecessary trauma and anxiety to any of you," said Sigmund to the assembled patients.

Coop was bound in his jacket once again, slumped over in his chair, and half asleep from the sedatives that the Psychobot Nurse had injected him with. Despite the heavy dose of medication, Coop was still able to glare at Sigmund hatefully.

"Every morning when I wake up and put this patch over my eye, I am reminded of how dangerous Coop can be," continued Sigmund. "He pecked out my right eye during one of his violent episodes, and ever since then I have insisted that he wear a protective face mask."

"Hey Doctor Looz?" said the tallest patient in the room. He was also the patient with the most stylish head of hair.

Sigmund rolled his left eye and sighed

impatiently. "What is it Elfly?" he asked.

"When am I gonna get out of here so I can start my comeback tour?" asked Elfly. "I'm no megala...mega? I don't wanna be king of the world." His shoulders jerked beneath his straight jacket and he deliberately rocked his head side to side. "I'm already the king of rock and roll!"

"Not now Elfly!" Sigmund scolded. "We go through this every session." Addressing the other patients, Sigmund explained, "Elfly has a different form of megalomania to the rest of you. He has delusions of being the greatest rock star on the planet, and if you had studied Elfly's case history as I have, you would understand why. In the circus he was known as the amazing Elfly because he was a man that could do what a fly could do. In other words, he was an amazing acrobat and trapeze artist. He learned to climb up and down walls with suction cups on his knees and hands. He dropped from great heights on to his head one too many times, however, and his illness is the result. Let's just say, his athletic prowess makes up for what he lacks in mental agility."

Right after Sigmund finished speaking, and if right on cue, Elfly jumped to his feet and started dancing, vibrating and hopping, despite the constraints of the straight jacket.

"You ain't nothin' but a hack doc!" sang Elfly, "dabblin' in my mind. You ain't nothin' but a hack doc, injecting my behind. Well, you ain't never cured a headache, and you ain't no friend of mine!"

"I like it Elfly. It's catchy. You're best song to date. It's about me and I'm flattered."

"Want me to sing it again?"

"Maybe next session. Well, look at the time. That's enough for this week." Turning to the padded door, he called, "Psychobot Nurse!"

The door crashed open and the ten-foot robot marched in.

"Take these patients back to their cells," ordered Sigmund.

Elfly was the first to hop toward the open door, and as he did so, he sang, "Well everybody in the mad house block, began to do the asylum rock!"

CHAPTER 16

RUST ROB

Howard climbed down a ladder on the side of his yacht and stepped on to the deck of the Porcelain Porpoise.

The legless robot watched Howard approach him through its one working electronic eye. All its programs worked together to register contempt and suspicion.

Upon arriving in front of the scowling robot, Howard greeted it, saying, "Hello there, I'm How..."

"I duz-nae care who ye be," interrupted the robot. "I duz-nae know whether ye be a pirate or a scallywag, a friend or a foe, but do ye this!" The robot pointed up and over to Little Klawd on the other ship. "Say ta yer giant puss 'avast', lest the puss sends us all ta the bottom o' the sea. Wait. Duz me one good eye deceive me? I know that puss! It be Lil' Klawd, only the puss ain't so lil' nay more."

Little Klawd, was still busy chewing on the skeleton of the former fish and at the same time he was sunning himself on the deck of the golden poot-a-maran.

Howard aimed his voice upward and shouted over to his cat on the bigger boat. "Stay Klawd, stay!"

Little Klawd yawned.

Turning back to the robot, Howard politely bowed and said, "Howard Looz, at your service."

The seagull on the robot's head cried, "EEK EEK," in greeting.

Howard then extended his hand and gave the robot's hand a vigorous shake, which unfortunately caused its rusty arm to break off.

"Aye, Figures," the robot grumbled.

"Erm... Uh... Sorry!" Howard apologised. "Would you like me to try and attach it again? I can pay for a new one if need be."

"Twas a bum arm ter begin with," replied the robot. "Rusted troo and troo."

Feeling awkward and not knowing what to do with the arm, Howard tossed it over his shoulder and into the sea.

"Now I be called a worse nickname than the ones I already 'as!" complained the robot.

"Really, what nickname is that?"

"I be called Rust Rob No-Pants. If I lose me one remaining arm, then I be called Rust Rob No-Pants-and-No-Sleeves."

"Oh," was all Howard could think of to say. "Er, so where is Stanley now?"

"Lookin' fer treasure I 'spect'! See this 'ere spool o' 'ose?"

A thick air hose dangled in the sea from a

large spool bolted to the bow of the boat.

"Follow the 'ose down an' ye'll fin' Stanley. 'E be 'alf a league below the Sy-kee-delic Sea, 'e is."

CHAPTER 17

BENEATH THE SEA

Stanley Siphonpipe Junior was in blissful ignorance of all that was taking place above the surface of the Psychedelic Sea.

He was exploring,

He was making a documentary film.

He was showing off the sunken treasure he had just discovered.

"I, Stanley Siphonpipe Junior have done it!"

He pointed his underwater movie camera (a camera that was not a robot and did not talk back) at his big, expressive face.

"Chalk another one up for Stan the man!"

Stanley Siphonpipe Junior truly was a man now, albeit a young man, having reached the mature age of twenty years old.

Stanley's whole head could be seen behind his transparent Plexiglas bubble helmet. An air hose leading to the ship above was connected to the top of his helmet. This enabled him to breathe the air being pumped down, while his exhales escaped in bubbles from tubes on top of his helmet.

Below the neck, Stanley was cocooned in a metal diving suit, which was designed to protect him from the many toothy denizens of the deep.

"What have I done? I'll show you!"

Stanley pointed his camera outward and panned across the seascape in front of him.

"First, let me tell you where I am; it just happens to be the unfathomable fathoms of the Psychedelic Sea. As far as the eye can see there are weird corals, which play host to hordes of hairy fish of every size, shape, colour and hairstyle. Yes, ladies and gentlemen, this is the sea's Great Hairier Reef. I mean, it's like an underwater city down here and these corals are like the apartment complexes housing every kind of sea creature you could ever imagine."

Suddenly there was a disturbance in the water and Stanley threw himself down on the sandy sea bottom just in time to avoid being trampled by an underwater stampede. A school of several thousand Psychedelic Squid raced by, swimming for their lives from a gigantic, white whale that was covered in colourful array of sea anemones. As the school of squid evaded the pursuing whale, they each squirted a trail of different coloured ink behind themselves."

"Good! They missed my air-hose this time."

Stanley stood to his feet, and with the camera pointed at his face, he said, "Before I was so rudely interrupted, I was about to tell you about the great discovery I made here in an unexplored corner of the Great Hairier Reef."

Stanley turned around and pointed his camera at a sunken ship off in the murky distance.

"I am pleased to announce that I have found the final resting place of the old chamber pot schooner, the Jolly Jakes, the infamous ship of Brown Squirt the pirate. Brown Squirt's ship was destroyed in a violent storm, and his treasure was lost –lost until now!"

Stanley panned down and pointed his camera at his feet. There resting in front of his feet was a treasure chest filled with gold, pearls and jewels.

"I have done it! I have found the treasure chest of Brown Squirt the pirate! I am rich! I can afford a new ship! I can afford to fix Rust Rob! Who needs Howard Looz? Who needs Livingston! I can fund my own explor...!"

He didn't finish. An enormous Great Blond Shark with long, blond hair appeared out of the colourful murk behind him and stopped to investigate the strange visitor to its territorial waters.

As a result of the shark's presence, all the hairy fish in the area suddenly swam away in chaos, bumping into each other in their panic to leave.

"And – there's a shark behind me, isn't there? Not again! Do we have to do this now? OK, let's get this over with."

The Great Blond Shark closed its gaping mouth around Stanley, bit down with the full force of its jaws and began to violently shake him from side to side in the same way that a vicious dog might shake a bone.

✳ ✳ ✳ ✳ ✳

CHAPTER 18

BAD HAIR CLAMS

"Oh 'tis a world o' danger down un'er," said Rust Rob. He tapped the spool of hose with pride. "The air 'ose be a lifeline, an' 'is divin' suit protecks 'im from the monsters o' the deep. Aye, I reeled 'im outa mure scrapes, than I cares ta tell ye. If me other arm goes, me reelin' days be o'er.

The hose began to un-spool rapidly and flail from side to side.

"What's happening?" asked Howard.

"AR! Do'er ya see that?" said Rust Rob. "Sumthin's got 'im. Its probably one o' 'em blasted Great Blond Sharks!"

✳ ✳ ✳ ✳

After several minutes of violently shaking Stanley, the Great Blond Shark grew tired of the effort.

Its attempt to eat Stanley cost it several hundred cracked teeth, and so finally, it spat Stanley out and swam away, tossing its long blond hair over its dorsal fin in a show of contempt.

258

"Is your brain made of cartilage as well?" shouted Stanley. "When will you stupid sharks learn that you can't bite through my suit?"

Pointing the camera back at his face, Stanley said, "That, ladies and gentlemen, was a Great Blond Shark, and believe me, they are not the brightest creatures in the Psychedelic Sea. I mean strike one; it has a brain the size of a walnut, and strike two, its blond. Anyway, as I was saying, I have discovered..." (He pointed the camera back down at the treasure chest) "...the treasure chest of Brown Squirt the pirate, which will fund ten thousand more expeditions like this one."

Without warning, a large, voracious, snapping clam with long, blue hair popped up from the sand underneath the chest, and swallowed the treasure; its gold, pearls and jewels before abruptly disappearing beneath the sand.

Stanley paused for a moment in stunned silence, pointed the camera at his face and explained, "And that ladies and gentleman was a Bad-Hair Clam. They eat anything that invades their territory. Please excuse me."

Cool, calm and collected, Stanley switched off the camera and tossed it aside. In the next moment, he lost his cool, lunged frantically for the Bad Hair Clam beneath the sand, and yelled, "Give it back you miserable mollusk!"

He found the hair of the clam, grabbed it and yanked the shellfish upward. Taking hold of its cement-hard lips, Stanley tried to pry the shell open.

In a sneaky maneuver the clam suddenly opened its mouth and bit down on Stanley's right hand, trapping it.

At that moment the sea bed began to shake and simmer as if being cooked, releasing millions of bubbles from the ocean floor.

Bad Hair Clams, thousands of them, emerged from the sand. The malevolent mollusks snapped their shells, opening and closing their mouths in a frenzy. The man in the metal diving suit was now the target of their angry eating-disorder.

One of the Bad Hair Clams opened wide its toothy shell and bit Stanley's bottom.

Other shells started to snap at Stanley's feet, making him dance and jump about. Before he knew it, there were Bad Hair Clams stuck on both of his feet, both his hands, his helmet and all over his body.

CHAPTER 19

THE DOOM OF THE PORCELAIN PORPOISE

Looking at the violent side to side motion of the air hose, Howard said, "Do you think you could reel Stanley up now? I would like to talk to him."

Dismissively, Rust Rob replied, "If Stanley was ter come back up urvery time 'e's set upon by therm monsters down thur, 'ed never get nurthing done. 'Ell come up when 'e's good an' ready. I'll wait fer the signal, so I will."

From the deck of Howard's yacht, Little Klawd also stared at the volatile movement of the air hose. It reminded him of kittenhood. It brought back memories of the boy Stanley Junior used to be who would dangle a ball of string in front of his nose. He understood very few words, but 'TOY' was a word he knew well. All his feline instincts shouted "PLAY!" He wanted to strike the hose, the 'TOY,' bat it with his paw, and make the maddening movement stop.

Little Klawd rose to his feet and prepared to leap.

"NO!" yelled Howard.

"AVAST LIL' KLAWD!" shouted Rust Rob.

The Giant Golden Saber Toothed Tabby leapt.

The force of eighteen tons of cat suddenly landing on the Porcelain Porpoise caused it to go halfway under the water before it bobbed back up, teetered, rocked and took in seawater.

Howard was knocked off balance and had to grab on to the side railings to keep himself from plunging into the sea.

Rust Rob fell hard on his corroded face. His other arm broke off.

At the same time, the seagull flew away as its nest and eggs slipped off Rust Rob's head and into the ocean.

"Bad kitty! Bad Klawd! Bad!" scolded Howard as Little Klawd danced on the rocking ship trying to find his balance.

"Curses! Just me luck!" cursed Rust Rob, as he slid from side to side. Unceremoniously, he tumbled over the side of the Porcelain Porpoise and into the Psychedelic Sea.

"Goodbye cruel world!"

＊ ＊ ＊ ＊ ＊

The Bad-Hair Clams were like clothespins from Hell and they clung on to every inch of Stanley's diving suit as he stumbled blindly through the minefield of snapping sea shells.

Had he been able to see, he would have witnessed Rust Rob sinking to the bottom of the ocean right in front of him.

Rust Rob did see Stanley however, and he gave him a withering look.

"Serves 'im right!" grumbled Rust Rob.

As soon as the robot touched the bottom, a Bad-Hair Clam appeared underneath and swallowed him whole.

✳ ✳ ✳ ✳ ✳

As Howard held on to the boat's rail for dear life, he shouted at Little Klawd, saying, "The ship is sinking! Stanley will drown! His air hose!"

Little Klawd stared back at him stupidly.

With sudden inspiration, Howard pointed emphatically at the air hose reel and yelled, "Look Little Klawd! Toy! Ball of string!"

Little Klawd lunged for the air hose spool, running over Howard in the process. The cat took the spool in his jaws and ripped it from where it was bolted to the bow of the boat.

Having been knocked down and almost squished to death, Howard lay flat on his back, barely able to move. He saw the fur of Little Klawd's underbelly, and then the cat's tail. Instinctively he grabbed Little Klawd's tail and held on for dear life.

With his new toy in his mouth, Little Klawd jumped out of Porcelain Porpoise and back on to the golden poot-a-maran.

Howard was also whisked away to the safety of his yacht.

In the meantime, the Porcelain Porpoise turned stern up and sank into the depths of the Psychedelic Sea.

The clams clinging to Stanley abruptly released him from their grip and dove headlong beneath the seabed. The thousands of other Bad Hair Clams in the vicinity disappeared in like manner.

"Got bored did you?" Stanley yelled after them.

He then noticed a growing shadow and looking up, he saw the Porcelain Porpoise falling downward through the water towards him.

"My boat!" yelled Stanley.

Not only did it look like the Porcelain Porpoise would fall right on top of him, but he also remembered that his air hose was attached to the ship. This meant that he would shortly run out of air and die if the sinking ship did not crush him first.

Just when all seemed lost, Stanley felt a surprising tug on his air hose, and in the next moment he was pulled out of danger and reeled up to Howard's yacht by Little Klawd and Howard.

CHAPTER 20

THE SURPRISE HOUSE GUEST

EXCERPT FROM LIVINGSTON'S JOURNAL
Privy the 25th

It was a shock to find Stanley Jr. sleeping on my living room couch this morning, especially since I was stumbling around in my underwear.

My eyes were still half-shut and I didn't see him there until I heard him say, "Are those bunny slippers?"

I shrieked and nearly fell over backwards.

I then scolded him saying, "Stanley, you nearly gave me a heart attack! When did you get in?"

Instead of answering my question he said, "I can't believe you actually wear bunny slippers."

I abruptly left the room and didn't return until I was dressed in my Sir Randolph Tickets uniform.

By this time, Stanley was gone from the couch and was now up, dressed and in my kitchen helping himself to a bowl of my cereal and to a glass of my chocolate flavoured milk.

"Help yourself," I said sarcastically, while standing in the kitchen doorway giving him my best irritated-scowl-with-arms-folded-across-the-chest routine.

"Breakfast of champions," Stanley enthused. "Yu wan' fum?" he asked with a mouthful of cereal.

"Not hungry," I grunted.

"So how do you like living in our old house?"

"The security is lax," was my terse reply.

"I beg to differ. Your new robots wouldn't let me in. They were standing around out front and they only let me in after Howard ordered them to stand down. He also instructed them to listen to me."

"I'll tell them that Howard was joking and to pay no attention to you."

"I like Pambot," said Stanley. "She's nice. Swats-er-whatever is a big one isn't he? I think they put more effort into making him strong than smart though. The skinny silver one's as cool as they come, but you must have felt sorry for the floating one when you decided to take him on.

Anyway, sorry about the surprise. Howard and I didn't arrive back from the Psychedelic Sea till around midnight. I didn't want to wake you, so I just came on in and made myself at home."

"That's what all the burglars say."

"So, where are we going, partner?"

Stanley Siphonpipe
Junior

"Partner?" I wanted to shoot the word down
in flames. "If and when I do go somewhere, I may
just let you tag along, but it won't be anything
like a partnership. Most likely you will be

pitching tents, building campfires, digging latrines and polishing my boots."

Without batting an eyelid, Stanley said, "Sorry Livingston, but I'm not your maid. I am an explorer and you need me or otherwise Howard wouldn't have gone all the way out to the Psychedelic Sea to get me."

"Need? HA!" I laughed, hoping to knock him down a peg or two. "As I explained to Howard, I've been exploring all by myself all these years, thank you very much. This was Howard's idea not mine, and the only reason I'm going along with it is because he pays the bills."

"You and I are going absolutely nowhere together until we test the Star Flush..."

"Wait. The Star what?"

PART THREE

THE FIRST INTERGALACTIC ADVENTURE

CHAPTER 21

THE TEST FLUSH

EXCERPT FROM LIVINGSTON'S JOURNAL
11:30 AM on Privy the 25th

"....And that is how you read Charade-oglyphics!" I explained as Directo-cam filmed my demonstration.

"Cut!" shouted Directo-cam. "I have an hour-and-a-half of footage showing you jumping up and down like an idiot in front of the Star Flush, yelling 'first word' 'second word' 'sounds like' and guessing what those butt-ugly stick-things are saying. Can we move on? When are we going to see a stupid, bleedin' test flush?"

Stanley caught my eye and said, "How can you stand to work with that thing? It's obnoxious!"

Directo-cam heard this and his lens eyes zoomed in and out angrily. He glared at Stanley and growled, "Are you talking about me punk?"

"Yes I am," said Stanley, standing up to the camera. "If I had my way, you would be back in the basement of the network switched off and hanging on the wall or where ever it is they put you at night."

"You know fatso, I could make you look fifty pounds heavier by going wide angle!" threatened Directo-cam.

"...And you can take a close up picture of my fist while I break your lens...."

Directo-cam made his theatrical lights strobe in Stanley's eyes, and said, "Here, have a cataract on me."

"Boys," I interrupted. "I mean boy and camera. Cut it out!" To Directo-cam, I said, "I just need to make my speech and then we'll proceed with the test flush."

Directo-cam cursed, while in-built censors bleeped over his swearing. He then yelled, "Places you morons. ROLL 'EM! OK everybody gimme a really big cheesy smile! I'm panning from right to left..."

I took my place standing with Howard and Stanley off to the right of the Star Flush, while the robot porters stood off to the left. (Oh yeah. Here is an important detail to insert here. It should be mentioned that Gigglebyte had some rain gear draped over his arms).

Directo-cam circled us, panning up and down and from side to side, filming the Star Flush from all different angles.

"OK Livingston, take your mark, and on my count, make your big boring speech. Five, four, three, ready, go."

Stepping forward, I smiled into Directo-cam's lens and said, "My fellow Cessestians – we the people of the planet Cessestial, have been entrusted with an incredible gift. For the first time in our history, we will be able to leave our own atmosphere, travel into space and explore other planets.

Young Stanley Siphonpipe Junior has courageously volunteered to be the first person from our planet to flush through the Star Flush.

I tried to talk him out of it. I said, 'No, I should go because I am older, wiser, and more experienced.'

But then Stanley said, 'Does a general go to the front line of the battle or does he order the soldiers under him to do that? Why needlessly endanger yourself?' he said to me. 'You're needed for command and control.' He begged me saying, 'Please, I want to do this more than anything. You don't need to prove yourself but I do.'

I admired the kid's spunk, his passion, his bravery, and I couldn't fault his logic, so reluctantly I've agreed to let Stanley go instead of me. We also decided to send one robot with Stanley and it was unanimously agreed that Gigglebyte..."

"Hold it! Unanimous nothing!" interrupted Directo-cam. "No one asked me for my opinion. So Stanley doesn't want to go with a professional movie-making robot, a veteran of hundreds of expeditions, but he's willing to take that untried, untrained, broken-down bucket of bolts? Is that it?"

"Yeah, well, I've been given a break," Stanley said to Directo-cam, "and I thought Gigglebyte could use a break too."

"Oh, he'll break alright," scoffed Directo-cam.

"Better a broken him than a functioning loud mouthed you. I wouldn't take you with me if you were the last robot on the planet!"

"I don't have to hover here and listen to this!" said Directo-cam.

"Yes, you do," I reminded the movie camera. "You're under contract. So no more insults from any bot and anybody and let's keep rolling."

Sulkily, the camera zoomed back and began filming from as far away from everyone as he could possibly get without losing focus.

In the meantime, Gigglebyte angrily blew black fumes out of his hover base, and muttered, "That's telling him!"

Gliding over to Stanley, Gigglebyte brought the rain gear to him (a plastic yellow rain jacket, a rain hat and windshield wiper rain goggles).

Speaking to whatever audience would someday see this taped presentation, I continued. "Let's talk about safety. Safety was uppermost in my mind when choosing a planet for our trial flush. When I consulted the Charade-oglyphics, I asked them to send Stanley and Gigglebyte to the most boring planet in the universe, and the planet they said that fit that description is called Skegness. They said, 'Skegness is a rainy miserable sphere that's completely dreary all the time and it's five galaxies away from here.'"

Turning to Stanley and Gigglebyte, I asked, "Are you ready?"

"Ready," affirmed Stanley after finishing putting on the rain gear.

Gigglebyte held up his metal thumb and said, "Flush away!"

Stanley and Gigglebyte then turned to face the Star Flush.

Blue disinfectant light started to spin faster and faster within the Star Flush bowl, while the Charade-oglyphics were jumping about on the screens around the upright lid.

"Howard, would you do the honors?" I said.

Howard ascended the stairs, stood in front of the control column, removed a thousand-puto bill from his toilet roll dispenser belt buckle, and then inserted the note into the money slot in the column.

"Charade-oglyphics, plot a course through the plumbing of the universe to the planet Skegness," I ordered.

The Charade-oglyphics worked feverishly, bouncing up and down as the dazzling light swirled and twirled within the bowl, creating a flushing noise that sounded like a hurricane.

"Jiggle the handle!" I shouted over the maelstrom.

Howard jiggled the turn handle. The light and noise increased until it was almost beyond the ability of Stanley and I to endure.

In fact, Howard didn't stick around to endure it. Instead, he leapt down the Star Flush stairs, and ran out of the laboratory.

Shouting over the noise, Stanley said, "This is one small flush for a man and a robot, but one giant turbo-charged flush for Cessestian-kind."

Stanley and Gigglebyte jumped into the swirling light of the bowl and disappeared from sight, accompanied by a thunderous FLUSH!

CHAPTER 22

SKEGNESS

Stanley and Gigglebyte experienced an exhilarating rush of motion through the invisible pipe-ways of the universe. They slid, twisted, turned and dropped at incomprehensible speeds, moving so fast that stars and galaxies raced by them.

All sound was swallowed in the vacuum of space. Stanley's whoops of delight never reached his own ears, and nor did he hear Gigglebyte's bad words.

A gray planet covered in thick layers of clouds then appeared in the distance.

Suddenly, they went into a state of suspended animation as if all time stopped, and then after what seemed an eternity, they resumed motion and began to spiral downwards through the misty atmosphere of the planet before starting to spin round and round faster and faster as if in a spin dryer.

Stanley was then catapulted up and out of

a vortex of spinning light and into the cold wind and freezing rain of an alien world. In the next moment, he landed face first in a puddle.

Gigglebyte shot out of the universal plumbing after Stanley, and also fell in the otherworldly mud. His stretchy head whipped off his neck and wound up behind himself facing his own bottom. His electronics cut out as a result.

Ten seconds later, his internal systems turned themselves back on and his voice droned, "Rebooting. Rebooting." He then moaned, "This just isn't right! No one should ever wake up and have to stare at their own booty." After untangling his neck and head from behind himself, he hovered upright and let the driving rain wash the mud off of his creaky lopsided body. "Yuck! GURR—OOOSS! Miserable! Welcome to Skegness!" he shouted over the howling gales and driving rain.

Picking himself up, Stanley wiped the mud off of himself as best he could and turned on his windshield wiper goggles so he could take a good look around.

Just behind him was the Skegness Star Flush, the gateway to the lackluster planet he found himself on. The lonely machine looked exactly like the Star Flush back in Livingston's laboratory, although this Skegnessian version was covered with plant matter, creepers, moss and lichens.

Having delivered the intergalactic travelers, the machine's Charade-oglyphics blinked off. The stairs withdrew into the Star Flush as the control column sunk back into the base ring. The lid then closed over the bowl and the machine darkened.

Surveying the new planet, this is what Stanley and Gigglebyte saw: Behind the machine was a flat field covered in brambles and tall, untidy grass lashed by the wind and rain.

In front of the Star Flush was an ocean beach that appeared to have been hit by an oil spill disaster. With no one to spill the oil, its presence could be explained by the natural fountains of oil seeping up from beneath the ground. Stanley counted twenty-two such fountains in the immediate vicinity, and each fountain created a sticky stream that blackened the beach and coloured the tempestuous ocean brown.

Over the roar of the dirty waves slamming against the shore, Stanley said, "Looks like a nice place to bring the family on a vacation."

"Yeah, all you need is a trailer park and a couple of tacky seaside arcades and this place would be perfect," said Gigglebyte. "Now remind me, of all the planets in the universe, why did we flush to this one?"

"The idea was to go to some place so pathetically dull that we would, arrive, look around, say 'nope, nothing to see...'

Stanley was interrupted by a strange bellow and thump sound that could be heard above the wind.

"Bellow, thump, bellow thump, bellow,

thump." The sound repeated over and over again.

Stanley's head automatically turned to look up the beach where the sound seemed to be coming from and he began walking in that direction.

"Stanley, what are you doing?" called Gigglebyte. "We're supposed to turn around and flush straight back."

"Are you kidding? We just got here," yelled Stanley, raising his voice above the wind. "I am the very first person from Cessestial to set foot on a different planet, and do you think I'm just going to turn right around and..."

"But Livingston said..."

"If he were here, he'd do the exact same thing."

"Which is?"

"Find out what's making that sound. I don't see the harm in taking a little stroll up the beach; maybe pick up an alien seashell or two. I want to see if there really is nothing to see, you see?"

"I see," said Gigglebyte.

CHAPTER 23

A STROLL ON THE BEACH

Heading toward the "bellow" and 'thump' sound in the distance, Stanley trudged through the wet, oily sand of the Skegnessian beach, while Gigglebyte hovered beside him.

Trying to strike up a conversation, Stanley asked, "So Gigglebyte, what were you doing before you took this porter job?"

"I was an actor."

"An actor?" repeated Stanley.

"An out-of-work actor. Yeah, show biz ain't for the timid. You gotta have a lot of self-belief or this industry will rip out your hard drive! Take us robots for instance. All the programmed talent in the world and what do they do? They always typecast us as robots! That is all we ever play, and believe me, I have a much broader range than that. I probably made more of a name for myself on the comedy club circuit though."

Stanley was incredulous. "You're a stand up comedian?"

"Was!" said Gigglebyte bitterly. "Was a comedian! I was fired, and pulled off the stage early. Story of my life!"

Stanley gave the robot a seriously worried sideways glance.

"They said I wasn't funny enough. Hey, is it my fault I don't have the most up to date joke programming? They said I had more in common with a vacuum cleaner because..."

After an awkward pause, Stanley helpfully finished the sentence, saying, "You sucked?"

"Riiiiiight. See! Even you know the punchlines, and you're not half as hilarious as me."

"Well, you're timing and delivery were a bit off there."

"Oh, not you too! Everyone's a critic. I hate critics! You try getting up there in front of a bunch of drunks night after night? One critic said my routine was just a lot of angry ranting and raving. Well hey; he obviously knows nothing about comedy, because comedy is angry. It's pessimistic. It believes that under the best of conditions, somebody will screw everything up! Well, I'll show them how funny I can be when I make my triumphant return to the stage. They're gonna have one hysterically hilarious ticked off robot on their hands!"

"I can see you're a laugh a minute," remarked Stanley, with a deeply concerned look etched on his face. "Er, the other robots aren't comedians are they?"

"No. Just me. Yeah, we were all members of the same robot employment agency, and that's how we all got to know each other. We've all had a bunch of other jobs, and we were sitting around on our butts doing nothing when I told them about this ad for a porting gig that I'd seen in the newspaper. Yeah, we each have our various functions, but I will probably be the only one who cheers everyone up if things get tough out here on all these planets you and Livingston are supposed to explore."

Changing the subject, Stanley said, "You have binocular vision don't you? Could you look out and try to see whatever it is that's making that noise?"

"OK, but I doubt I'll see anything in this weather."

He extended his head upward, transforming his eyes into binoculars.

Peering into the misty distance, he reported, "Yeah, I see more rain and fog, and oh wait! – I do see something. Yeah, there it is. Yep, that's what's making the sound."

"What is it?"

"It's some kind of big, hairy creature. I don't like the look of it – and it's stuck in some black gooey stuff. Hey, didn't those Charade-o-goof-ups tell us this planet was uninhabited?"

"Uninhabited by people!" explained Stanley.

"If my opinion counts for anything, which I know it doesn't, I recommend that we turn right around and head back to the Star Flush!"

✳ ✳ ✳ ✳ ✳

CHAPTER 24

THE ALIEN BEAST

Ten minutes later, Stanley and Gigglebyte arrived at the sad scene of struggle. A magnificent animal, a creature unique to the planet Skegness was fighting for its life, trapped in a pool of oil and tar.

The bellows and thumps drowned out the noise of the wind, rain and ocean waves.

Stanley was amazed by the creature before him.

Gigglebyte eyed it suspiciously.

The beast was a shaggy giant covered in long strands of reddish-brown hair which hung like curtains from its humped back.

It was a mammoth-sized animal and Stanley guessed that it weighed six or seven tons. It had barrel legs like an elephant although elephants didn't have deadly spikes around their feet like this creature did.

It also had a spike on the end of its long, armour-plated face, located just above its flaring nostrils.

Its eyes were bulging melon-sized googly

orbs mounted in periscope fashion high up on its bony forehead, and there was a strange fleshy appendage growing out the very top of its head; an appendage shaped like a castle turret and covered in hairs sticking straight up like the bristles in a brush.

It had cud-chewing teeth like a horse, but unlike any other mammalian creature in the universe, the animal had cheek pincers protruding from the side of its face that functioned like a pair of scissors.

Upon seeing Stanley and Gigglebyte, its bellow became more desperate and its eyes filled with fright.

Stanley tried to reassure the creature. He calmly called to the beast, saying, "You don't have to be afraid of us. We're not going to hurt you."

"What the heck is it?" asked Gigglebyte.

"It's whatever we want to call it. It's a brand new discovery, and I think I have the perfect name for it. Listen to the sound it makes."

The strange animal's bellow formed a trumpeting "GUMP" sound, followed by a low, reverberating "THUMP" from its vibrating throat.

"I'm going to call it a gumpathump," announced Stanley, "or to be scientific, a gumpathumpus Skeggnessius."

"Right. So, er, should we, er, take a sample now from gumper-whatever-you-said?"

"I think we should help it! The scientific samples can wait."

"Let me guess. You flunked the 'Let Nature Take Its Course' class at university, didn't you?"

"Yeah, I totally cut that class."

The gumpathump raised its head to the sky and gumped pitifully.

"Problem. How are we going to pull a big heavy gumpy…gumper…gumpybumpy…?"

"Gumpathump," corrected Stanley.

"…gumpathump out of the tar?" finished Gigglebyte.

"Hmmmm? It's a question of leverage. It will need something to hold on to while it pulls itself out. If there was something like a pole, or nail, or peg driven into the ground that it could grab on to with its cheek pincers, I'm sure that would do the trick and then…."

Stanley's voice trailed off. With sudden inspiration, he fixed his eyes on Gigglebyte. He sized the robot up from the top of his dented head to the bottom of his hovering base.

"Right, but where are we going to get?… OH NO! You're looking at the wrong bot!"

"Yes Gigglebyte, you will provide the leverage this creature needs."

"I should report you to the Society for the Protection of Abused Robots."

Stanley took a few cautious steps over to the gumpathump, coming alongside its strange head before carefully reaching out to stroke its face. The creature was jumpy and it jerked its head away at first, but then it gradually gained the confidence to let Stanley pet it.

Comforting the beast, Stanley whispered, "Don't worry gumpathump, it will be alright." He then called over his shoulder to Gigglebyte and said, "Gigglebyte, come here."

Gigglebyte hovered a few feet forward and stopped.

"Come closer."

Gigglebyte hesitantly hovered a further few feet nearer to the animal, and then stopped again.

"Closer than that. Get right in front of it."

Reluctantly, Gigglebyte hovered to within a few inches of the gumpathump's face. The creature responded by gumping and licking Gigglebyte's metallic head, which made him say, "OO! Gross! Yuck! Sick! Watch the slobber pal!"

"Dig a hole in the sand, turn off your anti-gravity hover base, and anchor yourself inside the hole."

"You forgot to say please!" grumbled Gigglebyte. He then dug a hole underneath himself with his mechanical hands, muttering and murmuring as he did so. Soon there was a hole big enough to insert himself. Once inside the hole of oily sand, he scooped the black grit back in on himself until he was buried up to his metallic chest.

"This is..." – His mind searched for a word. "...icky! I can feel tar up my tail pipe. I'm going to have to be taken apart and scrubbed bit by bit to get myself clean. You owe me big time!"

"If you help me get the gumpathump out, I will personally see that Howard Looz gets the cleaning bill," promised Stanley. To the gumpathump he whispered, "Shhhh! It's OK big fella – big girl – uh big whatever you are. We're here to help you. Let's try to get you out of this mess. I want you to bite my robot with your pincers and pull yourself out."

"Did you just say bite?"

"Stretch out your hand and grab its pincers."

"Are you crazy?"

"Just do it!"

Gigglebyte stretched out his hands so that he could take hold of the creature's cheek pincers. He gripped them gently, and to his surprise, the gumpathump allowed this. He then pulled them down carefully so that his metal body sat right between the bony blades of the animal's scissor appendages. Putting on a brave face, Gigglebyte said, "OK bring it on. Bite me. Do your worst."

The gumpathump hesitated. It lightly nipped, bit, tapped and tested Gigglebyte's body but seemed reluctant to squeeze him hard with the formidable weapons it had been equipped with.

"Do you see that? It doesn't want to hurt you," said Stanley. "These gumpathumps have a soft side to them."

Abruptly, Stanley stopped everything he was doing to listen. Something came to his attention; there were otherworldly sounds rising above the wind, the waves, the gumps and thumps. Eerie, distant shrieks pierced his ears and they seemed to be getting louder as each stressful second passed. The gumpathump tensed. A maddening fright filled its bulging eyes, and it pounded its front feet hysterically, while it gumped and thumped in terror.

"Uh oh," said Stanley, "Please tell me that's some alien atmospheric condition making that sound."

"Think about it," said Gigglebyte gloomily. "There's a big tasty easy-to-catch meal stuck in the tar. And it gets even better. This planet's pitiful excuse for daylight is disappearing fast. It's getting dark!"

CHAPTER 25

THE GUMPATHUMP-EATERS

The shrieks were now louder than ever coming from all directions.

Frantic, and frenzied, the trapped beast clamped down on Gigglebyte's head with its scissor pincers, and shook squeezed and bit the misshapen lump of metal in its grasp.

"N-N-Not M-M-My H-H-Head! S-S-SQUEEZE M-M-MY B-B-BODY!"

Unfortunately Gigglebyte's detachable head and stretchy neck gave the gumpathump no leverage, and so its desperate effort to extract itself from the tar was in vain.

Stanley tried to see into the dark, into the rain, mist and ocean spray, and though he could hear the approaching shrieking somethings or whatever they were, visibility was so poor, he could only detect indistinct shadows and shapes. They seemed to be large shadows however, but he also wondered if it were just his imagination. Finally one of the shadows took form. There was a lightning strike over the ocean. For an instant,

Stanley could clearly see something slithering along the turbulent surface of the Skeggnessian Sea. It was heading directly toward them. It was a gigantic fluke, a twenty-foot monster of a worm with small sharp spikes all around its translucent body. Its slimy, serpentine shape was as white and colourless as a parasitic tapeworm.

Another lightning strike. At the crest of a wave the worm's upper body rose up and Stanley saw its horrific head. Most of its face was just a mouth, a round leech-like sucker filled with a circle of needle sharp teeth. It had two narrow-eye slits on either side of its head, four eye-slits in total, which were blood red in colour.

Veiled once again in darkness, the worm shrieked.

As if this one worm wasn't bad enough, three more worm shadows rose up from the sea behind the first worm.

Arriving on the beach, the first worm lifted its rounded head and undulated in place while it looked around. After screeching one more time, it suddenly dove head first into the sand, burrowing and tunnelling until the end of its long body disappeared beneath the surface of the beach.

"N-not good," stammered Stanley. "N-not good at all." He looked to the flat fields bordering the beach. Lightning revealed half a dozen more worms approaching from this direction.

A quick glance back to the beach revealed that the other three worms had landed and then they followed the first worm's lead and dove beneath the sand. Stanley jerked his head back to the fields. The worms there were now gone as well, and were presumably somewhere underground.

"H–H–Help m–m–me or it w–w–will t–t–tear m–m–my h–h–head off–off!" pleaded Gigglebyte.

The gumpathump continued to shake the robot's corroded cranium back and forth and from side to side.

Taking decisive action, Stanley yelled, "GUMPATHUMP STOP!" Instinctively the creature understood, and it allowed Stanley to take hold of its pincers and push them down until they were firmly around Gigglebyte's metal torso.

Suddenly, there was a violent tremor. Thirteen monstrous worms exploded out of the sand and formed a circle around the trapped gumpathump.

One worm came up directly beneath Stanley. In less than a second, Stanley was fifteen feet in the air riding on the head of a terrible worm before he tumbled backwards down its slimy body. He ended up flat on his back, outside the circle.

The flukes screamed, hissed and prepared to attack, while Stanley could do nothing but cower and watch.

The gumpathump squeezed the robot hard, tugging with all of its strength until finally it began to emerge tail and all from the tar. With one final heave, the gumpathump pulled on the buried robot until all four of its feet stumbled out on to solid ground. It was good for the gumpathump but bad for Gigglebyte. His metal mid-section was crushed and all his electronics shut down.

Just as the gumpathump struggled on to its feet, a fourteenth worm erupted from the tar pool, missing the gumpathump's underbelly by a fraction of a second. It screeched and snapped at the empty air, while black tar dripped from its white body.

In the meanwhile, the other thirteen worms surrounded the gumpathump as their heads swayed backward and forward waiting for the perfect moment to strike.

"Rebooting. Rebooting." said Gigglebyte, as the robot switched himself back on. He then rocketed out of the hole and hovered over to Stanley's side.

To Stanley and Gigglebyte's relief, the horrid worms slithered around them as if they were not even there, taking no interest in them. The attention of the flukes was fixed solely on the gumpathump, and so Stanley and Gigglebyte ended up being spectators, watching in helpless horror as the predatory flukes moved in for the kill.

In the meantime, the gumpathump gumped and thumped defiantly, stomping its feet and snapping its cheek pincers as it looked wildly about for any weakness in the circle of pack-hunting worms.

Several of the monsters lunged at the

gumpathump's left hindquarters. It was able to dodge the wormy jaws, leaving them with mouthfuls of tar and hair.

Another worm tried to strike at the gumpathump's right hindquarters. The gumpathump aimed its spiky back foot at the worm's tender underbelly and kicked the fluke, ripping it open and mortally wounding it.

It was then that the gumpathump made a break for it, running straight at the worms that stood between itself and the field.

Two packworms then struck, aiming at the gumpathump's neck as it tried to run between the worms. The gumpathump was ready for them however, and reared up on its curly tail to bite the head off of one of the worms with its cheek pincers, while swiping, kicking and stabbing the second worm with its spiked feet, killing the other worm in the process.

Yet another packworm blindsided the gumpathump from the left and took a bloody bite out of its flank.

Stanley and Gigglebyte were sickened to see red liquid pouring down the translucent gullet of the colourless creature.

Fighting back though, the gumpathump turned on the blood-sucking worm and trampled it underfoot, leaving it injured on the ground.

Gigglebyte took a quick head count of the worms, and calculated that three of the flukes were now dead, and one was injured, which left nine packworms still in the hunt. "Wait. There should be ten worms," computed Gigglebyte. "Oh Oh! One of them is miiiiissing! Hey, where'd the worm in the tar go?"

He detected movement underneath the sand and then the missing worm burst out of the ground directly underneath the gumpathump.

Gigglebyte was already moving however, having made a snap decision to go to the gumpathump's aid against his hardwired better judgment.

"Curse my ethics program," he shouted as he jettisoned into the jaws of the worm underneath the gumpathump. It snapped its jaws, but instead of a mouthful of gumpathump flesh, it tasted metal.

In the meanwhile, the gumpathump charged forward one more time in an attempt to smash through the circle of predatory worms. It succeeded by running over two worms, but then another packworm was able to leap on to its back just as it was escaping. This worm bit the gumpathump repeatedly, burying its jaws into its hump. Despite the gumpathump's best effort to buck and kick it off, the worm clung on, and so with the monster in tow, the gumpathump ran off into the dark fields beyond Stanley's ability to see.

CHAPTER 26

BACK UP THE BEACH

The remaining packworms quickly dove beneath the sand in pursuit of the injured gumpathump leaving just one packworm behind, the fluke with Gigglebyte stuck in its mouth. Angrily, this worm shook its slimy jaws trying to dislodge the robot. When this didn't work, it tilted back its head, and swallowed Gigglebyte. With a screech, it then dove underneath the ground, leaving Stanley all by himself.

For a minute, Stanley was too traumatised to do or say anything.

"Goodbye, Gigglebyte," he finally whispered.

He had never missed a robot – a mere machine – an artificial personality before, but he now felt like he had lost a relative. The sudden isolation he felt, hit him like a ton of concrete blocks and he realised that he was now totally vulnerable and helpless on a desolate world, a trillion miles from anywhere.

"The Star Flush!" he thought. "I must get back to the Star Flush."

He left the tar pool behind and began the long slog back up the beach.

He moved as quickly as he could but unfortunately his squat body, short legs and big feet were not built for speed and especially not for speed across oil-soaked sand.

The stormy conditions and soggy cement-like sludge slowed him down to what almost seemed like a snail's crawl. Every step forward was strenuous and exhausting.

Many thoughts passed through Stanley's mind as he struggled onward. Again his memories returned to Gigglebyte with sadness. Not only did he miss Gigglebyte terribly, but the robot's self-sacrifice on behalf of the gumpathump also moved him with a mixture of admiration and grief.

He also felt sorry for the poor gumpathump and doubted that it would survive the night.

His focus then turned to the monstrous worms. He wondered if there were any more of the horrid things lurking about and the frightening thought also occurred to him that maybe, just maybe, they might be interested in a bite-sized snack like himself in absence of a gumpathump.

"But how can they see or smell from under the ground?" he asked himself. He immediately answered his own question. "They don't see or smell – they listen! They can hear every footstep I make."

The stretch of sand in front of him now looked as if it was full of land mines and he knew full well that one of the flukes could ambush him from underneath at any given moment.

He had no choice but to press on however, though he did so with trepidation, fearing that each step might be his last.

The minutes passed slowly as he trudged on and on, until at last, the Skegness Star Flush became visible in the gloomy distance.

"Oh thank Saint Valveless!"

His thankfulness was premature. Just when he thought he might escape from Skegness with his life, three packworms torpedoed upward out of the ground around him!

He froze in place, not daring to exhale.

The three worms oozed out of the sand jostling with each other to wrap themselves around Stanley as they sniffed him and stuck out their long multipronged tongues to taste him.

"Get Away!" shouted Stanley. He was ashamed of himself for giving into his fear. "What would my dad have done in this situation?" Stanley asked himself. "What would Livingston do? Surely not scream and lose his nerve."

Stanley then closed his eyes and waited for death, hoping that it would be quick and painless.

Several seconds passed, but nothing happened. There was no hiss, no strike and no bite.

"Why am I not dead?" he wondered.

Cautiously, he opened his eyes, and to his surprise he saw that the worms were no longer looking at him. Their attention seemed to be focused on the inland field.

Just as suddenly as they had popped above the ground, they now retreated beneath the sand.

A familiar sound reached Stanley's ears. It was the bellowing gump and rumbling thump of the gumpathump and it was galloping toward him from the direction of the field. No longer was there a fluke attached to its back (though there were several open wounds on its big, hairy body).

"Gumpathump!" Stanley shouted, overjoyed to see the beast. "You heard me screaming didn't you?"

The gumpathump slowed to a trot, stopped in front of Stanley and lowered its head to the sand.

"This is curious behaviour," Stanley thought. "What are you doing?" Stanley asked out loud.

The gumpathump did something almost impossible for any creature Stanley had encountered before with the possible exception of an owl. The gumpathump turned its neck around in a full circle, a maneuver that would have broken the spine of almost anything else. Its head was now facing straight up while the back of its head touched the ground. The brush-turret atop its head then swept the ground from side to side for some unknown reason.

"That's weird gumpathump!" remarked Stanley. "Oh, by the way, watch yourself. There are three worms waiting for you underneath the ground and – what are you doing exactly? Oh I get it. You're listening. That thing on your head is some kind of super sensitive hearing adaptation so you can listen for those..."

He didn't finish. The same three packworms that had ambushed him a minute earlier suddenly shot out of the ground underneath the gumpathump.

It was not taken by surprise. It reared up on its hind legs in order to dodge their snapping jaws, while its neck righted itself. When its heavy body came back down, it stomped its spiky feet on top of the boneless heads of two of the worms, crushing and killing them, while the third worm retreated underground.

The gumpathump nudged Stanley with its snout, lowered its head and gumped an invitation for Stanley to climb aboard.

Taking the hint, Stanley ran up the creature's bony face as if running up a flight of stairs. As soon as he was safe on the gumpathump's back, the ground around them started to quake and then hundreds upon hundreds of packworms emerged from the ground, filling the night with their terrible shrieks.

"Oh, no! There are millions of them!" shouted Stanley.

The gumpathump took several nervous steps backwards, turned its tail and then bolted toward the inland fields, galloping as fast as it could.

Stanley tried to hang on. Grabbing the

gumpathump's neck hair and using it like the reigns on a horse, Stanley tried to steer the beast, shouting, "Gettyup gumpathump! To the Star Flush!"

Glancing over his shoulder, Stanley saw the ground writing with worms in hot pursuit. Ahead of them, worms rose up to attack, and Stanley had to hold on tight as the gumpathump met every fluke it encountered with leaps, rear ups and pincer bites. Dozens of worms lost their ferocious heads to the gumpathump's deadly pincers.

"Whoa!" yelled Stanley when the gumpathump was about to run right past the Star Flush. The alien animal had no intention of stopping however, and so Stanley jumped off the creature's back, landed hard on the weedy ground, and after quickly picking himself up, he ran for his life toward the porcelain portal.

Abruptly, several packworms rose up in front of him, blocking his way. Before he had time to despair, the gumpathump suddenly doubled back and attacked the worms, biting off their heads.

Thousands of packworms now surrounded them and squirmed toward them from all sides.

While the gumpathump prepared to make its last stand against the approaching monsters, Stanley put his fingers under the closed lid of the Star Flush. The lid then opened. The Star Flush stairs extended and the control column ascended out of the base ring.

Stanley ran up the stairs, grabbed the flush

handle on the column, jiggled it and caused the Charade-oglyphics to light up on the screen monitors.

"Plot a course for the planet Cessestial!"

"NO" they gestured.

Exasperated, Stanley yelled, "No? What do you mean, No?"

"Insert money please" was the mimed answer.

"Money! But I don't have any money!"

CHAPTER 27

HOWARD'S ANXIOUS QUESTIONS

"Has Stanley returned yet?" asked Howard. His question was addressed to the Directo-cam.

The robotic movie camera had come searching for Howard and had found him sitting on a bench in the park.

"Nope. Nothing!" replied Directo-cam, and at that Howard deflated like a balloon. "For three whole hours! - not a word!" continued the movie camera. "For all we know, fat boy got sucked into oblivion. Stanley's probably stuck in a cosmic drainpipe somewhere in the universe causing universal clogging and in the meanwhile, we're all sitting around twiddling our thumbs, and I have four thumbs to twiddle. Anyway I thought you might like some company."

"I don't need any company," muttered Howard. "Go away. I want to be alone."

"You're worried about Stanley aren't you?"

"Yes I am!" snapped Howard. "We should

have tested the Star Flush on you first. Why did I ever keep that cursed contraption? I've sent a young man to his death and all for what?"

"Fame, ambition, pride, ego," suggested Directo-cam. "That's what makes me tick."

"Why am I even talking to you? Go away!"

"Listen Loozy Baby, I know this may not be the best time, but I have an idea for a major motion picture that I would like you to finance... It'll slay them at the box off..."

"Mr. Looz," interrupted a female voice from a short distance away.

Howard was grateful to see Pambot striding up the park path towards him.

"You are urgently needed back in the laboratory," she said upon arriving at the park bench.

Directo-cam's spot-light eyes flashed red in anger and he scolded Pambot, saying, "Excuse us! We were having a private conversation here, sweetchips."

"Not any more we're not," said Howard.

He promptly stood back up and began walking away with Pambot.

"We think we know why Stanley hasn't returned," said Pambot. "It is because Stanley doesn't have any money."

"So the thousand putos doesn't buy a return ticket?"

"Evidently not."

Howard had the funny feeling that he was

being watched, and when he looked back over his shoulder he saw that Directo-cam was right behind him.

"Back off!" he scolded.

Disgruntled, the camera then trailed Howard and Pambot from a few yards back.

"The problem is, Stanley doesn't have any money to put into the money slot on the other end," continued Pambot.

Howard thought about this and said, "Now let me get this straight, the thousand-putos just pays for a one way ticket. These Galactic Plumbers must be raking it in. Now didn't the Charade-oglyphics say something about a thousand basic units of a planet's money?"

"Yes," answered Pambot.

"We use the puto; what kind of money would Stanley need on an uninhabited planet? How are these Galactic Plumber people supposed to make any money from planets without any currency?"

"Livingston has been asking those very questions to the Charade-oglyphics for the last hour and the explanation they gave was that the Galactic Plumbers claim uninhabited planets as their own, thus increasing their real estate holdings. In regards to the Planet Skegness, it belongs to the Galactic Plumbers and because the planet is uninhabited, there is obviously no local currency; therefore, we can pay another thousand putos into the Star Flush on our end. Stanley and

Gigglebyte can then flush back to Cessestial. Livingston would like to ask you to put another thousand putos into the money slot."

CHAPTER 28

THE RETURN FLUSH

The gumpathump fought ferociously, killing every worm that tried to attack it, and yet, the worms kept coming.

In the meanwhile Stanley jiggled the flush handle frantically, and kicked the control column, shouting, "Come on! Work you stupid machine! I'm good for the money! We need to get out of here!"

The Charade-oglyphics mimed "No, No, A thousand times no! How many times do we have to tell you the answer is no! Who are you calling stupid? You're the one without any money!"

Suddenly, the Charade-oglyphics changed their message and began miming, "All right you can go now. You're return flush has been paid for. Plotting the return to Cessestial now. Calculations are in progress."

Disinfectant light exploded out of the Star Flush bowl creating a roaring sound louder than the stormy skies of Skegness. The multitude of flukes recoiled, turned their red eyes away, and slunk back away from the gumpathump into the shadows.

The light and sound also frightened the gumpathump and it bellowed in terror. Before it could run away from the Star Flush and into the waiting jaws of the worms, Stanley ran down the stairs, shouting "GUMPATHUMP!" He ran around in front of the beast, took hold of its face and forced it to turn around.

"Gumpathump, trust me. Come with me!"

The gumpathump hesitated.

Stanley ran behind the gumpathump. He pushed the creature toward the stairs of the Star Flush.

"MOVE IT! UP YOU GO! YOUR LIFE DEPENDS ON IT!"

The light terrified the flukes, but their instinct to kill overpowered their fear. The exposed hindquarters of the gumpathump were too tempting for the worms to pass up. They therefore rushed in to attack from behind.

One of the worms ran straight over Stanley, knocking him flat on his face. The slithering monster crawled over the top of him in order to sink its sucker jaws into the gumpathump's rear end.

From the wet ground, Stanley watched in revulsion as the gumpathump was set upon by dozens of the ravenous worms.

The gumpathump bellowed in pain, kicked, pinched and killed many a challenger, but there were four packworms it could not dislodge.

Gumping in agony, the gumpathump dragged its body in the only direction it could go, which was forward and up the stairs toward the spinning bowl of light.

In danger of being left behind, Stanley managed to take hold of the tail end of one of the worms attached to the gumpathump.

Bump. Bump. Bump. Bump.

Stanley felt each bump as he was dragged up the stairs. The next sensation was dropping and sliding across the galaxies.

The Star Flush bowl filled with light and began to spin.

"Stanley's coming home!" I shouted.

"Places everyone!" ordered Directo-cam.

Scurrying here and there, Howard, Brobot, Swatzanutter, Pambot and I returned to our places, standing at attention on either side of the Star Flush like a military honour guard.

Directo-cam hovered about, filming the ceremonial return of Stanley, and shouted, "Action!"

No one was prepared for the action that followed.

A huge, hairy monster, along with four white snakes suddenly erupted up through the bowl and landed hard on the laboratory floor in front of the Star Flush.

Stanley arrived as well, but he was holding on to the tail end of one of these terrible snake-things.

This all happened in a shocking second, and in light of this new development, I immediately dropped all pretence of bravery, screamed, turned tail and ran toward the laboratory exit.

AUTHOR'S NARRATION

Livingston ran.

Howard fainted.

The Directo-cam shouted, "Yeah baby! There's my money shot!"

Swatzanutter, Brobot and Pambot moved into defensive positions.

Pambot stood over the unconscious Howard, guarding him.

Brobot bent down on one knee and pointed his laser-shooting fingers at the alien animals, while Swatzanutter circled in front of the packworms, blocking their way into the rest of the laboratory.

Hissing and screeching, the four worms reacted like any cornered animals anywhere in the universe would react and they tried to fight back.

At the same time, the bloody and injured gumpathump rose up gumping and thumping in terror.

309

Just before Brobot shot it with laser fire, Stanley ran in front of the gumpathump waving his arms protectively and yelling, "Don't shoot!"

Brobot did shoot however, but not the gumpathump. One of the worms had risen up behind Stanley and was about to strike him, and so Brobot destroyed it in a burst of laser fire.

One of the worms slithered in the direction of Pambot and Howard. They were an obstacle standing in the path of its escape, and so it stood on its coils, bared its teeth like a deformed viper, screeched and moved to bite them.

"Eat this you son of a leech!" shouted Brobot as he fired on the fluke with a pulsating laser blast. It evaporated, just before its jaws could close around Pambot.

The two remaining worms charged at Swatzanutter.

"Not tooday ogly vorm!" pledged Swatzanutter as one of the flukes attempted to bite him. He grabbed the worm's upper and lower fangs, held its mouth open, turned it on its back and then pounded its head repeatedly against the floor until it stopped moving altogether.

In the meanwhile, the one remaining worm slithered past Swatzanutter and crawled toward the laboratory exit.

EXCERPT FROM LIVINGSTON'S JOURNAL

I made it to the door of the laboratory.
Retrieving the key from my pocket, I started to
unlock the door, which was very difficult to do
while hyperventilating, but then idiotically, I
fumbled the key.

Before I could stoop down and pick it up, I
heard a terrible screech behind me. Turning
around I saw one of the hideous white snakes
crawling toward me. I screamed, cowered and
closed my eyes. The snake then let out a hellish
wail and fell to the ground at my feet. My mouth
dropped open in surprise as I watched the snake
writhing on the ground as electric currents
surged through its body.

Holding the tail end of the snake-thing was
Pambot, and it was she that electrocuted the serpent
with electricity channelled through her hands.

In the very next incredible moment, a voice
was heard inside the dead thing; it was muffled
and said, "Rebooting. Rebooting. Help! Can anyone
hear me? Would somebody get me out of here!"

Pambot ripped open the belly of the snake
with her hands, and then Gigglebyte spilled out
of it drenched in stinky slime.

"I'm free! I'm free!" shouted Gigglebyte.
He hovered upright, did a double back flip

somersault in the air and then moved to embrace Pambot.

She held up her arms defensively, and said, "Don't even think about it!"

PART FOUR

WHAT CAN GO WRONG, WILL GO WRONG

CHAPTER 29

EVIL SCHEMES

Sigmund Looz gazed out the window of the stone and mortar room that he called an office inside the Septo City Insane Asylum and looked lustfully up at the stars of the night sky and the three moons of Cessestial.

"Ah, the moons, the planets, the galaxies! The universe!" sighed Sigmund before turning to face his two guests. "As a psychiatrist, I think I know 'crazy' when I smell it. I ask you, don't megalomaniac patients like the pair of you think that thinking too small reeks of weakness and timidity? Doesn't it smell as putrid to you as it does to me? It seems absolutely insane not to obtain something one wants, unless it is absolutely impossible to obtain it!" He paced from the window to his desk wringing his bony hands in between bouts of emphatic waving, pounding and pointing. "When something truly is out of reach and impossible, then the thought of taking it really is just a foolish notion, a delusion, a whim, a fleeting fancy."

He leaned over his desk and leered at the two guests seated in front of him. "I am going to confess something to you. Call it doctor-patient confidentiality." He turned his back on his guests and walked over to a large portrait of his father, Armitage S. Looz. It was hanging on the gray wall on the left side of his office. "My dear departed father would have run over my own mother in a turbo-charged racing pooter to get his hands on the object my brother has come into possession of. Talk about dumb luck! Yes, it has come to my attention, that there is a device, a machine and an object of alien origin, which can transport people across the vast distances of the galaxies, even across the universe to the millions of other planets that are out there. I am not supposed to know of the existence of this, 'Star Flush', but I do. Let's just say, I have an inside man, a spy, an informer, and I am telling you that this Star Flush is light years beyond what I was attempting to do with the Space Vacuum Cleaner."

Returning to his desk, he took a seat on a corner of it and grinned at his guests.

"Our old friends, the brat who almost became my son, along with the idiot who helped put us in here.... Yes, I'm talking about young Stanley Siphonpipe Junior and that vagabond fraud Livingston, or what was his real name?"

"Vincent Sludgepool," replied one of the guests.

"That was it! Yes, the fraud Livingston and young Stanley are supposed to go through this Star Flush and explore the universe! They intend to use the Star Flush politely, and with cowering diplomacy to step into other worlds and tiptoe around in the name of exploration. They would arrive as snivelling, whimpering beggars and leave the same way! Pathetic! A misuse of this fantastic weapon, and yes the Star Flush will be a weapon at our disposal. I say weapon, because it is the battering ram that will break down the walls that separate world from world!"

Sigmund Looz placed his hand on a small model battering ram, picked it up and stroked the realistic looking toy. There were other models of ancient weaponry, torture and execution, both miniature and full-size replicas, decorating his office. Completing his private museum of warfare and capital punishment were two toilet-style electric chairs and his two guests were strapped in these chairs.

"It's as if the door of a house has been left unlocked. It's an irresistible invitation to thieves, beckoning them to enter the house, to rob, to pillage, to plunder.

However mere stealing is beneath the likes of you and I. It is an unimaginative use of this fantastic device. Yes, we will steal, but it is for a higher good. We will bring our sovereign rule and reign to the ends of the universe, and it's not a crazy dream! It's a reality!" He tilted his head back and cackled, until a fit of wheezing made him stop. "Excuse me. Lung infection. It's all this damp air and mildew I breathe in day after day in this decrepit place. Never mind.

Why am I telling you two all this? I have some good news and some bad news. The bad news is that you are both incurable. The good news is that I am about to leave my post here at the asylum. I am quitting. I resign. I am taking you with me! I shall turn in my official Septo City Asylum doctor's jacket and replace it with..."

He stopped, removed his doctor's jacket, crumpled it up and discarded it in a waste paper bin near his desk. He traipsed over to an antique wardrobe (which was next to his iron maiden), threw open its doors and removed a black cape. He put on the cape, fastening it around his neck until the heavy cloth fell over his shoulders and draped down to his knees.

"Do you see this cape? This was the cape worn 600 years ago by Vlad the Incontinent. It's nice to own a little piece of history and this shall be an appropriate replacement for my jacket. Now where were we? Oh yes, I was telling you that I wanted to take both of you with me, because I intend to harness your twisted minds in the plot I am hatching."

Addressing the guest on the left electric toilet, he said, "You and I have had our differences

Coop. Our relationship is built on mistrust and hate. You ruined my wedding day and you later poked my eye out. I in turn have made sure that you were wrapped up in a straight jacket and controlled by medication. Yet, now, I grudgingly admit that I need you.

Perhaps we can help each other for our mutual benefit. You Coop, are surprisingly strong, clever, devious, and you would even kill if necessary without a sense of remorse. Let us just say that taking over planets will require someone with absolutely no conscious and sense of right and wrong. Aside from that, you were raised on the local military base and I will need your help to obtain a pooter. Not just any pooter. A deadly, weaponized pooter. The military, I am sure, will have explosive devices and the like that we might borrow as well. Of course, the pooter I speak of will be guarded by those blasted birds your father created, as will be the bombs, but there is no one who knows more about genetically engineered guard poultry than you. I will rely upon your expertise to get past such vicious creatures in order to obtain my prize."

Looking to the guest on the right electric toilet, Sigmund said, "And as for you my deranged Elfly; you have all the right moves. I couldn't ask for someone who is more pliable, eager to please, easily motivated, oblivious to reality and yet athletically coordinated for some of the tasks I have in mind."

"Thank yu very much, Uh huh huh!" mumbled Elfly. "Hey, I'm hungry! Can we send out for some burgers and fries?"

Switching Elfly's electric toilet on with the press of a button on his desk, Sigmund sent just enough electrical current into Elfly to make his wavy hair smoke and his body to twitch.

"Yowlsey! Yowlsey! Yowlsey."

After shocking Elfly, Sigmund shouted, "Psychobot Nurse!"

The heavy wooden door of the medieval office crashed open and in stomped the ten-foot, mechanical monstrosity.

"Nurse, unstrap these patients," ordered Sigmund. "We're leaving!"

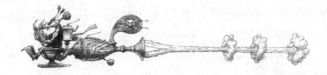

CHAPTER 30

MEDICAL ATTENTION

EXCERPT FROM LIVINGSTON'S JOURNAL
Privy the 27th, 6:17PM

In the aftermath of the invasion of white-snakey things, not to mention the big, hairy something-or-other with the weird face, Stanley and Gigglebyte explained everything.

It was clear that Stanley had narrowly escaped with his life, and to be honest, I was a bit put out with him because he hadn't turned around and flushed straight back as I'd told him to. He said he was only trying to do what I would have done. Appealing to my ego and vanity worked and I found it impossible to stay angry at him.

After listening to all this, and looking around at the dead (I now knew they were called) packworms, Howard offered to make arrangements to have the horrid things frozen.

"Shouldn't we just bury the things in the backyard or something?" I replied.

"Don't you want them for scientific analysis?" asked Howard.

"Just kidding" I lied. "Of course I want to study them. Yes, good idea, Howard. Go ahead and make those arrangements."

After Howard left the laboratory, I told all the robots, including Directo-cam to go recharge their batteries because it was going to be a big shopping day tomorrow.

"Shopping! Forget it!" complained Directo-cam. "I've got important footage to edit, thank you very much."

At that, Directo-cam promptly vacated the premises, as did Pambot, Brobot, Swatzanutter and Gigglebyte.

While all this was happening, Stanley was attending to the hairy creature that he called a gumpathump and gave it first aid, putting disinfectant and bandages on its wounds.

"Now, that you've patched it up," I said, "why don't you flush whatchamathump back to where it came from?"

Stanley was horrified. "We can't send it back!" he protested. "It will die and there are hundreds of gumpathump-eating worms waiting for it!"

"Well, we can't keep it."

"Why not?"

"Because."

"Because why?"

"It will shed all over the furniture and it's not potty trained."

"She needs a vet" insisted Stanley, "And I think I know a good one. The gumpathump is a she by the way."

Stanley then went over to a phone-monitor-camera set-up mounted on the laboratory wall and tried placing a call to his mother. She wasn't home.

By using the citywide computer network of computers and cameras, he soon tracked her down to Looey's, a fancy restaurant in the ritzy district of town. Connecting to one of the restaurant's tableside phone-monitor-cameras, Cesselia appeared on our monitor.

She looked stunning. She was dressed formally, wearing a glamourous black evening gown. Her red hair was done up and she was decked out in a glittering jewel necklace and earrings.

My heart leapt for joy upon seeing her!

I then saw that she was with someone and this someone was a horribly handsome, despicably dapper, pathetically, perfect man. He was a blond-haired fellow with a rugged muscular body and top it all, a tan.

"Mom, come down to Livingston's lab, quick! It's an emergency!" said Stanley.

This was all he needed to say to her. Less than twenty minutes later, Cesselia entered the laboratory followed by the detestable dapper dandy.

"What is that horrible thing?" was the first thing Cesselia said upon opening the laboratory door and seeing a dead electrocuted fluke sprawled out on the floor.

Stanley met his mother with a quick embrace and said, "Thanks for coming, Mom. Sorry to pull you away from your dinner like that, but I really do need your help. Or I should say there's an animal that needs..."

"Stanley you're dirty – you're bruised and bleeding! What happened to you? What is this thing?" asked Cesselia, repeating her initial question.

"It's um er a carnivorous predatory worm that hunts in coordinated packs. I call it a packworm, but it's dead..."

"A pack.....worm?" she repeated. "I've never heard of such a thing."

Taking off her dress shoes, she got down on her knees and started examining the worm, poking her fingers at its slimy dead eyes, and looking into its awful round mouth full of teeth.

"But that's not the animal I mean, Mom."

Looking up to her blond companion, Cesselia said, "I've never seen anything like this before. Jacques, in all your travels have you ever encountered anything like this?"

The man she called Jacques was a foreigner. His accent was romantic, melodic, easy to listen to and poetic – making me hate him all the more. He sounded like he was from the country of Urinoir, where it was wee wee this and wee wee that.

"No, zis is truly amazing," said Jacques. "If I am not miztaken, zis creature is new to science, wee? I would gladly leave any restaurant in ze middle of any meal, no matter how expenzeeve to see sush a wonderful curiozity."

Glaring at Jacques, I coldly said, "And you are?"

With a courteous bow, he replied, "Oh, do forgeeve me. I have not introduzed myzelf. I am Jacques Poosteau, and you need no introduction because you are ze world-renowned explorer, Leevingzton. I wash all your shows and never meez an epizode."

"Just great!" I thought in disgust. "He's charming as well!" I felt like flushing to the planet of the packworms and trying to eat one of them out of self pity.

Jacques turned to Stanley Junior. He took his hand and shook it. "And you must be Stanley Junior. Your beaut-ee-ful muzzer has told me all about you. She eez so proud of you, and you too explore under ze wat-air, wee wee?"

Stanley grinned and said, "Yeah, I've done a bit of diving here and there. Pleased to meet you Mr. Poo..."

"Please, call me Jacques."

"Jacques," said Stanley, finishing his greeting.

Rudely interrupting their friendly little back-pat session, I challenged Jacques, saying, "And how would you know if something is new to science?"

Looking up from the dead worm, Cesselia said, "Livingston, Jacques is a marine biologist."

The hits just kept on coming! "Perfect," I said to myself. "He's smart too."

"I am by no means an expert on zese matters like yourself," confessed Jacques humbly. "I can only presume it eez new to science as I have never seen one of zese before. So tell me, eez it new?"

"Maybe," I answered, petulantly

"Where did eet come from?"

"Far away."

It was then that Stanley saved me from all the awkward questions by gently pulling his mother up from the worm, and saying, "We don't have time for this, Mom. I'll tell you all about the worms later, but now I need you to come see a sick animal."

Stanley took his mother, Jacques and myself to the other end of the laboratory. Waiting for us there was the Star Flush, another dead packworm and an awe-inspiring alien animal. Each thing on its own was amazing, but to be confronted by all three strange sights at once was overwhelming for Jacques and Cesselia. Their mouths dropped open. Their eyes shouted, "HOW? WHAT? WHERE? WHY?"

Before Cesselia could say a word, Stanley took her by the hand and led her to the gumpathump.

"I promise, I'll explain everything later," promised Stanley. "Mom, all you need to know right now is that this is a wonderful, intelligent creature called a gumpathump, and it saved my life."

"Saved your life? You weren't hurt were you?" asked Cesselia.

"Mom, I'm fine. I'm covered in mud and a few bruises and scratches. Nothing serious. Please, Mom, the gumpathump! Help her!"

Cesselia's medical training took over. It was a marvel to watch. Cesselia snapped out of her worried-mother-mode and instantly became a focused, clinical doctor. She even forgot that she was dressed in a sexy black dress. Ignoring the dirt, blood and mud caked on the gumpathump's body, Cesselia put her head against its chest in order to listen to its heartbeat.

"Call for an emergency airlift now!" she ordered. "I need to get this creature to the hospital."

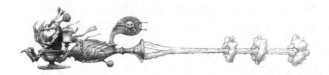

CHAPTER 31

PREPARATIONS

EXCERPT FROM LIVINGSTON'S JOURNAL
Privy the 28th

It's full steam ahead on the Star Flush expedition. There's no getting out of it now. I have to go and I have to pretend that I want to go.

The test flush was a success. Nobody died. I take that back. Stanley and Gigglebyte almost died. Some monster worms died. Memo to me: we're going to have to press the Charade-oglyphics for more details about the planets they recommend to us, because they neglected to mention that Skegness was infested with man-eating worms.

I've already had an interesting conversation with the Charade-oglyphics about where to go next. I requested a planet that was relaxing, sunny and where I could top up my tan.

"Are there any paradise planets?" is what I

asked the Charade-oglyphics.

"Oxnard," is what they spelled out. They told me that Oxnard is a tropical planet that is warm all year round, the natives are friendly, and one day the ox will lie down with the nard.

"What's a nard?" I asked.

Their ambiguous reply was: "A nard is something that oxen don't want to lie down with at this present moment in time."

"Oh," was all I could think of to say. "I guess I'll have to flush to the planet Oxnard in order to find out what a nard is."

So today was the big shopping day, the day to prepare for the expedition.

Star Flush security was the first thing on the shopping list and Howard's biggest concern. He therefore dispatched Stanley Junior to Paranoid Paul's Security System Warehouse. The time was about 9 in the morning when Stanley left. Stanley hired Paranoid Paul himself to fit the new security system in the laboratory.
Stanley returned with Paranoid Paul and his team of technicians about an hour later. Stanley took them into the laboratory, set them to work, and then left them to it.

Fortunately I didn't have any direct dealings with Paranoid Paul, because according to Stanley, he turned out to be the rudest person he'd ever met.

Anyway, the only thing we needed to do after Paul and his team arrived was to go out and get supplies for the upcoming expedition.

Because Howard had pressing business matters to attend to, he left it up to Stanley and I to go make the necessary purchases. To help us with such a venture, Howard sent his Limoutrine and driver. Best of all, he gave us his credit card to use!

It was just after ten in the morning when the Limoutrine descended in front of the laboratory.

Pambot, Brobot, Swatzanutter, Gigglebyte, Stanley and myself were there to greet the Limoutrine.

The driver's door opened and Howard's robot chauffeur, Maurgrease, stepped out. He marched over to us with his metallic nose held high in the air.

Bowing to both of us, the very properly programmed robot said, "Good morning Mr. Livingston and Mr. Siphonpipe."

Maurgrease was made of brass that was polished and shiny; I could see my reflection in his frame.

"Good morning to you," I said. "Let's cut to the chase. Do you have something to give us Maurgrease?"

"Yes, Sir. I have been instructed to give you this gold credit card belonging to Howard Looz."

A golden coloured plastic card was ejected from Maurgrease's slit of a mouth.

"Those were the magic words I was waiting to hear!" I said, before snatching the card from the robot's metal lips. "Ka-Ching! Ka-Ching!"

I held up the card to the sunlight, read

Howard Looz's name several times, smiled a billion puto smile, and then put the card safely in my wallet.

"Maurgrease, today is your lucky day!" I announced. "You and our robot porters are going to the exclusive robot health spa, Engine-ama. I think, we'll ask the good folks at the spa to give you a new personality."

"Sorry, Sir. I will have to decline your kind offer, Sir, because I will be your chauffeur for the day."

"Sorry Maurgrease, but I'm going to drive," said Stanley. "You hop in back."

"Excuse me, Sir? Did you say,..." Before Maurgrease could finish his sentence, Stanley ran around the Limoutrine and jumped into the driver's seat. "...'back' Sir? – I must protest, Sir. Wait Sir! This is most irregular, Sir! It is I that should do the driving, Sir."

"Reeeee-laaaaax!" sang Stanley, "I think your screws are too tight. It will be more fun if I drive. I'm ordering you to enjoy yourself and hop in back with the other robots."

I then joined Stanley in the front of the Limoutrine, while Pambot, Brobot, Swatzanutter and Gigglebyte piled into the plush pink, furry back seats.

Taking his instructions literally, Maurgrease reluctantly jumped into the craft, landing on the laps of Pambot and Brobot.

Stanley started the Limoutrine's motor and

revved its rocket engines. The Limoutrine blasted off with an explosive backfire. All the robotic passengers were thrown backwards because of the G-Forces being violated. Within moments the Limoutrine was going supersonic speeds through the air.

* * * * *

The first stop, as promised, was the Engine-ama Robot Health Spa, and we booked all the robots (including Maurgrease) for servicing, cleansing and an oil engine-ama.

After the spa, Stanley and I spent the rest of the day racing from shop to shop buying supplies with Howard's credit card and ordering next-day delivery.

Stanley bought new T-shirts, stretchy spotted trousers, five pairs of hiking shoes, a brand new purple backpack, a tent and all the camping equipment one could ever need.

Because I hate camping, I bought a waterproof canopy bed with waterproof blankets, sheets and a pillow. I also bought an antique, wooden wardrobe to hang my clothes up in, a portable, gas-powered oven, and a portable bathtub and shower with a water heater.

I was surprised to learn that Stanley wanted to go into a saddle shop. "Why do you need a saddle?" I asked.

"For the gumpathump," he replied.

"Oh no, we're not taking that shaggy beast!" I protested.

"Livingston, she's smart, she's tough, she can help us carry our stuff around and we could use a good beast of burden."

I finally gave in, and said, "Oh all right, but it had better smell a lot better than it did yesterday."

Stanley made special arrangements with the saddle shop to have a saddle, reigns and a carrier basket made that would fit the size and dimensions of the gumpathump. Again it was a rush-order so we paid that much extra for it.

After the saddle shop, we just happened to wander into the Robot Shack Electronics and Gadget Superstore. There, I spied a gizmo like the thing that Stanley's father had worn in his wide-brimmed leather hat. It was another Journal-Keeper, a top of the range model. It looked like a miniature computerised typewriter hooked up to a video camera and there were wires and suction cups dangling beneath it.

To Stanley I said, "These things are great! Your dad had one of these in his hat." What I didn't say was, "And by the way, I kept your dad's hat and the journal but didn't give it to you because his account of the Plague Isle adventure would expose me for the fraud I am."

"I sort of know how these things work," I said to the pimple-faced kid behind the counter, "But tell me about this make and model and what makes it so special."

The kid proceeded to explain that using the latest brain-reading technology, the Journal-Keeper could measure brain waves, detecting if a person was happy, sad or mad, and so write about a person's day in that mood. It would, first of all, sample a person's writing so it could keep the journal in a person's unique writing style. It would then record everything the person experienced and store all that information on its hard drive in the form of a diary. The Journal-Keeper could later be hooked up to a printer, and out would come a diary that looked like a person actually wrote it all down by hand.

"Oh, and it can be easily attached and worn under the hat of your choice," said the kid, and that clinched the deal.

"I'll take it," I said, not bothering to look at the price tag. "Here, install the Journal-Keeper in my pith helmet." I handed the kid my helmet and Howard's credit card.

After the gadget shop we went to the bulk quantity food store because we figured we were going to need a lot of food and beverages to keep us going out in the universe. We bought enough food to feed a small army for a few years, and right along with the groceries we bought a refrigerated freight box to keep it all in.

The smartest way to haul the freight box around would be on a tractor, and so the next stop was the Dear John tractor shop. There we bought a bright green hover tractor that could easily haul the refrigerated box on its flatbed platform, along with all the fuel we would need for our expedition.

The last stop of the day was Larry Looter's new and used pooters. By this time, it was around five in the afternoon.

As we flew over the city in Howard's Limoutrine, we noticed that there was a lot of smoke in the air.

"Must be a fire somewhere in the city," I casually remarked, but then we both forgot about it because when we arrived at Larry Looter's, the dazzling sight of hundreds and thousands of shiny new pooters, the neon billboard sign, the flapping triangular flags hanging over the lot and the myriad of balloons made us forget about everything else.

Stanley brought the Limoutrine down on to the tarmac, and then Honest Larry Looter himself ran out of the sales room to greet us.

"Welcome friends to Honest Larry's Super Duper Pooter Sale of the Century! You couldn't have picked a better day to come. I'm Honest Larry, and I'll eat my hat if I can't find a super duper deal for you. What can I do for you boys?"

Honest Larry's smile was almost as big as the cowboy hat he was wearing, and he shook both our hands as if he had known us all of our lives.

"You just look around to your heart's content, yu hear!" said Honest Larry. "And you can take any of these babies out for a test poot. It just so happens we're having a sale on Winabogoze."

Conferring with Stanley, I said, "I like Winabogoze. That's better than sleeping in a tent."

"We need something small, light and with lots of speed," he said.

I gave in, figuring that I'd bought enough of the things I wanted for one day, and so I said, "OK, have it your way. This is your area. You do the talking."

Turning back to Honest Larry, Stanley said, "We're actually interested in racing pooters. Can you show us the fastest pooter you have? Price is no object."

"Now you're talkin'! Boys, you just made my day!"

Honest Larry took Stanley and I straight over to the racing pooter section of the lot.

"How fast does that one go?" Stanley asked, pointing out a very sleek, black and white striped racing pooter.

"You mean the C.C.C.?"

"Yeah, the C.C.C." said Stanley, "The Cooking Combustible Commode."

"Oh yeah, ain't she a beaut! That's a four cylinder rocket engine she's sitting on, is our lady of the speedway, Cindy C. as we like to call our C.C.C.s, and this particular C.C. really is a bad girl. She goes from zee-roh to two hundred and fifty in three-point-two seconds, and her top speed is seven-hundred and seventy-five miles per hour."

Honest Larry reached into the pocket of his plaid suit jacket and took out a set of keys.

"Why don't you try Cindy C. out and see what she's made of! I could knock twenty grand off the price with a trade in of that Limoutrine you got there, and tell you about our poot-now-pay-later-plan."

"No thanks, we'll just pay up front if that's all right?" I said, just before I whipped out Howard's credit card. He took the plastic, looked at the name on the card and his smile got even bigger. "Have her delivered to the Livingston laboratory in the Looz Towers Park by tomorrow."

"Mister, I'd have her shipped to the moons if that is what you wanted. Thank you! It's been a pleasure doing business!" said Honest Larry, while shaking my hand and Stanley's hand firmly.

The smoke we'd seen earlier was now drifting into our nostrils, so Stanley asked, "Hey, uh, what's with all the smoke?"

"Haven't you heard, son? Oh it's terrible! Just terrible!" said Honest Larry, dropping his salesman face for the moment. "Some of them lunatics at the Insane Asylum have escaped and set the place on fire. They killed a whole bunch of people. It's just plain awful! I'm surprised you haven't heard about it, 'cause it's all over the news. The Septo City Insane Asylum is on fire!"

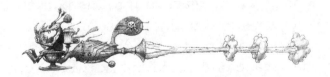

CHAPTER 32

PARANOID PAUL

AUTHOR'S NARRATION
Privy the 28th, 11:00 PM

Howard Looz descended into the night time gloom of the Looz Towers Park.

Apart from the bright lamps of his pooter, there was very little light in the park apart from the dim illumination of the surrounding city and the yellow lamps lined up along various paths in the park.

He brought his craft down in the grounds of Livingston's laboratory. Usually the lights were on at night, but currently the laboratory was just as dark as the rest of the park.

Howard parked his golden pooter next to where his own Limoutrine was parked, and then switched off the engine and head lamps. As he got off his Bumley, Stanley appeared out of the shadows and greeted him with a "Hey Howard. Sorry to call you so late. The installation of the security system took a little longer than expected, but it's ready to show you now."

Howard was silent.

"Howard?" said Stanley.

Howard snapped to attention. "Sorry."

"Are you feeling all right?"

"No."

"What's wrong?"

"I think my brother was in that fire."

Though there was no love lost between Stanley and Sigmund Looz, the thought of someone, even an enemy, dying in such a horrible way, made him wince in pain. "Oh right, er sorry. Do you know that for sure, Howard?"

"I mean Sigmund and I haven't spoken to each other in years" confessed Howard, "but still, family is family, and when I think of the horrific way those people died – all the other doctors, as well. There were at least twenty, along with ordinary medical doctors, nurses, orderlies and robotic assistants. It's a tragic loss of life – I mean locked in a room while the building was set on fire – It doesn't bear thinking about. I fear that my brother will only be able to be identified by his teeth. And then there is the fact that hundreds of dangerous inmates of the asylum have all been turned loose at the same time! No one should feel safe."

"Horrible!" Stanley agreed. "I don't know what to say."

"You can say that the security system is installed around the Star Flush!"

"That's why I asked you to come down here." Yelling over his shoulder, Stanley shouted, "Paul, show Howard the security system."

Like the dramatic opening of a theatrical production, dome-top searchlights atop the laboratory switched on and swept the area.

A new titanium door opened with electronic buzzes and clicks, and then a fellow wearing a large helmet and a black-padded uniform stepped cautiously out of the doorway, before the door slammed shut behind him.

From a distance, Howard and Stanley watched the man.

The uniformed fellow looked carefully to his right and left as if he was about to cross a busy highway. He tossed something into the bushes, and made a mad dash away from the door.

After walking, stopping, looking, walking, stopping looking, walking, stopping and looking the uniformed man arrived in front of Howard and Stanley.

Howard greeted the man, saying, "You must be Paranoid Pa...."

"SHHHHH!" interrupted the man. He held up his hands in a keep quiet gesture. He then jumped, spun around, stopped to listen, looked about and sniffed the air.

Turning back to Howard and Stanley, he whispered, "It's probably nothing. I just get the sense that we are being watched."

Stanley rolled his eyes impatiently and said,

"Paul, I think you are being...."

"Paranoid!" finished Paul. "That's what keeps me alive, Stan!"

Warily, Stanley said, "Howard, meet Paranoid Paul of Paranoid Paul's Security System Warehouse."

Paranoid Paul was dressed from head to toe in black body armour and he wore an over-sized helmet on his head with three small revolving satellite dishes and rear view mirrors. Paul was also armed to the hilt with laser guns, bazookas, grenade-launchers, and on his utility belt there was an electrically charged baton.

Howard extended his hand and said, "Howard Looz. Pleased to meet you."

Ignoring Howard's outstretched hand, Paranoid Paul said, "So Looz, you are now the proud owner of a new state of the art, top of the line, custom installed security system. Let me show you what security measures we've put in place."

"Er, right" said Howard, as he awkwardly withdrew his hand. "Yes, by all means, proceed."

"We will start out here with Phase One," explained Paul, referring to the Looz Towers Park. "You really ought to think about losing all these trees, flowers and bushes. Too many places for the enemy to hide. Cut them down. Build a concrete and steel security wall, around the perimeter with electrified razor wire around the top of the wall."

Howard was taken aback. "This is a park! Absolutely not!"

"That's what your subordinate, Stanley here said. Oh well, don't say I didn't warn you. The next best thing is to post guards outside the laboratory."

"What about our robots?" suggested Stanley.

"Bad idea Stan," said Paul. "Let me come up with the ideas please. Who is the professional here? Hands up if you are a security expert!"

Only Paul raised his hand.

"I thought so. I'm in the major leagues pal and I don't need advice from a rookie. Should I tell you why robots are a bad idea Stan? Pay attention and you might learn something. Question. How do you know you can trust the robots, huh? Who programmed them? Even if they are trustworthy, a plasmatronic immobilizer could easily stop a robot in its tracks. A criminal with just a little knowledge of robotics could open the brain case of an immobilised robot and program the robot to suit his or her own evil ends. Didn't you tell me these robots were like luggage carrying bellboys or something and travel with you wherever it is you go? Hardly makes for a consistent and vigilant watch, does it Stan? Bad idea, fatso."

Stanley felt like punching Paranoid Paul in the face, but all the weapons Paul had to hand made him think better of it.

"So what do you suggest?" asked Howard.

"I've been through this with Stan. Since you rejected Plan A: The fortified wall proposal, to save a bunch of stupid flowers and trees, I recommend PLAN B: Trained guard animals. With a bit of training, a tame house pet can be made into a lethal weapon against any perpetrator or trespasser. I hope you don't mind Looz, but I took the liberty of training your giant cat."

"Little Klawd?" said Howard.

Apologetically, Stanley explained, "Er yeah, Little Klawd was hanging around the park and Paul insisted on teaching him a few things."

"Like what?"

"LIIIIITTLE KLAAAAAWD!" called Paranoid Paul.

The ground of the park rumbled with impact tremors. Foliage shook, branches broke and the gigantic tabby parted the trees as he entered the laboratory grounds.

Upon seeing Stanley and Howard, he purred, yowled and plopped down on his belly in front of his two masters. Both Stanley and Howard greeted their cat with lots of petting, stroking and childish pet talk such as, "Hey Little Klawd! Hey big fella! Nice to see you big guy."

"Step aside," ordered Paul. He barged in front of Stanley and Howard, shoving them out of the way. "You people make me sick the way you treat this animal. You'll make a big sissy out of him treating him like that!"

Addressing the cat, Paul said, "OK Little

Klawd, remember what I taught you. What do you do if you see, smell or hear any unauthorised personnel near this building?"

Paul made a claw-swipe gesture and Little Klawd responded by jumping to his feet with his back arched and his claws extended. He hissed, spit and roared.

To Howard, Paul said, "Now Looz, I want you to tell your cat that you're a burglar."

"Why would I say that?"

"To demonstrate what I've been teaching your cat. Just do it!"

With absolutely no enthusiasm, Howard dully said, "Hello Little Klawd. I'm a burglar."

WHUMP! Little Klawd swatted Howard to the ground and pinned him there.

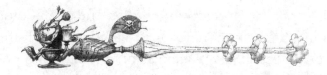

CHAPTER 33

PHASE TWO and THREE

"At ease Little Klawd," commanded Paranoid Paul. "Good job. You can let Mr. Looz up now. You'll make a fine guard cat."

Little Klawd lifted his paw up off of Howard.

"OOOOOOOOOH!" groaned Howard, as he staggered to his feet.

"Little Klawd is 'Phase One', perimeter security. 'Phase Two,' is roof top security," explained Paranoid Paul. "Say the thieves try to come by air, perhaps by pooter or parachute and want to break in through the roof. You are a lucky man Looz, because I have installed a fail safe rooftop security system. The whole dome is now charged with ten thousand volts of electricity, and it's equipped with anti-pooter plasmatronic immobilizers surrounding the dome. If any pooter flies within five thousand feet – BAM! BAM! BAM! The pooter engine dies and the pooter falls out of the sky. The beautiful thing is that all your own security is plasmatronic proof, so no one can throw the same trick back in your face.

Stanley shrugged and said to Howard, "Its better than the anti-pooter laser guns Paul wanted to mount on the roof."

Continuing with his demonstration, Paul led Stanley and Howard down the path leading to the newly installed titanium laboratory door and said, "Phase Three is doorway security. Phase Three will only come into effect in the unlikely event that the perp makes it past Phase One: Little Klawd, or somehow survives Phase Two: The Roof. However, Stan's choice of doorway security was not my first choice. My recommendations were summarily dismissed by lard-pants here."

"He wanted a rapid fire laser gun nest and to plant land mines!" complained Stanley. He then yelled at Paul, saying "And don't call me lard-pants!"

Several seconds later, when they had almost reached the laboratory door, Paranoid Paul abruptly stopped, and this caused Stanley to run into Howard's back. Paul then used one of his guns to draw a line in the path in front of him.

"OK Looz, put your toe across the line," whispered Paul.

Howard was suspicious. "Why? What happens when I cross that line?"

"Phase Three happens," answered Paul.

Carefully, Howard put the toe tip of his right shoe over the line, and suddenly, something with knife-sharp talons leapt toward him!

"SQUAWK! SQUAWK! SQUAWK!" screeched a fowl creature with a blood-curdling crow.

Paranoid Paul took his electrically charged baton and batted the talons of the bird down before they could tear into Howard's face. The enormous bird was knocked to the ground, but then it immediately jumped back up, ready to attack again.

It was a vicious, genetically engineered guard rooster that was bigger and stronger than any guard dog and twice as nasty.

It lunged at Paranoid Paul and tore into the padded sleeve of his uniform with frenzied pecks and bites.

Paul fought back, shocking the bird with his electric baton while yelling "Down! Down Rex! Down!"

The bird reluctantly backed away with unspent violence in its yellow eyes.

"Guard poultry," explained Paranoid Paul, "Killer chickens that the military uses in combat. They make great watch-chickens. I mean this bird will tear you limb from limb if it gets a chance." Paul then reached into his pocket, retrieved some raw bloody meat, and tossed it to the ravenous rooster.

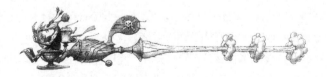

CHAPTER 34

PHASE FOUR AND FIVE

"Rex is only part of the doorway security," explained Paranoid Paul. "As you can see, I've installed a titanium door and fixed it up with intricate locking mechanisms that only Stan here will be able to unlock."

"Why only Stanley?" asked Howard.

"Because blubber-boy here will have the one and only remote control to unlock the door and its programmed to respond only to his fingerprints."

Stanley grumbled under his breath and his nostrils snorted in anger.

"That's all well and fine, but couldn't a thief try to break in through the walls or windows of the laboratory?" Howard inquired.

"Tomorrow we install titanium panels in the walls and titanium bars in the windows."

"Tomorrow?"

"Yeah Looz, tomorrow. I'm on over-time as it is. I finish the job tomorrow, but there is still enough security to stop an army, believe me."

Out of yet another pocket, Paul produced a remote control device and handed it to Stanley.

"Don't lose this, tubby. Hurry and press the green button before Rex decides to rip somebody's guts out."

Stanley pressed the green button while giving Paranoid Paul a spiteful look. The lock mechanisms in the new titanium door made clicking and buzzing sounds as it opened outwardly.

Paul, Howard and Stanley stepped into the darkened laboratory. The door then automatically slammed shut behind them and the lights of the laboratory turned on.

"Your remote control sends signals to that control box we installed on the ceiling up there," said Paul. He was pointing up to a plastic box in the centre of the dome, four stories above them. "The control box controls everything. The lights, the door, roof top security, and Phase Four and Five, which I am about to tell you about. Oh yeah, and it's plasmatronic immobilizer proof because of the non-conductive materials it is made from. I am confident that the perps would be stopped by Phase One, Two or Three of your security system. But there is extra security with Phase Four and Phase Five. OK chubby, press the orange button."

"Look, if you call me chubby one more time, then I'll..."

"You'll what?" challenged Paul as he reached for his electric baton.

"Then I will do exactly... NOTHING! ZILCH!

ZERO! ...about it! But I will be REALLY, REALLY ANGRY!"

"Please! Just press the orange button, so we can all go home tonight," pleaded Howard.

Stanley pressed the button and a crisscross array of harmless laser beams appeared, zigzagging across the laboratory.

"This gentlemen, is Paranoid Paul's ultimate burglar alarm," boasted Paul. "Besides these laser beam trip-lights, there are motion sensors in the floor. If anything or anybody should break the beams of laser light then WHAM! BAM! Searchlights turn on from above. The alarms go off. We're talking noise people. I mean sirens, alarms, bells, a foghorn, explosive sound effects and the sound of a brass band. It will be a wall noise for Mr. Burglar!"

"Lots of noise? Is that it?" complained Howard.

"Is that it? Is that it? No, that's not it! I wanted to install cannons that fire napalm but Stan here doesn't like the smell."

"Right," said Howard. "So no cannons. No skin-burning acids. What did you install instead as a deterrent?"

"What else?" snapped Paranoid Paul, taking offense at the question. "What else? In the almost nonexistent chance that said perpetrator makes it past Phases One, Two, Three and Four, there is always 'Phase Five!' Once the alarms kick in, so does Phase Five and I guarantee that Phase Five is not for the faint of heart. Push the blue button."

Stanley pressed the blue button on the remote and this shut off the alarm tripping laser beams.

"Now press the black button marked 'Are you sure?'"

When Stanley pressed the black button, the laboratory was consumed by a blaring, trumpeting series of horn blasts like the warning signal of an oncoming freight train and then something charged like a bull from the back of the laboratory, stomping down the central computer aisle. It was a metal monster with flashing, revolving red lights and metal legs pounding the ground, a rectangular machine, completely covered in black plated armour and spikes. Four long elastic tentacles tipped with metal pincer-hands spilled out of a hollowed out slot on top of the machine, and four ray guns were mounted on each corner of the machine, elevated above its open slot.

"This is Phase Five," shouted Paranoid Paul over the horn blasts. "This is a Molecule Scrambler. Since Stan here doesn't like anything that shoots, blows up, slices or dissolves and permanently solves your perpetrator problem, I have installed my most effective, non-lethal burglar deterrent. Terrifying isn't it?"

Howard stared with his mouth open, thinking that "terrifying" was somehow an inadequate word for what he was looking at.

"When an intruder is detected, The

Molecule Scrambler will capture the trespasser with its tentacles, place the perp in its scrambling slot, aim those four nasty ray guns at the criminal, and then Pow! It's over Mr. Burglar."

"You said this was non-lethal?" Stanley reminded him.

"Oh, the criminal is still there. He's just floating around as a zillion disconnected molecules. You can keep the burglar floating around as harmless molecules for as long as you want, kind of a no mess, no fuss prison. Think about it. Prisoners that take up virtually no space, don't eat, don't give you lip and don't try to escape."

"Can their molecules be reassembled?" asked Stanley.

Paul looked at Stanley as if he were stupid. "Well, DUUUUUH, YEEE-AH! Is their lard in your ears as well as your rear end? On your remote control you have the reassemble button, the white one. The four ray guns will then shoot a kind of a reversing ray and the person, place, or thing will either reassemble right in front of the Molecule Scrambler, or if you program your remote control right, you can send the person, place, or thing to a different location. I'll demonstrate."

Speaking to the machine, Paul said, "Molecule Scrambler, disintegrate Howard Looz."

"What?" cried Howard. He turned to run, but the Molecule Scrambler quickly chased him down. One of its tentacles grabbed him as he screamed for help. The machine's tentacle then dropped him into its scrambling slot. Once Howard was deposited like a piece of bread into a toaster, the ray guns blasted him, causing his molecules to fly apart in a burst of light.

"Now all you need to do is send him to a specific place somewhere within a five mile radius and his molecules will reassemble as normal," explained Paul.

"How do I do that?"

"Simple. Just type in the name of the place with the keypad on your remote control."

"So if I type in, Penthouse Suite of Howard Looz, Looz Towers, 182nd floor, I could send Howard home?"

"That's what I just said, didn't I?"

Stanley typed out the address of Howard Looz's penthouse suite.

"Now what?"

"Press the white button and the Molecule Scrambler will do the rest."

Upon pushing the white button, the four ray guns swivelled upward dragging Howard's ball of molecules with them. The molecular ball was then fired in a beam of light toward the ceiling and it disappeared.

✳ ✳ ✳ ✳ ✳

Howard's glowing ball of molecules appeared inside his penthouse. They took shape and became the solid, molecule-reintegrated, reassembled Howard Looz.

Howard fell flat on his face, shivered, quivered and said, "Yeah, that'll work!"

Back in Livingston's laboratory, Paranoid Paul continued his instructions to Stanley.

"The Molecule Scrambler will be automatically sent into action if the alarm is tripped and the perps will end up zapped into a quadrillion little quarks. Unlike robots, the Molecule Scrambler's programming can't be tampered with easily. It is immobilizer proof. You would have to rip open its back panel to attempt to mess with it and the Molecule Scrambler will only obey your voice and my voice."

"Since ownership is transferring to me, how do we cancel you? – I mean its obedience to your voice?" asked Stanley.

"Molecule Scrambler, turn off your horn siren!" commanded Paranoid Paul.

The Molecule Scrambler obeyed, becoming blissfully quiet.

"Delete your obedience program with the voice imprint of Paranoid Paul," ordered Paranoid Paul. "Activate your obedience program to Stanley Siphonpipe Junior's voice imprint. You will no longer respond to the voice of Paranoid Paul."

"Tell it to do something," said Stanley.

"Molecule Scrambler, switch off," ordered Paranoid Paul.

The Molecule Scrambler remained switched on.

"See now tubs, it doesn't listen to me any longer. It's all yours."

"Good," said Stanley. "Molecule Scrambler! Capture Paranoid Paul and disintegrate him."

"Why, you no good, double crossing..."

The Molecule Scrambler stomped forward, picked up Paranoid Paul in one of its tentacles, dropped him into its scrambler slot and then zapped him with its ray guns, disintegrating him.

Stanley chuckled to himself as he typed in the address of the Septo City Sewer.

✳ ✳ ✳ ✳ ✳

A moment later, Paranoid Paul's molecules reassembled over the sewer, and he fell into the stinking wastewater.

When he came back up for air, he spluttered and shouted, "That's it! I quit. Looz can get someone else to finish the job for them. See if I care. They'll pay for this! Wait till they see the bill!"

As an aside, Paul remarked, "Man, I have got to learn to be more paranoid!"

✳ ✳ ✳ ✳ ✳

Stanley was still chuckling as he used his remote control to set up the new security system. He shut the lights off, opened the titanium door and made a dash into the park before Rex the guard rooster could attack him.

Just before the door closed, someone else slipped out of the laboratory.

Paranoid Paul's paranoid instincts had been correct; there had been somebody watching!

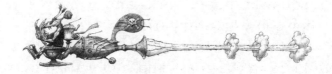

CHAPTER 35

NIGHT SHIFT

Privy the 29th, 11:06 PM

"Shhh, calm down," whispered Cesselia while addressing an agitated Rot Rat with a broken leg. Enclosed behind a wall of electricity in a large bar-less cage, the rhinoceros-sized rat limped back and forth across its enclosure while squeaking and shaking in fear.

With a reassuring smile, Cesselia spoke to the creature as if it were a person that needed to hear her comforting words. "It's just a storm," she said. "Surely you've been through storms before."

Another crack of lightning exploded above the Septo City Pet Clinic causing thunder to rumble through the interior of the animal hospital. The Rot Rat trembled all the more at the sound, and its frightened squeaks joined the howls, squawks, hoots, barks and whinnies of all the other convalescing patients.

A squall from the Psychedelic Sea had blown in from the coast and had settled over

Septo City bringing with it a violent electrical clash in the upper atmosphere, along with torrential rain.

"Secure the patient," Cesselia ordered.

Cushioned electronic hands emerged from the back of the Rot Rat's cage, taking a firm hold of the rodent. It squealed in anger at this indignity.

"Electronic barrier off," commanded Cesselia. She then removed a hypodermic needle from her white medical jacket, stuck her gloved hands inside the cage and injected the large rat with a sedative.

"There now," she whispered, as the beast's eyes closed. It slumped over on its side into an induced slumber. "You need to sleep and get off your feet so you can recover big guy. Your leg needs to recover so you can have half a chance of escaping from Little Klawd out in that big cat-box you call home."

Cesselia restored the electronic wall to the Rot Rat's cage. She disposed of the needle and gloves. She then retreated to her office, sat down at her desk, took a look at the pile of paperwork, sighed and made a valiant attempt at starting to fill out forms and reports.

Beginning the first report, she got as far as filling out her name before her eyes and her pen strayed. She gazed out her rain-battered window while she absentmindedly doodled.

A picture of the Star Flush began to form on the side of the report, and as Cesselia drew, she recalled her visit with Stanley earlier in the day.

It had been then that she finally learned the whole incredible truth about the gumpathump, the packworms and the indestructible porcelain machine that she had found Little Klawd trapped in.

Stanley told her that the machine was called a Star Flush. He explained as much as he knew about where it had come from and how the machine worked.

Stanley then recounted his adventure on Skegness, and informed Cesselia that he intended to go on another Star Flush expedition.

Reliving the conversation in her mind, Cesselia could hear herself saying, "What do you mean, you're going on another Star Flush expedition? You just got back! I could cut you out of my will you know. Don't do this to me! I worry about you when you're just across town and now you're telling me you're going billions and trillions of miles out into the universe. It's not like you can phone home if you get into trouble."

Stanley dismissed his mother's frets with a grin, and said, "Hey it's me."

Playfully, she then slapped his face in a teasing manner, while scolding him, saying, "Wipe that smirk off your face young man. This isn't funny. 'Hey, it's me' doesn't reassure me in the slightest. Your father always said, 'Hey, it's me,' as well until…"

A wave of grief came over her.

In his own defence, Stanley said, "This is what I do, Mom. I'm an explorer just like dad was. It's what I've always wanted to do. You should be proud of me. I made history. I was the very first person from our planet to explore another planet!"

"Who said anything about not being proud? I'm up to my eyeballs with pride, which is also why I hate you so much for making me worry!"

"I love you too," Stanley said before leaning over and pecking her on the cheek with a kiss. "I flush out with Livingston tomorrow morning on our first big intergalactic expedition. Privy the 30th, a truly historical occasion! You can come see me off if you want to."

"When?"

"Nine sharp."

"Split shift. I'll be working all night, but of course I'll come. Even if I look like death warmed over, I'll come." Cesselia then added, "But you might have to keep me from punching Livingston and Howard in the nose for making you do this!"

Following on from this exchange, Stanley made her promise not to tell anyone, not even her new boy friend, Jacques Poosteau.

The subject had then changed, moving on to the gumpathump, and upon declaring the creature well enough to leave with Stanley, she said, "Its wounds have healed at an amazing speed, which makes me believe that this kind of animal must need to patch itself up fast on that horrific planet where it comes from. All I did was clean her up, disinfect her, give her a few injections and I made sure she had plenty to eat and drink – Oh, in regard to eating, I assumed she was a vegetarian and so I tried lots of different kinds of plants, grasses and leaves. She seemed to like everything. She will have no problem feeding on the plants in and around the park. You'll need to get a big trough of water though. You might want to build her a barn or a pen or something. Wandering freely around the park probably won't be a good idea, unless you can train her to stay close to home. Though not ideal, chaining her to a tree might have to be a temporary measure until she is used to everything. Other than that, she's ready to be discharged, so I'll arrange an airlift for her back to Explorer's Cottage."

The memory of events earlier in the day were interrupted when the phone–computer–monitor on her desk suddenly began to ring, and she smiled as Stanley's face filled the monitor screen.

"Stanley," she sang in greeting, "I was just thinking about you. I don't see you for months on end, and then I see you twice in one day. To what do I owe this unexpected honour? Don't tell me you've brought home another stray from another galaxy to fix"

Actually I need some advice about the current stray," Stanley replied. "The gumpathump won't be quiet. She keeps bellowing and howling at the top of her lungs and I want to know how to calm her down and make her stop."

"Where is she?" asked Cesselia.

"Chained to a tree outside like you told me. She's been gumping and thumping for hours."

"Try earplugs."

"Earplugs?"

"You're just going to have to put up with the noise until she gets used to her new surroundings, – that is, unless you want to go out and pet her all night."

"In this weather? No thanks! This is almost as bad as the Planet Skegness."

Cesselia glanced out the window and shivered, saying "I'd hate to be an animal tied to a tree tonight. Burrrr! From what you told me though, she's used to this kind of weather. But think about what she's been through – blood loss and injuries, a trip through that space-ringy-thingy that you eventually told me the truth about..."

"Star Flush," Stanley corrected her. "And it wasn't like I voluntarily told you about the Star Flush – it was more like a confession under duress after torture and interrogation."

"It was a matter of national security. No, let me rephrase that. It was matter of your mother's security, which is far more important."

"You grabbed my ear and twisted it!"

"That a mother's prerogative, not torture."

"Well, it hurt."

"You can't be a mother for twenty years

without learning how to coax the truth out of your stubborn and obstinate children – or in my case, my stubborn and obstinate son."

"Threatening to tweak my nose with a pair of pliers was a bit drastic, don't you think?"

Cesselia laughed and said, "Well you should know better than to try and keep things from me."

"Yeah, but you can see why Howard wants the Star Flush to be a secret?"

"Yes I can," she fumed. "It's because he's a Looz, and to him it's just a new money-making business venture. He lied to me. He told me it was some top secret thing that they had been working on at Looz Enterprises, when it had actually fallen from the sky. I'm going to tell him off next time I see him!

Anyway, as I was saying, it must be a traumatic experience for any animal to travel through space at millions of miles per second. The poor thing then arrives in a strange new world, gets put in a cage here in this hospital, gets drugged up with medicine, and now she's tied to a tree in unfamiliar surroundings. Her behaviour is totally under...."

Suddenly the electricity in the clinic cut out, which killed the phone-computer-monitor and plunged the whole hospital instantly into darkness.

'...standable." finished Cesselia. "What? Stanley. Hello Stanley,"

The clinic erupted with the noise of barks,

howls, squawks, roars, yowls, chirps, crows and squeaks.

Initially Cesselia was startled, but kept her calm. She knew that in the event of a power cut, the animal cages would instantly revert to a battery operated back-up system, which would keep the animals secure until power could be restored.

"Hmmm? That's strange," she said out loud. "Must be the storm."

Her next logical thought was about switching on the emergency generators located in the basement of the clinic. Deciding that this was indeed the course of action she would take, she opened her desk and fumbled through it until she found a flashlight. She turned the torch beam on, stood up, turned around and then jumped in fright as her light struck the face of a grinning bald man.

"Hello Cesselia."

"Coop!" gasped Cesselia.

"Sigmund sends his warmest greetings."

Coop lit a match and dropped it into Cesselia's wastepaper basket.

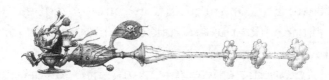

CHAPTER 36

THE ROT-RAT

Using a leafy, bottle-shaped tree as an umbrella, Little Klawd tried to keep his great bulk from the worst of the rainstorm while he did his bit for security and stood watch over Livingston's laboratory.

Being a cat, he could watch and sleep at the same time. He was gifted with the ability to close his eyes and nod off while still being totally aware of what was going on around him. He was conscious of every lightning flash and every thunder rumble. There were also alarms and fire sirens, but these background noises did not concern him.

Gradually a different kind of sound came to his attention, and even though it was much softer than every other noise, it instantly snapped him out of his slumber. It was an incessant snuffling and grumbling low-pitched squeal that was rather like the squeak of a mouse, but only if the mouse weighed a ton.

Upon detecting the frightened "please-don't-eat-me-I'm injured" type squeal he jumped to his feet fully alert. It was the unmistakable sound of a Rot-Rat running away in peril. The squeaks confused him though, because they were boldly approaching him rather than fleeing in terror.

Then out of the drizzle it appeared. It was the strangest Rot-Rat Little Klawd had ever seen, and he wanted to strike it dead with his claws. He moved to swat, but then his befuddled instincts told him to investigate the creature first.

The rhino-sized rodent fearlessly headed toward him and maneuvered itself into a position just below his face. There it stopped, and looked up defiantly at him as if it was tempting fate or wanted to commit pesticide. Its squeaks were relentless, driving him crazy with desire to chase the creature. Yet, the Rot-Rat did not run, it did not blink and its nose did not even twitch. Something was not right about it. It did not smell exactly like a Rot-Rat, at least not a living one. Nor did it move like one, but instead it stood upright, rolling across the ground on its hind end, while its arms and legs dangled limply from its stiff body.

Beneath the squeaking, Little Klawd discerned a humming noise and a ticking, which he associated with the machines of people, though putting two and two together was beyond his feline mental abilities. He therefore failed to see that the Rot-Rat was in reality a robot in disguise and it was playing pre-recorded squeaks.

This fraudulent Rot-Rat was the handiwork of Sigmund Looz's Psychobot Nurse, and was made from spare robotic parts, the skin of a dead Rot-Rat (that the Nurse had had to hunt down and kill), and crucially, a bomb stolen from the local military base.

While Little Klawd and the robotic rodent stared each other down, the vermin impostor stretched its mechanical arms upward. They lengthened and hydraulically extended until they reached up to the giant cat's whiskers. It then yanked these hairs, almost ripping them from Little Klawd's face, making him yowl in agony. Rage and killer instinct took over Little Klawd's feline mind.

In the very next moment, the robotic Rot-Rat suddenly sped backwards on its wheels, before spinning around and racing away from the cat.

Infuriated, Little Klawd bolted with a leap after the Rot-Rat and chased the creature through the park, leaving his lookout post unmanned (or uncatted to be more precise).

※ ※ ※ ※ ※

Red lights illuminated the empty grounds of Livingston's Laboratory. A black pooter, mounted with guns, landed on the rain-soaked grass in front of the building.

A moment later, a small brown tractor driven by a tall fellow in a rhinestone jumpsuit hovered up behind the black flying craft. The tractor was hauling refrigerated freight, fuel, furniture, torture devices, a ten-foot robot and two passengers on the platform behind it.

Lightning flashed as Sigmund Looz rose up off of the deadly pooter. He stood up proudly in the face of the storm as if he were its lord and master. His long black cape flapped in the wind, while he waited for Coop, Elfly and the Psychobot Nurse to join him.

Coop was also dressed from head to toe in black and wore a matching backpack. He stepped off the tractor platform carrying Cesselia over his shoulder. She was bound and gagged.

The Psychobot Nurse followed Coop off the platform.

Elfly switched off the tractor engine, stood up and sauntered on over to the others.

Sigmund glanced at Elfly and did a double take when he noticed what Elfly was wearing.

"You idiot! I told you to wear black!" scolded Sigmund. "Burglars don't wear glitter."

"Burglar? Nuh uh," said Elfly. "I'm the king of rock and roll, and you gotta admit that this is one snazzy suit. I visited my Mama today and she had my suit ready and waiting for me."

Sigmund was exasperated. "Where's your utility belt?"

"I'm wearing it."

"Are you telling me that the gold thing with all the jewels is the utility belt I gave you?"

"Mama painted it gold and glued a few jewels on it, but yeah it's the same belt with all the same tools. How do you like my new boots? Mama went out and got me these as a coming home present!"

Elfly held up one of his lanky legs and pointed to a gold tipped boot made of white leather that was sporting a shiny gold star on each ankle.

"And look at my do," Elfly continued, pointing to his poofed-up pompadour hairstyle. "It's waterproof."

Drops of water slid off the oil-slick that grew out of Elfly's head.

"Oh shut up!" snapped Sigmund. He bit his lip, took a deep breath, and closed his eyes in order to control his temper.

Needing to turn away from Elfly, he looked to Coop and then to the woman who was slumped over his shoulder. Sigmund's smiled perversely at the sight.

"Good work Coop. I hope she wasn't too much trouble." He noticed scratches across Coop's face. "Ah, I see she put up a fight."

Upon hearing Sigmund's voice, Cesselia kicked and screamed as best she could despite the ropes and the gag in her mouth.

Sigmund laughed. "That's what I love about you Cesselia! You're so feisty!" Circling behind Coop, he found Cesselia's face. His eyes clouded over with a dreamy expression. Speaking as if in a trance, Sigmund said, "Cesselia, you're just as beautiful as I remember you. My dear sweet Cesselia, your beauty mesmerises me." His finger brushed gently against her cheek and she jerked her head away in disgust. "At last we are reunited and soon we will marry. We will be like the first two people in paradise, the father and mother of a new race. You will soon forget everything in this corrupt world, including your mistake, your one blemish, your lump of a son, Stanley Junior. He will very shortly cease to exist at all. "

Cesselia's eyes widened in horror. She shook her head vigorously, pleading "No!"

"Its nature's way," said Sigmund. "The male lion takes over the pride and kills the cubs so that he can sire his own cubs. I'm that lion and you are my lioness."

Leaving the distraught Cesselia, he circled back around to face Coop. "You know what you must do. Be quick about it. Take your revenge on your old school friend Livingston, and while you're at it, rid the world of young Stanley Siphonpipe Junior. I will have no rival for Cesselia's affection, not even the affection a mother reserves for her child. Speaking of the mother, give her to the Nurse while you go about your business."

❋ ❋ ❋ ❋ ❋

The robotic Rot-Rat raced out of the park, and entered the residential neighbourhoods of Septo City.

Little Klawd was close behind it. He was almost hit by a pooter delivery truck as he leapt out of the park and into the busy city skyways.

The rolling robotic rodent turned sharply several times, changing its direction while ducking down small streets and alleyways.

Little Klawd's paws slipped on the wet concrete as he tried to match each abrupt swerve and turn. He slammed into the side of a tubular towering tenement.

At last the mechanised-menace sped out of the city and headed into the adjunct wasteland – a wasteland, which Little Klawd knew well because it was also his five hundred square-mile cat-box.

The Rot-Rat led Little Klawd on a twenty-mile chase into the miserably wet wilderness.

Suddenly, the Rot-Rat stopped. Its squeaking ceased and then its eyes began to pulsate with red light.

Little Klawd dug his paws into the soggy sand to put on the brakes. The sudden cessation of squeaks and chase left his feline instincts bewildered.

The ticking in the creature's chest now seemed ominous. Just as an animal can sense seismic activity before the tremor occurs, so Little Klawd knew that something terrible was going to happen.

And then something worse than terrible did happen! The robotic Rot-Rat exploded! A cloud of fire and shock waves rent the air, sending sand flying outward in all directions.

The gigantic tabby was blown three hundred yards through the air and into the crest of a tall sand dune. This crumbled and fell on top of Little Klawd, burying his still body as surely as if he'd been placed in a grave.

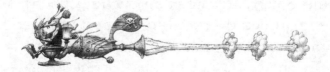

CHAPTER 37

THE INTRUDER

The gumpathump was finally able to sleep despite the chain that bound her to a dragon palm tree in the grounds of Explorer's Cottage. Remarkably, it was the wild weather that enabled her to relax. She therefore snoozed away in her own unusual manner, with her head twisted at an impossible angle so that the fleshy-brush appendage atop her head swept the ground, enabling her to listen out for packworms. She could only hear worms that were too small to be of any consequence, and so she slumbered peacefully. In the background of her dozing mind, she could also hear Livingston's snores in one room of the nearby cottage, while Stanley sighed and yawned in another part of the cottage.

Gradually, she became aware of a different noise characterised by faint vibrations in the ground. Something was approaching. She therefore woke up, rolled over and jumped to her feet, ready to run. Even if she had wanted to run away though, she could not because of the massive collar and chain that tethered her to the tree.

The stealthy footsteps drew near to her, stopped and then a flash of lightning illuminated Coop suddenly and terribly beneath the dragon palm. His face was ghostly white with prominent red gashes across his cheek.

The gumpathump was startled by the abrupt appearance of the man, and she reared up on her hind legs and tail bellowing in fright while champing her cheek pincers together.

Coop put his finger to his lips and whispered, "Shhhhh! If you continue like this I will have to silence you. Do you want to wake the dead in that condemned house?" His voice soothed her and she calmed down. "There now," he whispered. "That's more like it. It would be a shame to slaughter such a unique creature. There is nothing like you in the whole of our world. Amazing. The first traveller from another planet to our planet. Yes, I know much about you. What is it that you are called? Gumpathump is it? It is not your fault you have been brought here against your will and tied like a witless beast. I know what it is like to be bound. Your only crime is that you belong to those that I have come to eliminate." Coop removed a black disk from his backpack. "Do you see this, Gumpathump? It makes quite a noise. It will create a lot of heat and light. Twenty minutes from now, it will explode, and you will go mad with terror. I would rather set it off in two minutes, but that would bring meddling authorities to the park before we'd had a chance to leave through that Marvellous machine, that Star Flush which brought you here. For your sake though, I will put this explosive device on the far side of this condemned building, and this should reduce most of the injuries you will suffer. There will be no hope for those inside the building however, so please don't waste your time crying for them."

Coop left the bewildered gumpathump, and moved toward the cottage.

Pambot, Swatzanutter, Brobot and Gigglebyte stood at the door of the cottage, acting as sentries. They were inert, motionless and powered down, but when their electronic senses detected the intruder's presence, they switched themselves on.

"Stop. Identify yourself. You are trespassing on private property," said Pambot.

Gigglebyte hovered up into the air, looked at the stranger and said, "Yeah, like she said. You don't want to make her angry pal, and you don't want me to backfire in your direction either!"

Swatzanutter shook his fists, while uttering the threat, "Leeeeeeave now tressposser or I keek yur boooooooott!"

Brobot aimed his laser-fingers at the man and shouted, "Go ahead! Take one more step! I dare you! I've got a laser beam with the name 'ugly man' written on it and it's aimed at your ugly head!"

Coop stopped, removed his backpack and

said, "Oh I'm sorry. Is this private property? I think I took a wrong turn here in the park. Perhaps you could give me directions. I think I have a map of the park here in my bag."

Instead of fetching a map, Coop took out a contraption that looked like a hand–held gatling gun. It was a plasmatronic immobilizer and rather than firing bullets, it sent pulsating discharges of ionised gas with such explosive amounts of anode current that it could cripple anything electronic within a 500 yard radius.

"Oh here's my lighter, but where oh where is my map?"

Coop calmly aimed the plasmatronic immobilizer while pretending to fumble for the map. He pulled the trigger and released a power surge that hit the area like a silent bomb blast, causing the four robots to shut down where they stood or hovered (as a result Gigglebyte dropped abruptly to the ground).

Casually, Coop proceeded to the far side of the cottage and planted the black disk underneath the windowsill of Livingston's bedroom.

Red digital numbers lit up across the face of the disk, and these numbers began to count backwards.

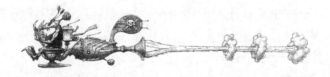

CHAPTER 38

REX

Coop rejoined Sigmund, Elfly and the Psychobot Nurse. Cesselia was in the Nurse's steely embrace.

"Mission accomplished?" asked Sigmund.

"In only a matter of minutes Livingston and young Stanley will cease to exist!" answered Coop.

Coop's chilling reply caused sobs of agony to erupt from Cesselia's muffled mouth.

"It's called going out with a bang," said Sigmund. "We will be half way across the universe by the time the bomb explodes. Let the plan commence."

Lightning crackled overhead as they approached the secure titanium door of Livingston's laboratory. The dome-top searchlights switched themselves on and swept the grounds upon electronically sensing their presence. Within two yards of the laboratory door, they halted, while the Psychobot Nurse scanned the bushes on either side of the entrance with her light-beam eyes.

To Coop, Sigmund whispered, "Do you see it?"

"I would be very disappointed if I could," Coop replied. "It is waiting in ambush."

"You have a magnificent way with these freaky fowls as you proved during our visit to the military base," said Sigmund. "Take care of the bird as you see fit." To the Psychobot Nurse, Sigmund said, "As soon as the bird is subdued, dear Nurse, cut a hole in the laboratory wall."

To Cesselia, Sigmund apologised, saying, "My darling I'm sorry to do this to you, but we're going to have to put you on the ground for the moment. I know it's cold and wet, but before you know it, you and I will be sunning ourselves on the paradise planet of Oxnard together."

Commanding the Nurse, Sigmund said, "Nurse put Cesselia on the ground, and be gentle. The last thing I want is a black and blue bride."

The Psychobot Nurse lowered Cesselia on to the rain-saturated grass.

In reaction to the chilling ground and the wretched water that soaked her through and through, Cesselia shivered and wriggled like a worm, trying to generate any body heat whatsoever to combat the discomfort she had to endure. She also tested the ropes that limited her movement to rolling. Despite her misery, she preferred the relative freedom of the ground to the shoulder of Coop or the embrace of the Psychobot Nurse.

Coop removed his shoes and socks, preferring to be barefoot for what he was about to do. He closed his eyes, and when he opened them again, his eyes looked strangely like the eyes of a bird. He arched his back and made eerily authentic clucking and crowing noises. With his bare feet he scratched at the mud while his head bobbed forward and back, forward and back, forward and back. In this bird-like manner he moved ever closer toward the laboratory door.

Suddenly the Guard Rooster attacked Coop, leaping out of the bushes in a surprising blind-siding move.

Its red comb, membranous display fan and hanging wattle gave it the appearance of a fierce warrior decked out in war paint.

It screeched as its talons flew forward, aimed at Coop's back.

The rooster was caught off guard however as Coop turned on it and caught its talons in his hands. He then held the monstrous chicken upside down.

It crowed in a bloodthirsty rage while Coop crowed back at it, matching it in volume and in its frightening lust for blood. Screeching in anger, it sank its beak into Coop's thigh, and drew the blood it was after. Despite the injury, Coop continued to hold the upside-down bird steadily, and he spoke to it, saying, "We are not so unlike you and me. We are brothers. I was cared for under the wings of a mother hen like you – that is until the social workers took me away from my home in the coop. Now let the blood rush to your head my fowl brother. You are feeling sleepy. That's it. Sleep my friend."

A languid expression filled the eyes of the topsy-turvy fowl. It fell into a catatonic sleep as it hung in Coop's upraised hands.

Seeing that the bird was temporarily out of action, Sigmund said, "Nurse, please operate on this building; make a large incision in its wooden walls."

As an aside he remarked, "It was so thoughtful of that security expert fellow not to return and fortify this building."

The Psychobot Nurse stomped forward. Panels in her chest opened and two buzzing surgical saws emerged. These saws cut through the bushes, before they made contact with the wooden walls of the laboratory, just to the left of the titanium door. Upon completing her incision and withdrawing her saws back into her chest, an oblong plank of wood fell outward and away from the laboratory wall leaving a gaping oblong hole in its place.

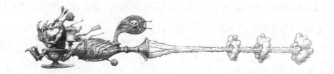

CHAPTER 39

THE WARNING GUMP

Something was amiss and the gumpathump knew it. She had witnessed the angry exchange between the stranger and the robots. She felt the shock wave of anode electricity. She had seen the stealthy visitor disappear around the cottage before she sensed him walking away. She sensed impending danger just as surely as her brush appendage could sense a packworm deep underground. She therefore resumed the bellowing gumps and her cottage-shaking thumps that had prompted Stanley to call his mother earlier in the evening.

As a result, Stanley was soon up and out the cottage door, and he was none too happy about it. Wearing pajamas, rubber boots and a rain jacket, Stanley stormed out into the storm.

"This is miserable!" he complained. "Hey bots," he wearily said to the four immobile robots near the door. "Some night, eh?"

Having been shut down, they were unable to reply, but Stanley was too tired to register the fact that the robots had been completely deactivated. He walked by them without a second thought.

He made his way over to where the gumpathump was tethered, and he scolded her, saying, "Gumpathump, what is wrong with you?"

She sensed displeasure in Stanley's expression and tone, and so she lowered her vocalizations to a whimper.

"I thought you liked the rain? Is your chain too tight?"

Groggily he checked the chain to make sure the gumpathump was not tangled up and he found everything in order.

"You need to calm down girl."

He reached up to the gumpathump's face and stroked her on the side of her wet head.

"That's it, Gumpathump. Everything is OK. I'm right inside the house. OK, now. You lie down and go to sleep."

Slowly, he backed away.

"Shhhh. Quiet now. I'm going back to bed. Good night Gumpathump. See you in the morning."

He turned away and began trudging back across the slushy ground toward the cottage.

Instead of calming down, the gumpathump gumped and thumped louder than ever. She reared up and brought her front feet crashing to the ground, causing mud to splatter all over Stanley.

"Great! Just great!" shouted Stanley. He spun around, pointed at her and yelled, "Stop that right now Gumpathump! There is nothing wrong! I am going back to bed. I don't need this Gumpathump. I'll wear earplugs if I have to. Good night!"

Stanley stomped into the cottage and slammed the door behind him, leaving the gumpathump to bellow, cry, pound the ground, and run skittishly back and forth, pulling on her chain.

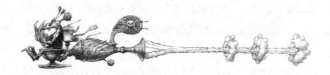

CHAPTER 40

ELFLY'S BIG ENTRANCE

"ELFLY! ELFLY! ELFLY! WE LOVE YOU ELFLY!" screamed the fans.

"Elfly, Pay attention!" shouted Sigmund.

Looking down into the front row of the packed auditorium, Elfly saw Sigmund scowling at him from a front row seat.

The interruption of his fantasy concert brought him back to the present reality. His delusion dissolved and he stood in the harsh rainstorm of the present, just as if he'd woken up from a dream.

He was cold, his jumpsuit was soaking wet and Sigmund was toe to toe and face to face with him, glaring at him.

Glancing to his right, he saw Coop holding an upside-down rooster.

Peeking over Sigmund's shoulder, he saw the Psychobot Nurse standing near the hole she had made in the laboratory wall.

Behind him on the ground, he saw the pretty lady who they were going to bring with them on their trip to the stars. He seemed to remember that they had called her 'Cesselia' or something like that.

"Elfly, you're on!" yelled Sigmund.

"I'm on?"

"Yes, it's your cue to go on stage. Just like we rehearsed, remember? You must switch off the alarms like we planned. Quickly now! Let's go through your check list."

"Yeah, let's rock and roll!" agreed Elfly.

"Screwdriver?"

Elfly pulled out a screwdriver from one of the many pouches in his golden rhinestone belt, took a quick glance at it, and then put it back in the pouch.

"Uh huh," he answered.

"Headlight?"

"Nuh Uh. My hair is too greasy for those lil' varmints to make a home in."

Sigmund slapped him on the side of his head and growled, "Light! Light I said – the band to go around your head with the light attached to it, you idiot!"

"Oh yeah."

Elfly retrieved a jewel studded silver band out of one of the pouches, and this had a small round lamp sewn on to the front of it. He pulled the band over his considerable head of hair without messing up a single strand, and then he turned the lamp on. This made Sigmund blink and shade his eyes in irritation.

"Don't turn it on yet! Wait till you are inside the laboratory," scolded Sigmund.

Elfly switched the headlamp off.

"Suction-cup gloves and suction-cup kneepads?"

Elfly removed these items from several more pouches.

"Uh huh."

"Put them on."

Elfly put on the suction-cupped gloves and kneepads.

"Is that everything?" asked Sigmund.

"Well I've got some fries in one of these here pockets in case I get hungry."

"Fries?" Sigmund snarled. "Of all the..." Sigmund reached into Elfly's pouch and removed the offending fries, tossing them on the wet ground. Attempting to be patient, he said, "Let's go through your blocking Elfly. You enter through the hole in the wall. You could say it's like the backstage door if you want. You will then make a spectacular entrance by climbing up the walls and into the dome, four stories above the floor. There you will find a plasmatronic proof control box made of polycarbonates and polybutenes."

"poly-whatcha-ma-call-it?"

"Plastics and rubber substitutes but let us not get bogged down in technical vernacular. Just worry about the box. You will then remove the sealed lid of the box with your screwdriver. You must be very careful not to drop the screws, for even something as small as they will trip the alarms. You will then be able to manually switch off all of the alarms and therefore disable the Molecule Scrambler as well."

Elfly gave Sigmund the thumbs up and said, "All right big boss man, it's all right."

Sigmund then stepped aside as Elfly swaggered toward the laboratory and entered through the man-size hole in the wall.

Once inside, Elfly stood for a moment, mesmerised by the sight of the crisscross beams of red laser light. He let out an impressed wolf-whistle.

"These lights sure are sparkly!" he remarked. "They remind me of my half time gig at the Super Toilet Bowl!"

"Get going," ordered Sigmund from the other side of the hole.

Elfly switched on his headlamp. He then threw himself hard against the inner wall of the laboratory, nearly cracking his head and breaking his nose as he did so.

"OW! My purty purty face!"

"Stop playing around! You're wasting time!" barked Sigmund.

Elfly's suction-cupped gloves held the wall as did his suction-cupped knees, and so he began climbing up the vertical and upward curving walls of the laboratory, crawling like an insect as he ascended.

Ten strenuous minutes later, he reached

the centre of the domed ceiling and he found the control panel Sigmund told him about.

"I've arrived baby!" shouted Elfly. "Mama said someday I'd reach the top."

CHAPTER 41

THE DRAGON PALM TREE

Movement.

There was a slight shift in the dragon palm as the gumpathump tugged on her chain. With another pull there was even more shifting, more creaking and more tilting. The great alien beast dug her spiked feet into the mud and pulled with all her might while bellowing as loudly as she could. This was followed by another huge shift in the tree as its roots lost their grip in the saturated soil. The tree teetered and groaned.

Using her tonnage and muscular bulk, the gumpathump strained her shoulders, legs and back to pull down the tree and so the tree began to up end.

It was at that precise moment that Stanley threw open the cottage door again, and marched outside in a fit of temper, shouting, "What is with you Gumpathump! I can even hear you with earplugs in my ears."

He saw the tree falling straight towards

him and he yelled out in fright.

The gumpathump took a running leap toward Stanley, grabbed him with her cheek pincers and tossed him aside, throwing him through the air.

Part of the tree fell like a hammer on the gumpathump's back, pinning her to the ground, while the upper half of the tree crashed down on to Explorer's Cottage, causing its walls and roof to collapse.

CHAPTER 42

THE CONTROL PANEL

"Oh, I've got a dirty, dirty feelin'. I'm kneelin' on the ceilin'," sang Elfly as he removed the first screw from the control panel. He did this with one hand, because his other hand was suction-cupped to the dome above him. Nimbly, he transferred the screw from his hand to his mouth so he could hold it between his teeth.

"HOOOOW IIIIS IIIT GOOOOING?" Sigmund yelled.

This distracted Elfly.

"AAAAAARGH!" spluttered Elfly after swallowing the screw. He then coughed, gagged, and then broke out singing, "Well you ain't never swallowed a rivet and yu ain't no friend of mine!"

After regaining his composure and ability to breathe, Elfly sang, "Viva laaaaab-or-a-tooooory!"

Returning to the task at hand, Elfly removed the other screws, transferred each one safely to his mouth and pried open the lid of the control box. It swung upward on stiff hinges, and locked in place.

All that was left to do was turn each switch off.

CHAPTER 43

AMIDST THE RUBBLE

Stanley woke up in a mud puddle feeling sore, wet and chilled to his bones. Feeling dizzy and disoriented, he wondered what had happened to him and why he was lying outside on the soggy ground.

Suddenly, it all came back to him and he remembered the falling tree and the heroic maneuver by the gumpathump.

"No! Oh, no, Gumpathump!"

He staggered up, regained his balance and ran over to the fallen tree and to the gumpathump underneath its bulky trunk. The gumpathump's eyes were shut and she was completely still.

In distress, Stanley tried to lift the tree off of her, but it was far too heavy for him and would not budge. Tears filled his eyes as he tenderly petted the gumpathump's face.

In response to his touch, the gumpathump's eyes opened with a blink, while her mouth and nostrils flared open with an intake of air.

"Gumpathump! You're OK! You're alive! Don't worry, I'll get this tree off of you with, er, uh, little help from…" Stanley raised his voice and shouted, "Swatzanutter!"

There was no answer back and when he looked to the place where the front door of the cottage had been, he could only see scattered thatch and a pile of rubble.

"Swatzanutter! Pambot! Gigglebyte! Brobot! Any Bot!"

There was still no reply.

"Livingston!" shouted Stanley.

Stanley remembered that Livingston had been asleep in his bed, but now Livingston's bedroom was buried somewhere underneath the remains of the cottage.

The robots would have to wait. Right now, he needed to make sure Livingston was OK.

To the gumpathump, Stanley said, "I'll be right back." He then left her whimpering in pain, while he wandered around the ruins to where he thought Livingston's bedroom was. Having made an educated guess as to where Livingston was located, he started digging through the rubble, tossing aside the thatch and broken pieces of the walls. All the while he called Livingston's name.

Then in the midst of the ruined bedroom Stanley heard a snore.

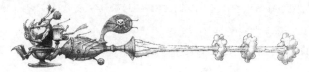

CHAPTER 44

THE STRANGE CLOCK

EXCERPT FROM LIVINGSTON'S JOURNAL

I woke up to Stanley's persistent shakes. My eyes opened. With a snort, my nasal passages also opened. Gradually I realised I was covered in dust and rubble. I then noticed my bedroom was gone and in place of the room was the chilly open air with its drizzle.

Stanley was saying something, but I couldn't hear him. His mouth was moving but no sound came out. I then remembered that I had been wearing earplugs in an attempt to sleep through the racket the gumpathump was making.

After I removed the earplugs, I said, "What did you say?"

Urgently Stanley repeated himself saying,

"Hurry Livingston! A tree's fallen on top of the gumpathump!"

I shook myself and sat jolt upright.

"Tree? Is the gumpathump OK?"

"I don't know. Come help me move the tree!"

My mind was not fully awake yet, and I wasn't thinking all that clearly.

"I'm coming, I'm coming. Er, have you er seen my slippers?"

This annoyed Stanley and he shouted, "We don't have time..."

"I'm barefoot," I shouted back. "My feet will get cold and I'll probably get a splinter."

"I don't care about your feet."

"I do."

In frustration Stanley dove into the rubble, furiously tossing anything and everything aside in a hurried search for my slippers, while I tried to help from the safety of my debris-covered bed.

Stanley then found a curious object. He brought up a black disk-shaped object from underneath some thatch and plaster. There were glowing numbers counting down backwards on it.

"What's this?" asked Stanley.

"I don't know. I don't think its mine. I've never seen it before."

"I don't like the look of it. It's ticking."

In my sleepy stupor, I asked, "Is it a clock of some sort?"

"Yes and the digital numbers are counting down from thirteen, twelve, eleven..."

A worried look came over Stanley's face as the numbers continued to count down: Nine, Eight, Seven …

"S–S–Stanley, I–I–I think you should get rid of whatever it is!"

"I think you're right!"

Stanley stood up in what was left of the bedroom, and threw the black disk as far as he could throw it.

BOOOOOOM! While it was still in mid-air, the disk exploded in a mushroom cloud of fire and deafening noise.

There was flying rubble, dirt, pain and then I blacked out.

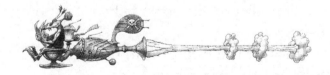

CHAPTER 45

CHAOS

AUTHOR'S NARRATION:

Sigmund turned to face a firestorm rising from the direction of Explorer's Cottage.

"So ends the miserable lives of Stanley and Livingston," he announced over the din.

Coop malignantly grinned from ear to ear while Cesselia wailed through her gag; her tears joined the stream of rain that ran over her face.

* * * * *

Elfly failed to flip any of the switches off. The explosion distracted him, and he reflexively tilted toward the sound, with a "What the hey?"

It was then that a remnant of a fry slipped from its place in the pouch of Elfly's belt and fell straight through several of the alarm-tripping laser lights.

Immediately, a storm of complete and utter mayhem was unleashed.

SIRENS! BELLS! FOGHORNS! The TRA-RA-RA-BOOMTY-AY of a brass band cooked Elfly's eardrums.

The Molecule Scrambler woke up like a grizzly bear coming out of hibernation, and with its horn blaring it charged through the laboratory searching for intruders.

* * * * *

The topsy-turvy cockerel in Coop's hands awoke with a vengeance as the shock waves of heat and noise passed through the park. It screeched, kicked, flapped and pecked at everything in sight, before escaping from Coop's clutches. It fell on its head, rolled on to its feet and jumped up ready to attack.

Coop was ready, and when the vicious bird leapt towards his eyes, he caught the cockerel by its throat.

The man and bird then fought each other with kicks, punches, pecks, bites and scratches.

They were so locked together in combat that when Coop tripped and fell through the hole in the laboratory wall, so too did the rooster.

* * * * *

All the noise made Elfly twitch and jerk. His suction-cupped hands pulled away from the ceiling, causing his upper body to swing downwards.

Hanging precariously by his knees, he looked straight down at the drop below him and moaned, "I gotta go potty Miss Claudy!"

Eventually his suction-cupped knees lost their grip as well.

"MAMA!" he cried just before making the four-story plunge.

Elfly broke his fall (as well as every bone in his body) when he fell on one of the specimen shelves on the way down.

The shelves were empty apart from a single specimen jar, a container with a green-eyed maggot. The shelves cracked and splintered into pieces as Elfly crashed through them, and this caused the specimen jar to topple to the floor and shatter. The pickled monster maggot slid across the laboratory floor on a slick trail of formaldehyde.

In the meanwhile, Elfly's irreparably broken body followed the maggot down on to the floor, where he landed with a bone-breaking thump.

※ ※ ※ ※ ※

The Molecule Scrambler detected the sliding motion of the pickled maggot.. With one of its tentacles, it picked the maggot up and placed it inside its scrambling slot. Its four ray guns blasted the maggot with their molecule disintegrating beams.

At the same time, another tentacle picked

up Elfly's shattered body. He too was dumped inside the slot and blasted.

Elfly was reduced to a ball of white light containing his disconnected molecules, and these molecules then merged with another ball of light composed of the atoms of the green-eyed monster maggot.

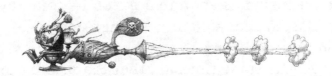

CHAPTER 46

METAMORPHOSIS

Coop and the rooster continued to grapple with one another, while violently crowing, pecking, kicking, scratching and striking each other.

The Molecule Scrambler detected their intrusive presence.

Coop and the ruthless rooster were so engaged in their cockfight that they didn't see the machine racing towards them. Before they realised what was happening, they were ripped away from each other by powerful tentacles. They were dropped together into the molecule disintegrating heart of the scrambler and blasted at the same time.

✳ ✳ ✳ ✳ ✳

Sigmund Looz watched in horror as his plans unraveled before his one good eye.

"Psychobot Nurse!" he screamed. "Disable the Molecule Scrambler! Destroy it!"

While the Molecule Scrambler was still firing its destructive rays at Coop and the rooster, the Psychobot Nurse stepped through the hole in the wall. She stomped over to the Scrambler, grabbed it by its metal legs and upended it.

Despite the upheaval, the ray guns continued their process of disintegration. The molecules of Coop and the ferocious fowl flew apart inside the overturned scrambler slot and then they re-emerged from oblivion as another ball of merged molecules, before disappearing.

While the Nurse tried to destroy the Molecule Scrambler, its ray guns were occupied,

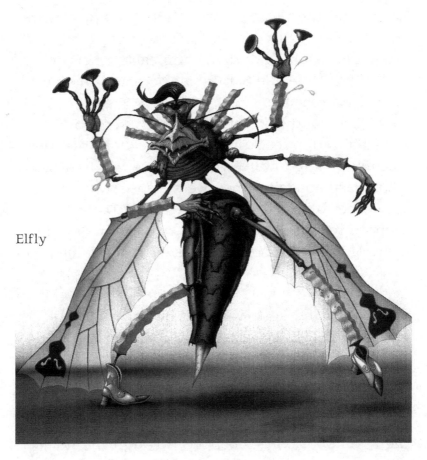

Elfly

but its tentacles were not. With its tentacles, the machine fought back, lashing the Psychobot Nurse repeatedly.

The Nurse grabbed the tentacles with one hand and smashed the spinning red light with her other hand. This caused an eruption of sparks and smoke. The Nurse then ripped the machine open, laying bare the wires and controls inside it.

Believing it was now safe to enter; Sigmund stepped into the laboratory, through the hole.

"Find the reintegration switch!" shouted Sigmund.

The Nurse found the reintegration switch inside the guts of the Molecule Scrambler and turned it on. This caused the four ray guns to fire rays at the ball of molecular light. Its guns spun outwardly in unison, sending the ball out in front of itself. There the light orb started to take shape and form.

Sigmund watched in amazement as the molecules solidified.

He had expected to see his lunatic henchmen Coop and Elfly restored to him as before, but the Molecule Scrambler had instead created something else altogether. Instead of either Elfly or Coop, there was now a man-sized maggot. It was a slimy sluggish white worm with skin that seemed to be made out of the fabric of Elfly's jump suit. Rhinestones were imbedded in the skin of the pupa along with greasy fries that stuck out of the thing's back intermittently. On the thing's face, there were two lamp-like green eyes. Strangely enough, at the very top of the maggot's head, there was a hair-do just like Elfly's, which hadn't changed much at all, despite the freak accident.

Revolted at the sight, Sigmund screamed, "Nurse! Finish destroying the Molecule Scrambler and then destroy this monster - this - this abomination of nature!"

Obeying the command, the Psychobot Nurse thrust her fist into the heart of the scrambler and started pulling wires. Small electrical explosions erupted in the machine sending up a cascade of sparks The Molecule Scrambler then ceased all of its functions, becoming dark and silent.

Sigmund kicked the Elfly-worm and ranted, "Fool! You failed in the one task I needed you for. All you had to do was flip a couple of simple switches and you completely and utterly botched it up! Idiot! You deserve whatever has happened to you, Elfly. Did you really think I would take an imbecile like you with me through the Star Flush anyway? I fully intended to crush you like a worm after I was through with you. How convenient that you have become a worm. It makes the task of squashing you so much easier..."

Before Sigmund's eyes, the jump suit skin of the Elfly-worm hardened, becoming a dry, brittle cocoon. Even though the laboratory was filled with noise, he heard a sound above it all which he hated more than all the other sounds. He heard Elfly singing. It came from inside the cocoon.

"I'll find me a ladybug, and lose my antennas over you," sang the voice. "I'll chase you' round all over town, and bring you some doggy doo."

To Sigmund's dismay, the cocoon began to roll from side to side and to split apart down the middle.

"Our mandibles connect. Our six arms entwine. Greatest case of buggy lovin' you'll ever find. It's called a bug's life."

"Psychobot Nurse, step on it!" commanded Sigmund.

The robot brought her heavy foot down on the cocoon, just as a six-foot tall insect escaped out the top end of the cocoon and flew up into the air.

"What a life," sang the insect. "That's good enough for me. You heard me say it now. It's called a bug's life. It's called a bug's life."

Sigmund stared up at the insect with both awe and consternation.

Looking down at Sigmund, the insect said, "Hey there Doc. Look what happened to me. I've been changed into a big ol' bug. What do you know about that? And I can fly! I can fly!"

The insect buzzed around the laboratory, marvelling at its new abilities.

"Elfly! Come back down here! I'd like to talk to you."

Returning to Sigmund, Elfly hovered just above him and said, "I don't know how it happened. I just remember falling from the ceiling, and the next thing I know, I got me two more arms and these purty wings on my back. What the heck happened?"

There were guitar motif patterns embroidered into the very fabric of Elfly's new wings. Rhinestones decorated his exoskeleton segments, as did the occasional fry. The white boots with the golden stars were now melded into the bottom of his hind appendages, and his hairdo was now mounted on top of his green-eyed fly face.

Sigmund smiled slyly and answered the insect by saying, "Elfly, your molecules have been scrambled with the molecules of a fly that somehow got into the scrambling machine. You've just experienced what every caterpillar experiences as it changes into a butterfly. It's called metamorphosis. Do you know what this transformation means Elfly?"

"Er, I have to eat poop?"

"No, it means that all is not lost. It means that you may be of some use to me yet. Look at you. You can fly. You are a fly, a fly that will do my bidding. Someone with your special talents is just what I need, especially since I lost Coop. Sorry to say, but Coop won't be coming with us through the Star Flush. He died inside the Molecule Scrambler and his atoms have been scattered to..."

Sigmund didn't finish. The lights went out.

The alarms were silenced.

"What? Is there a power cut?"

"Beats me," answered Elfly. "There ain't nobody in here 'cept me an' you and a 'bot named...."

"BOO!" shrieked a disembodied voice.

CHAPTER 47

THE PHANTOM FOWL

Elfly darted downward, landed on Sigmund's back, wrapped his six arms and legs around him, and in fright he yelled, "It's a ghooooooooooooost!"

"Buzz off!" barked Sigmund while he swatted Elfly away.

Elfly flew frantically around the laboratory several times before leaving through the hole in the wall.

Laughter filled the laboratory.

"Who's there?" called Sigmund. "Show yourself!" To the Nurse, he said, "Do you see anything?"

"I detect the sound," said the Nurse, "but according to all my instruments, there is nothing making the sound."

Without warning, Sigmund ascended upward to the top of the laboratory dome like a rocket.

"Hello Siggy," said a mocking voice.

It was Coop's voice, though Coop was nowhere to be seen.

"Coop? Is that you?"

Poultrygeist

"In a matter of speaking," said the voice.

Glowing light gathered in front of Sigmund and congealed into a form that certainly was not Coop. He gasped in horror. What appeared before him was hideous. The ghastly thing was a combination of everything Coop had been and everything the genetically engineered rooster had been. Its ethereal make up looked like red flames, making it seem solid and physical one moment and like an apparition the next. The spectral being clutched him around his throat with talons instead of hands.

"As you can see Siggy, I have been reborn," said the entity. "I am no longer the man known as Coop. I have evolved. I have become god-like.

But am I a ghost, I ask myself? I do not believe so. I am alive – more alive than I have ever been. Yet, I am like a ghost.

My last memory is being dropped into the scrambling machine alongside my fowl brother. Something must have happened to our molecules inside the contraption. Was the scrambling process disrupted?"

Sigmund took a deep breath and gathered his devious wits about him. "Yes," he replied. "The Psychobot Nurse turned off the machine in mid-reintegration."

"That explains it. My molecules phase in and out of one frequency to another. In this material dimension, in which you see me now, I am subject to certain limitations, for instance if you should strike me now I would feel it. However ...." (The entity disappeared, though its voice carried on speaking).... "When my molecules phase out, I am no longer subject to the laws of physics in this material dimension. My molecules may pass through this aspect of time and space without obeying any of its rigid physical laws. Yes, I am like a spirit!" The monstrosity reappeared. "I am an inter-dimensional, egg-toplasmic entity of diabolic intellect! I have given myself a new name. Hear my new name and tremble! I am Poultrygeist! Cock-a-doodle-booooooo! ...

And just as I have been changed, our relationship must change Siggy. Once I was your pitiful patient subject to your abuse and torment. Now you will be subject to abuse and torment. You want to rule planets do you? No, it is I that shall rule, and I shall rule over you. I therefore command you to bow in fear and trembling before me or I shall drop you to your death."

"I do tremble before you Poultrygoose!"

"Poultrygeist!"

"Sorry. But would it not be better for millions to bow before the great and mighty Poultrygeist. Shouldn't the multitudes deify you? Worship you? Think of it. Yes, you could bring whole planets into subjugation and if you will permit me, I could take care of the more mundane details – the day to day running of a planet for instance – you know, tedious tasks like administration – while you become the supreme being of a new interplanetary religion – and while I grovel before you in worship and fear, allow me to humble myself before you and petition thee as well. Hear my prayer. If it be thy will, I would like you to go get my brother Howard, for are you not a god who sits in judgment on the insubordinate who refuse – and

Howard will refuse, I can assure you – to bow his self-righteous knee to you? After all, my brother is the richest and most powerful man on the planet and it is he that should be the first to pledge his obedience to you."

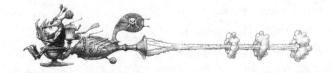

CHAPTER 48

THE ESCAPE ATTEMPT

Cesselia had been left on her own.

Sigmund was inside the laboratory and so was Coop, the robot and the fellow in the rhinestone jump suit. There had been a terrible explosion, a fight with a guard rooster, all kinds of alarms, sirens and bells. However, in the chaotic madness of everything that had transpired, Cesselia had been left on the wet ground outside the laboratory. She knew she would have no better chance to escape than at that present moment.

Fearing that her captors might return any second, Cesselia rolled across the laboratory lawn toward the cover of a flower bed.

She was able to wriggle like a snake into the middle of a floral bush despite the thorny stems that scratched her and tore right through her clothes and skin.

Now concealed, she used the thorns around her to cut through the ropes binding her wrists. Soon individual strands of the ropes began to tear and then suddenly, her hands were free.

She removed the gag from her mouth. She gasped, coughed and gulped the air.

The ropes binding her feet were next on the agenda. While she was untying these ropes she heard a voice that filled her with dread.

"Yoooooo Hoooooo Cesselia," sang Sigmund. "Oh, Cesselia! Come out, come out where ever you are! You probably thought I forgot about you, didn't you?"

Frantically, Cesselia picked at the knotted rope around her ankles.

"How could I forget my beautiful bride, heart of my heart, soul of my soul?"

At last the knot around her ankles came undone, and she removed the ropes from around her feet.

"What kind of game is this? Hide and seek is it? You could not have gone far my darling, so I guess that you are hiding somewhere, perhaps in these bushes."

Instinctively, Cesselia searched for something with which to defend herself, and her fingers found a rock imbedded in the soil.

"Don't you realise what awaits us across the galaxies my love, my dar...?"

Cesselia leapt like a ferocious animal out of the flower bed. With the stone, she smashed Sigmund across the side of his skull.

Sigmund slumped over and fell backwards on to the ground.

She gave Sigmund a kick in the ribs before stepping over his unconscious form. Instantly, she began moving in the direction of Explorer's Cottage, slowly at first, but as strength returned to her numb legs, she was soon flat out running as fast as she could.

With all her thoughts focused on finding her son, be he alive, or injured, or dead, she had been slow to notice the buzzing sound. The strange noise gradually came to her attention. The sound caught up with her, and it seemed as if it was right on top of her. Something took hold of her. She saw her feet leave the ground. She looked up and screamed in terror when her eyes met the glowing green eyes of a monstrous fly.

"Hey where you goin' in such a hurry darlin'?" said Elfly. "Dontcha know we gotta get ready to go on a trip to the stars?"

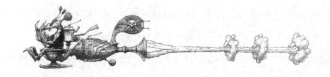

CHAPTER 49

THE APPARITION

Howard Looz tossed and turned in his bed, troubled by his dreams. On the edge of his sleepy mind, he thought he heard a tapping sound.

He felt a gust of wind blow through his bedroom.

Lightning flashed and thunder roared outside his open window.

"Open Window? I didn't leave the window open."

Forcing himself to get out of bed, Howard wandered over to the bedroom window. Its silky white curtains billowed in the howling wind and rain. He fought the elements to pull the pane down, and upon succeeding he re-fastened the inside latch.

"How did the window open from the inside?"

The curtains fell back down over Howard's head, trapping him for a moment, and as he turned and tried to free himself from the curtains, he saw a shadow move toward him. Someone was there in the room with him.

The silky material before him distorted the image, giving it a ghostly visage.

"WHO'S THERE?!"

Howard gasped. The intruder was now only inches away, but he or she or it didn't look right. It didn't look like a person. The image on the other side of the curtain was grotesque.

Howard screamed. The curtain was ripped away. It was a ghost! A monster with the face of an evil bird.

Howard fainted, falling to the floor like a dead man.

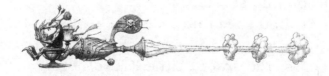

CHAPTER 50

THE BOMB SITE

Little Klawd woke from the sleep forced on him by the concussive bomb blast. He emerged from beneath the sand dune that had buried him.

Every muscle, limb and bone within him felt sore and stiff.

Vaguely he remembered chasing a strange looking Rot-Rat, and then there had been a flash and a terrible noise.

He shook the sand off.

Putting one weak paw in front of the other, he began limping toward Septo City in search of his masters.

✳ ✳ ✳ ✳ ✳

Little Klawd arrived at a scorched crater in what used to be the grounds of Explorer's Cottage.

Having no speech with which to ask questions, he could only yowl to express his confusion and sense of loss.

Beyond the crater was a pile of rubble where the cottage had been standing, and after a leap across the crater, Little Klawd began investigating the ruins of Livingston's home.

He found the gumpathump lying on her side, stuck under a fallen tree. Using his head, he pushed the tree off of the gumpathump. He then licked her face until she wakened and was able to stand to her feet.

Leaving the gumpathump, he followed an unmistakable trail of scent, and found Stanley and Livingston under a pile of thatch and drywall. Bending over them, he licked their faces until they too opened their eyes.

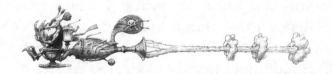

CHAPTER 51

THE TRAITORS

Howard coughed and woke up. The air smelled of smoke. Before him was a hellish scene of fire and mayhem. He felt dizzy. Where was he? How did he get here? Was he dreaming? Was this a very vivid nightmare? These questions along with a dozen sights and sensations bombarded him all at once.

The dying drizzle of the night's fading storm convinced Howard that he was not dreaming. The cold raindrops felt real enough.

He noticed that he was upright, wearing his business suit. How or why he came to be out in the open surrounded by dwindling bonfires (or whatever they were) was too much for him to comprehend. His knees buckled and he almost passed out from nausea, but then he noticed that a horrid arm was supporting him; it encircled his chest and lifted him up with a yellow – was it a claw? A deformed hand? Howard couldn't be sure. His eyes followed the arm and he twisted his neck to look over his shoulder, regretting doing so the moment he did it. Directly behind him, he saw the ghastly face with the beak he had seen in his bedroom. He turned away with a frightened whimper and a shudder.

He saw the Star Flush; it was before him, its lid standing open in a fog of smoke and mist. Strangely it was outside the laboratory, exposed to the elements.

He made the mistake of glancing to his right. There he saw the surreal image of a large fly perched atop a hovering tractor.

"How y'all doin'?" said the insect.

He closed his eyes and shook his head in disbelief, but when he opened them again, the fly was still there. In back of the fly on the tractor platform, he saw Cesselia. She was tied to a cylindrical fuel tank and her mouth was gagged. She caught his eye and they exchanged a look of mutual dread.

He then heard a familiar voice calling his name, saying, "Howard, Howard, Howard."

He heard approaching footsteps and then his brother, Sigmund, walked out of the smoke and stood in front of him.

"Sigmund," he said in surprise, not believing his own eyes. "I thought you were dead! Thank goodness you're still alive!"

His brother's face was more serious, more wrinkled, and more drawn than he remembered, and there was now an eye-patch covering one of his brother's eyes. There was also a bump and bruise on the side of his head.

"It's been a long time, hasn't it, brother?" said Sigmund.

"I thought you died in the fire at the asylum! Have they captured you too? I still don't know if I am dreaming or if I am awake."

"Pinch yourself then Howard. This is no dream."

"Have we been kidnapped? Have you and I – and – and – Cesselia been taken against our wills by these – these – things? – these thugs in horrible masks? What are they going to do with us?"

"We? You keep using the words 'We'. It has never been 'We'."

"I don't understand," said Howard.

"When 'We' arrive on the planet Oxnard, I shall explain everything."

"Ox? – Oxnard?"

"To be honest, I had never heard of the place either, until just a short while ago. The Charade-oglyphics are quite conversational once you get the hang of speaking with them. Yes, the Charade-oglyphics told me that Livingston, and that no good son of Cesselia's, Stanley Junior, wanted to go to the planet Oxnard. It is a tropical paradise, a lush green planet, from what I've been told. Think of it brother! We will finally export Looz Enterprises to the ends of the universe – Only it won't be 'We,' or 'Us.' It will be 'Me!'

"Sigmund, you can't do this!"

"Oh but I can!"

"This is madness!"

Sigmund backhanded Howard in the face with a stinging slap.

"Don't you talk to me about madness! You know nothing about the diseases of the mind. When you have worked in an asylum for as long as I have then you can lecture me on the subject of madness."

"Sigmund, please! Don't do this! You don't know how to use the Star Flush."

"Oh but I do."

"But how could you? Who taught you?"

"Who? Livingston taught me."

"Livingston? You mean to say that Livingston's a traitor? He sold our secrets to you?"

"A fool, yes, but a traitor, no. 'Was' a fool I should say. Did I mention that Livingston is dead?"

Howard was stunned to hear this news and he looked at his brother with an expression of dismay.

"Oh yes," continued Sigmund. "There was a terrible accident over at his cottage. Sadly, Stanley Junior died along with him."

Upon hearing these dreadful words yet again, Cesselia screamed curses at Sigmund in muffled anger and grief.

Turning to her, Sigmund soothingly said, "There, there my darling. I understand that you are angry, and that is why I will forgive that matter of the bump on the head. Hush now. You're getting yourself all worked up. I know that you grieve now, but I promise you that you'll forget about your defective first child when we have other children to replace him."

In rage, Howard suddenly lunged forward and punched his brother in the mouth, drawing blood in the process.

Poultrygeist pulled Howard back, tightening his grip around him.

For a moment, Sigmund was stunned, but then he smiled, tasted the blood on his lips and started to laugh. "If you must know," he boasted, "the traitor from your little organisation was the same one who showed me all the boring educational films about the Star Flush. You don't know how many times I had to watch Livingston demonstrate how to read Charade-oglyphics. Yes, it is this employee of yours who has been generously sharing all kinds of valuable information with me. That is how I learned that there was a Star Flush in the first place and how I discovered all the security arrange…"

Sigmund stopped in mid-sentence. Looking beyond Howard, he said, "Ah here comes the little prima donna now!"

A glaring spotlight approached, and behind the invasive beam hovered the robotic movie camera, Directo-cam.

"Hey, Siggy! There you guys are!" said Directo-cam. "Sorry I'm late. I had to make sure I had enough batteries for the trip."

The movie camera zipped over to Sigmund

and panned the scene, shining his theatrical light in the faces of all those present.

"So who's the ugly bird and the bug?" he asked. "What happened to the other two lunatics you had working for you?"

Poultrygeist tensed and his talon-hands dug into Howard's stomach.

Sigmund gave Poultrygeist a sly glance and held up his hand to say, "Wait and be patient."

"Directo-cam!" scolded Howard. "How could you? You betrayed us!"

The camera swerved around so its spotlight was pointed directly at Howard's face.

"No Howy, it was you who betrayed me! Hey this Star Flush gig would have made my career, but no, Stanley didn't want me tagging along! So bye-bye, Directo-cam. Thank you very much. Don't call us. We'll call you. Don't let the door hit you on the way out!" In a self-righteous snivel the camera said, "Sorry Howy, but your brother Siggy appreciates my talent. He offered me a sweet little job that I would have been crazy to turn down. This gig is going to make history man!"

Panning to the right and left, the camera looked around and said, "Wow! What happened to this place? No way. Don't tell me you burned Livingston's laboratory to the ground?"

"I vaporised it actually," Sigmund replied. "After we moved the Star Flush outside of course. My brand new pooter..."

"You mean the black one I saw parked back

there? The one with all the fancy gadgets and weapons?"

"I call it the Pooter of the Apocalypse," said Sigmund. "My new weaponized craft was acquired from the local military base earlier this evening. I had no intention of using it until I was about the business of conquering unsuspecting planets. Our intention was to leave peacefully without making a lot of noise, but our plans went awry. I therefore decided to test my pooter's weapon system and as you can see there is nothing left of the laboratory but smoke and burning embers."

"Ah man, I wish I could have been here to film it," said Directo-cam. "Gratuitous violence is right up my street, baby! But, aren't you worried about the fire brigade and police coming to investigate all these fires and explosions and what not?"

Sigmund laughed. "Septo City's finest have their hands full tonight. There is a pet clinic on fire across town and those that were not busy there responded to the explosion of Explorer's Cottage. When they arrived – well, let's just say they had a little run in with the Pooter of the Apocalypse when I shot them out of the sky."

"My, my, Siggy, You've been a naughty boy," said Directo-cam. "Well, what are we waiting for? Let's get this show on the road."

"What are we waiting for? That's a good question. What we're waiting for is the guest presenter, the friendly face of our interplanetary exploits, the host of our intergalactic TV specials."

"You mean someone like Livingston?"

"Oh, he's much better than Livingston. His name is Jacques Poosteau."

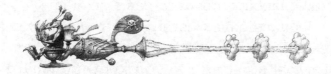

CHAPTER 52

THE GUEST PRESENTER

At that very moment, and right on cue, Jacques Poosteau arrived.

"Hey there Sig, how do I look?" asked Jacques. His foreign accent was now noticeably absent.

"Like a star," replied Sigmund.

With a fedora hat on his head and a brown leather jacket over his khaki coloured shirt, Jacques was indeed the picture-perfect explorer.

"Now all I need is a whip," he said.

It was then that Jacques noticed Cesselia. Her eyes were ablaze with anger and wet with tears.

Turning to Sigmund he said, "Ah Sig, do we have to tie her up like this?"

"Believe me Jacques. You wouldn't want to untie her right now. Look at her. I think she would scratch your eyes out. Not long ago she nearly cracked my skull open like an egg. I still have a throbbing headache as a result."

Jacques gave Cesselia a sympathetic smile, and said, "I'm sorry, babe. I really do like you, kid, but I'm just an actor. Do you know how hard it is to get acting gigs? I was hired to play the part of the charming, sophisticated, marine biologist, Jacques Poosteau. My real name is Harrison Turd.

Sigmund here figured that if you took a shine to me, then no other fellow would have you. I was supposed to wine you and dine you until Sig could have you all to himself. In return, I was paid a nice little fee and he promised that I would be the star presenter on these fantastic intergalactic trips he told me about."

"And what a star you are and will be," added Sigmund. He put his hand on Harrison's shoulder and led him away from Cesselia and over to the Star Flush.

"And you too Directo-cam," called Sigmund. "Come! It is time."

Directo-cam joined Harrison and Sigmund in front of the Star Flush.

"You two will make history and everyone will know your names. Follow me."

Harrison and Directo-cam followed Sigmund up the stairs of the Star Flush. Standing in front of the control column, Sigmund took a thousand puto bill out of his pocket and inserted it into the money slot.

He pushed the handle down.

A blinding blue light began to whirl and twirl inside the porcelain bowl. Its great suction ripped a hole in the fabric of space and time.

"Charade-oglyphics, plot a course to the Whipyo Asteroid," shouted Sigmund over the flush.

"Whipyo Asteroid?" repeated Directo-cam. "Sounds fun."

"Oh you'll love it," said Sigmund.

"I thought we were going to another planet?" said Harrison. "Someplace called Oxnard?"

"No, we're going to start small and work our way up to the planets," explained Sigmund.

"Gotcha," Harrison smiled. "I'm with you."

"No, you're with the Directo-cam!"

Sigmund pushed Harrison and the movie camera into the swirling bowl of light.

✳ ✳ ✳ ✳ ✳

Harrison and the Directo-Cam emerged through another Star Flush at the outer edge of the universe.

They found themselves riding a dark, bumpy mass of rock and metal through the void of space, an asteroid absent of all heat, air and light.

Harrison immediately froze to death while smiling for the camera.

"Hey it's cold out here," said the Directo-cam, though his words were inaudible in the vacuum of space.

He surveyed the asteroid with his bright movie lights. "Get a load of this place," he said to Harrison. "Harrison? Harrison? Are you OK Harrison?" He reached out to touch Jacques, and then the actor tipped over and shattered into a million ice cubes.

"Oops," said Directo-cam.

Directo-cam noticed that the brown bumps and lumps of the asteroid had eyes. Hundreds of mineral based life forms and rocks that cannibalised other rocks began to move toward the Directo-cam. Their jaws were filled with granite crunching teeth. They had claws designed to rip, hold and pulverise other rocks.

They surrounded Directo-cam hungry with the desire to absorb his inorganic nutrients into themselves.

Directo-cam screamed without being able to make a noise, because in space, no one can hear you swear!

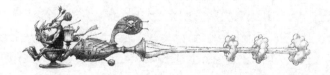

CHAPTER 53

THE BOLD EXIT

"Sigmund rejoined Howard and Poultrygeist.

"He should never have called me Siggy baby," said Sigmund.

The Molecule Scrambler marched on to the grounds of what had been the laboratory and made its way to the Star Flush accompanied by the Psychobot Nurse.

"Excellent. Now, I do believe we can be on our way."

"What? You're stealing our Molecule Scrambler as well?" said Howard.

"Using for the greater good is perhaps a better description than stealing. Initially we wanted to destroy it, and we did pull a wire or two, but then I had second thoughts. Such a machine could help us in our, I mean er, Poultrygeist's conquest of other planets you see. I mean, we will really mix things up with a Molecule Scrambler, and so I asked my Psychobot Nurse to repair it and download her obedience program into its electronic brain."

Looking down at Howard's toilet–roll belt buckle, Sigmund said, "My dear rich brother, I thank you for putting up the thousand putos for this journey. Allow me." He ripped a thousand–puto bill from Howard's belt buckle, ran up the stairs and placed the money in the control column.

Once again, Sigmund pushed down on the flush handle, and again there was a tumultuous noise and yet another whirlpool of light.

"Charade–oglyphics, plot a course to the planet Oxnard."

Descending the stairs, Sigmund said to the Psychobot Nurse, "Do you have our one last bomb, dear Nurse?"

The Psychobot Nurse opened her metallic chest and produced another black disk with digital numbers, and she handed this disk to Sigmund. He, in turn, took the bomb and placed it on the basin of the Star Flush.

"We might as well burn our bridges behind us," he said. "We wouldn't want anyone else to follow us through the Star Flush."

After Sigmund pushed buttons on the disk, digital numbers began counting down from sixty seconds.

(...59...58...57...)

"You first, Nurse."

The Psychobot Nurse marched up the stairs, dropped into the swirling light and disappeared.

(45...44...43...)

"Molecule Scrambler!"

The machine marched up the stairs and also stepped into the light.

(30....29...28...)

"Elfly and my dear Cesselia! See you in paradise my darling."

With Cesselia tied to the fuel tank in the back, Elfly drove the hovering tractor up the stairs.

There was a look of defiance on Cesselia's face and just before she disappeared into the Star Flush bowl, she slipped her wedding ring off her finger and tossed it aside.

EXCERPT FROM LIVINGSTON'S JOURNAL

Both Stanley and I were in our dirty pajamas, running through the piddling rain toward the laboratory.

We didn't know who planted the bomb on the cottage or why they did it, but we did know that the Star Flush was just the kind of something that the worst kind of people would kill for.

Little Klawd and the gumpathump trotted along with us; it would have been nice to have had the robots with us as well, but we were in too much of a hurry to activate them, so we just left them lying in the rubble of the cottage.

The first thing we noticed when we entered

the laboratory grounds was that there was no laboratory. The storage shed with all our supplies was still standing, thank goodness, but that was little comfort in light of seeing the smouldering wreckage of what had been my laboratory.

The next thing I noticed was the Star Flush. It was in full-on flush mode, with its spinning bowl of light and its rip-roaring noise.

The final thing we noticed was that there were a couple of shadowy figures in front of the Star Flush that we could only see in silhouette.

AUTHOR'S NARRATION

(11....10...9....)

To Poultrygeist, Sigmund said, "Your worship, if you please."

To Howard he said, "See you in paradise, brother."

Poultrygeist floated forward with Howard in his clutches, and they then descended into the Star Flush.

(4...3...)

EXCERPT FROM LIVINGSTON'S JOURNAL

I saw a misshapen figure, (who seemed to be carrying someone or something else,) and it/he/she entered the Star Flush. They looked like they were floating or hovering.

There was one remaining figure. I saw someone, a man I think, and he got on a pooter, and then he rocketed straight up and then took the pooter down for a nosedive into the bowl. I thought I could hear him laughing.

AUTHOR'S NARRATION

(2...1...)
BOOOOOOOOOOOOOOOOOOOOOOOOOOOOM!
The time bomb exploded with fire and a blast that shook all the skyscrapers in Septo City!

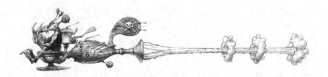

CHAPTER 54

THE SMOKE CLEARS

EXCERPT FROM LIVINGSTON'S JOURNAL

It was the second time that night that I'd been knocked unconscious by a bomb blast.

As before, I had no idea how long I'd been out cold. Whether it was seconds or minutes, I didn't know.

I opened my eyes wondering where I was. The ground felt furry. I realised I was lying on top of Little Klawd. The big cat seemed to be asleep beneath me.

My ears hurt. They were ringing and I couldn't hear a thing.

"Oh yes," I remembered. "We had been running for the Star Flush and then BOOM! There had been an explosion."

I then thought, "Where's Stanley?"

I sat up, and from my perch atop Little

437

Klawd, I looked around. Then I found him. I saw Stanley lying on his face in the mud. He was about twenty yards off to the right of me.

"Was he OK?" I wondered.

I watched him until I was sure I could see him breathing.

The gumpathump looked the worst off. At first I thought she was dead. She was flat on her back with all four feet sticking up in the air. Her neck was completely screwed up. Her head was twisted around, facing up, and her eyes were closed.

"No animal could end up looking like that and survive," I thought. But then I noticed that she too was breathing.

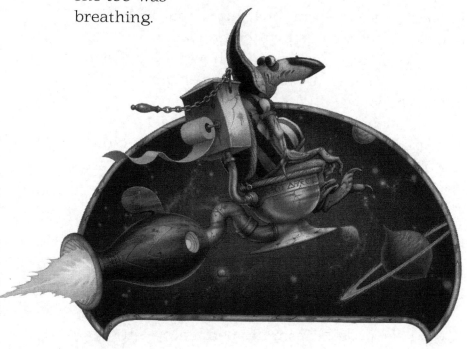

"The Star Flush!" I remembered. "Oh no, they blew up the Star Flush!"

I expected to see nothing but a hole where the Star Flush had been.

I looked into the haze, drizzle and smoke, but then I saw it. Yes, there was a crater, but in the crater, there was also a Star Flush!

Little did I know then, but because of the Star Flush, Stanley and I were about to have an intergalactic adventure of epic proportions – and I, Livingston, despite being a fraud, liar and an impostor would end up righting many a wrong in the universe.

THE END

THE STORY CONTINUES IN VOLUME 3

THE FANTASTIC INTERGALACTIC ADVENTURES OF STANLEY & LIVINGSTON

✳ ✳ ✳ ✳

THE PARADISE PLANET WAR

VISIT THE RODNEY MATTHEWS SHOP AT

WWW.RODNEYMATTHEWS.COM

FOR UPDATES
ON STANLEY AND LIVINGSTON NEWS, VISIT

WWW.STANLEYLIVINGSTONADVENTURES.COM

✳ ✳ ✳ ✳

ORDER A SIGNED COPY OF THE COVER ART

High quality artwork-matched images printed on art paper
with archival non-fade inks. Each open edition print is
personally signed by Rodney Matthews.

'A VIEW TO SEPTO CITY'
From the book, 'The Fantastic Intergalactic
Adventures of Stanley & Livingston'.

Regular size – 28 x 21 inches

VISIT WWW.RODNEYMATTHEWS.COM
TO PLACE YOUR ORDER

✳ ✳ ✳ ✳

ABOUT RODNEY MATTHEWS

This year (2010) Rodney Matthews celebrates his 40th year as a freelance designer and illustrator of fantasy and science-fiction.

Previously, he was employed at Ford's Creative, an advertising agency in Bristol U.K. He was trained in commercial and graphic design at the West of England College of Art, 1960. Since that time, Matthews has forged himself an international reputation in fantasy art.

He is perhaps best known for his record album cover art, having painted around 100 subjects for artists including Thin Lizzy, Nazareth, Asia, Magnum and Rick Wakeman. Around 100 of his images have been published worldwide in poster and limited edition print formats (selling millions), besides many editions of calendars, jigsaw puzzles, snowboards, T-shirts and illustrated books. Recently, Templar Publishing released a Rodney Matthews illustrated 'Alice in Wonderland' collector's book.

Rodney's original artworks have been widely exhibited in the U.K. and Europe, including the prestigious Chris Beetles gallery in London's West End. His admirers include John Cleese, who has purchased 6 original Matthews works to date, one of which was a commission from 'The Wind in the Willows.'

In 1998, Matthews and Gerry Anderson (Thunderbirds, Captain Scarlet, Space 1999 etc.) completed a 26 episode animation series, 'Lavender Castle.' It was produced at Cosgrove Hall Films in Manchester England. Following that, Matthews contributed concept art for the 'Magic Roundabout' movie. His talents have also graced the video game industry with overall concept designs produced for Sony/Psygnosis UK, Sony 989 Studios, San Diego and Midway, via developers - Traveller's Tales.

Rodney Matthews is still active in many of these genres, and by the way of full circle, has recently produced some interesting advertising imagery for an electricity company.

ABOUT MARCO PALMER

At age 16, Marco was given his own humour/opinion column in a newspaper called the Toppenish Review in Toppenish, Washington.

At age 17, Marco moved to Ventura California and finished his senior year of high school with scholarship money awards for creative writing.

He was one of the youngest students to attend a screenwriting course taught by Paul Lazarus (a former Vice president of Columbia Pictures and Warner Brothers) at the University of California at Santa Barbara. Mr. Lazarus said that Marco had a unique gift in comedy writing and thought he had a future writing for comedians like Mel Brooks, Woody Allen and Marty Feldman.

For the next twenty-two years, Marco wrote for and performed with fellow actor and comedian, Rodd Christensen.

Marco relocated to Great Britain in 1991.

While in Britain, Marco married a British girl and became the father of three boys.

Rodd and Marco travelled extensively around Great Britain performing in schools and festivals.

Together Rodd and Marco produced two musical/comedy CDs of their work (JURASSIC CHURCH, THE ACTS FILES) a video, and two collections of their comedy sketches (MIC and DASHING THROUGH THE SHOW)

Rodd Christensen went on to star in the BBC children's show Balamoray as Spencer the Painter, while Marco has been writing, working in education and earning a degree in English Literature.

✳ ✳ ✳ ✳ ✳

ON COLLABORATING WITH RODNEY MATTHEWS

Why do I always end up working with people named Rod? Rodd Christensen and I were looking for an artist for our 'Jurassic Church' album cover back in 1993 and I read an article about another Rod, a fantasy artist named Rodney Matthews.

"That's the guy!" I said after reading the article.

I wrote to Mr. Matthews about our project and the rest, as they say, is history.

While Rodney was working with Gerry Anderson on Lavender Castle, I submitted ten speculation scripts for his cartoon series. I made Rodney laugh, and he thought I would be a perfect match for the material should Lavender go to a second series. Despite the show being in television markets around the world, America did not pick up the show. American television outlets thought the humour was too British.

Rodney thought that hiring an American writer could have helped crack the American market place, but it was not to be.

At the same time, Rodney pulled out some art work for an idea he had about two explorers called Stanley and Livingston. Rodney's original concept was to base them loosely on the real David Livingstone and Henry Morton Stanley, but instead of exploring Africa, they would explore distant planets and have all kinds of adventures.

I was asked if I wanted to have a go at writing a screenplay based on this concept, and the answer was "Are you kidding? Of course!"

Rodney had originally conceived of Stanley and Livingston as travelling in a space ship.

I suggested we do something different, and brought up the wormhole, tunnel in space, portal to the planets type idea. "What about a Star Flush?" I said. Rodney thought that was funny, and ran with that idea. He then invented pooters and together we created the bathroom-esque culture of Cessestial.

It has been a fun collaboration process. Often times I will describe things based on what Rodney has drawn, and then Rodney will draw pictures based on what I have written. I will then rewrite as the pictures are refined. I will call Rodney and say, "How does the Star Flush operate? Or what does the Psychobot Nurse look like? Rodney will then say something like, "I can see the Psychobot Nurse looking like those Nazi women who worked in the concentration camps," and I will write based on such a description.

I consider it a wonderful privilege to collaborate and brainstorm with my favourite artist in the world, and it has been a pleasure working on the three volumes and counting of The Fantastic Intergalactic Adventures of Stanley and Livingston with my good friend, Mr. Rodney Matthews.

In the future we hope to put together a special edition of these books with full colour illustrations through out, and we are working on a project Rodney has written himself called the Gasbags. I laughed till I cried at Rodney's very silly poems about the Gasbags. Keep checking out the two websites, www.rodneymatthews.com and www.stanleylivingstonadventures.com for updates on these projects and more.

☀ ☀ ☀ ☀ ☀

SPECIAL THANKS

Thanks to the many who helped get this project off the ground. Thanks for the helpful critiques, advice and those who gave of their time, labour and resources to these novels.

Thanks to: Mike Jolley at Templar Publishing.
Thanks to literary agents: W. Gail Manchur and Andrew Whelchel III for their encouragement along the way.
Thanks to Robert Lambolle of Read and Right for the critique which turned the story around.
Thanks to Open University writing professor, Jules Horne for her helpful critique.
Thanks to Beverly Bryant of Woodmill High School for her editorial advice.
Thanks to Yendor Matthews, Chris Nutt, Ken Eaves and George Russell for their help with the www.stanleylivingston adventures.com website.
Thanks to the staff and pupils of Woodmill High School, Dunfermline Fife, Scotland UK.
Thanks to the many friends and members of my family who volunteered to be guinea pigs while reading various drafts of the story.
Thanks to Rose Gorell of centre Glass, Ventura California for her investment in this enterprise.
Thanks to Randall Miller for dialogue advice in regard to the character Brobot.
Thanks to the late Karin Matthews, our inspiration for Cesselia.

✳ ✳ ✳ ✳ ✳

Review of Rodney Matthews' illustrated
ALICE IN WONDERLAND
by Lewis Carroll

Rodney's new book, 'Alice in Wonderland', was published at the end of 2008 by Templar Publishing. It contains 14 colour illustrations and 14 monotone pencil drawings.

This 95 page book from Templar's 'Collector's Classics' series comes as a hardback (ISBN: 978-1-84011-488-1), and a jewelled slip-cased edition (ISBN: 978-1-84011-483-6).

JOHN CLEESE: Masaccio, Michelangelo, Manet, Monet, Matisse, Munch, Mondrian, and Matthews. All my favourite artists begin with 'M'. Except for Mantegna (I don't mean that Mantegna doesn't start with an 'M', it's just that he's not one of my favourite artists. Neither is Macke; bloody rubbish, if you ask me). And so Rodney Matthews is generally acknowledged to be among the greatest artists that have ever lived.

Need I say more? Please buy this book, and all his other works, because then my immense collection of his stuff will become even more valuable. Especially when he dies.

John Cleese, 2008